THE CLAIMING WORDS

BY TRICIA DRAMMEH

RED LIZARD PRESS

Red Lizard Press
1050 E Piedmont Rd
Suite E-119
Marietta, GA 30062

Copyright © 2012 by Tricia Drammeh

All rights reserved, including the right to reproduce this book or portions thereof in any form whatsoever. For information, address inquiries to:

Iconic Publishing Subsidiary Rights Department
1050 E Piedmont Rd, Suite E-119, Marietta, GA 30062

First Red Lizard U. S. trade paperback edition- 2012

Red Lizard Press and colophon are registered trademarks of:
Iconic Publishing, LLC.

Red Lizard Press is an imprint of Iconic Publishing, LLC.

Cover design by Catherine LaPointe

Edited by Jano Donnachaidh

Dedication

To my husband, Aaron-Haruna.

Acknowledgments

I'd like to thank my family for all their love and support, specifically my mom, Diana, and my sister, Kristyn, for undertaking the monumental task of reading the first draft. With all my heart, I thank my children for their patience. Christopher, Dena, Khadeja, and Ahmed —I love you all.

Thank you, Shanon Borus Holloway, for your sharp eye and steady camera.

A heartfelt thank you to Lisa Wiedmeier for giving me a gentle shove in the right direction. Huge thanks to Keith Smith for focusing on the details, to Jacoba Dorothy for looking at the big picture, and to Tockica Jedna for her honesty, kindness, and wisdom.

Thank you to Jano Donnachaidh whose brilliant editing and tireless efforts transformed my manuscript into a novel we can both be proud of.

To all my friends and my online family. Your support and encouragement mean the world to me.

A final thank you to my husband. Your claiming words still have me spellbound.

The Alexanders have always kept their secrets hidden…

When sixteen-year-old Jace Alexander moves to the small town of Oaktree, Georgia, he attracts the attention of every girl in school. Shy, introverted Alisa Cole immediately casts Jace in the leading role of her latest fantasy, but she assumes he'll never return her interest. After she saves Jace from a Hunter, everything changes. Her accidental discovery of Jace's secret propels her into a world of magic and danger. Alisa's newfound courage is put to the test when Jace introduces her to his intimidating older brother, Bryce, and she decides she would rather battle a Hunter than endure another moment under Bryce's intense scrutiny.

Jace and Bryce aren't the only ones with secrets…

Rachel Stevens is the girl who has it all. She's beautiful, popular, and in possession of an ancient power which endangers not only her, but those sent to protect her. Jace is drawn to Rachel—and he isn't the only one. The Demon Re'Vel will do anything to claim her—even if it means waging a war with the entire Alexander family. As layers of secrets are peeled away, revealing the truth of her heritage and her family's betrayal, Rachel struggles to resist an immortal suitor who stalks her in her dreams. With the Alexanders fighting to protect her, can Rachel escape the power of the Demon and his Claiming Words?

THE CLAIMING WORDS
By Tricia Drammeh

CHAPTER ONE
ALISA

From my lonely seat in the back of the classroom, I watched my conniving cousin flirt with the guy I loved. Hopeless pain held me in place as Becky tossed her mane of golden, highlighted hair behind her. She crossed her legs, revealing about five inches of tanned thigh, and leaned forward until her cleavage was displayed to its best advantage. I felt a jolt of jealousy, but recognizing this feeling as irrational and unjust, I immediately set about beating the green-eyed monster into submission. After all, Jace and I had never actually spoken. It was only the first week of school, and he probably didn't even know my name. So far, our relationship was fairly one-sided.

He flashed an easy smile her way, and I sighed in resignation. Becky always managed to entice the hottest guys in school, whereas I routinely repelled them. With great difficulty, I tried to stop looking at our new student's tall, athletic form. I absentmindedly doodled in my notebook and tried to conjure up a favorite daydream to get lost in. It was pointless to fantasize about Jace Alexander. He was so far out of my league; he would probably reject me even in my fantasies.

"So, where are you from?" Becky asked our new student.

"We just moved from Denver. Before that, we lived in London," he replied. Was it my imagination, or did he lean back in an attempt to escape her overzealous attentions?

"Ooh, London! That's so interesting!" she purred. I wondered if she even knew where London was. "I have cheerleading practice after school, but if you want to hang out later, I can give you my phone number."

I couldn't help but wonder what she planned to do if Jace actually asked her out. My Aunt Leanne would never allow her only daughter to date an African-American guy. I guessed Becky just liked the chase.

"Sure, I..." he trailed off when Becky shot me a nasty glance over her shoulder.

"What are you looking at, freak?" my cousin snapped in my direction. Laughter filled the half-empty classroom. I blushed and looked back down at my notebook, embarrassed to be caught staring at a guy who would never return my interest.

"Actually, I can't today. But thanks," Jace said when Becky turned to face him once more. He didn't press her for the phone number she offered. I settled back against my seat and tried to calm my nerves. By lunchtime, the whole school would be talking about how I'd tried to scam on the hottest guy in school. By the end of the day, the story would be inflated and embellished to the point where everyone would believe I'd asked Jace to marry me; Becky would make sure of it.

When the bell rang, Becky followed Jace out into the hallway, and I knew it was only a matter of time before he succumbed to her feminine charms. It hurt my soul to watch them together, but I couldn't figure out why. By the end of the day, the whispered rumors had turned to open laughter at my expense, but that was okay. I was used to being tormented by Becky's followers. And, besides, Jace didn't laugh at me. Not once.

***

The temperatures during the second week of school reached record highs, and the walk home was beyond miserable. I'd been too apathetic to take my driver's test; consequently, I was practically the only junior in my high school forced to either take the bus or hoof it. I cut through a field behind the school to get home faster. The hot sun beat down on my short, dark hair, and I felt a line of sweat slither down my back.

I noticed two figures just ahead of me, and nearly turned back. Most of my fellow classmates despised me, and since the feeling was mutual, I tried to avoid contact with them whenever possible. When I recognized Jace, I cursed the fact that I had no social skills to speak of. He seemed different from the people I'd grown up with, and might have stopped to speak to me. He'd managed to resist Becky, after all.

Jace wasn't the only person who'd resisted my cousin; I could only hope he would be able to hold out longer than the last guy. Back in middle school, Becky and I both liked the same boy, but when he expressed interest in me instead of her, my popular cousin retaliated by spreading vicious rumors about me. Too shy to fight back, I remained silent while the whole school turned against me. Long after the boy moved away, long after Becky fell in love with someone else, the repercussions of that ill-fated crush continued to haunt me.

I thought about Jace and how I might be willing to go through the whole love-triangle drama all over again on the off-chance that he might return my interest. Walking slowly through the field, a vague fantasy began to form inside my head: Jace asking me out, our whirlwind courtship, eventual proposal, and elopement to Vegas.

I squinted and peered into the distance, but couldn't identify the person who stood just a few feet away from Jace. Oaktree, Georgia was a small town and I knew almost everyone, but I didn't recognize this guy. They circled each other, and at first, I thought the two guys were messing around. Cautiously, I drew closer and realized I'd misinterpreted the situation. Jace leapt to the side as the large man lunged at him. I let out a startled shriek.

Jace looked over his shoulder and shouted, "Don't come any closer!" I staggered back a step and almost tripped over my own feet.

The attacker took advantage of Jace's brief distraction. He flew toward my classmate and pinned him to the ground, clenching one hand around Jace's throat. Jace struggled for about a minute, and then stopped. I found it odd the attacker paid absolutely no attention to me. Generally, psychos went for defenseless females, or so I'd thought.

I briefly considered calling 911; the attacker didn't seem to care what I did. Jace, however, seemed to need more immediate help. Without considering the consequences of my actions, I sprinted forward and swung my heavy book bag at the man's face. I hit him dead on, and he turned his attention to me for a second or two. His blood-red eyes bore into mine, and I recoiled in horror.

Apparently, I'd distracted the red-eyed man enough to cause him to release his death grip on my classmate. Jace scrambled away from his attacker, and leapt to his feet. They faced off once again. Jace, face screwed up in concentration, crouched low and sprang toward his enemy in a crouching roll. The attacker bared his teeth and leapt out of the way effortlessly. Red-eyes certainly seemed to have the advantage in the battle. In fear and disbelief, I watched as he formed a ball of fire in the palm of his hand and hurled it at Jace. My classmate put his hands up, palms facing outward, and the fireball sizzled into nothing.

Jace disappeared and abruptly reappeared in a spot behind the attacker. With supernatural speed, he jumped at the man and hooked his arm around his neck. He wrenched the man's head to the side, and Red-eyes slumped to the ground. Jace wiped at the sweat on his face with the back of his hand, and then kicked the man viciously in the ribs. He reared back to kick again, but stopped when he saw me.

We stared at each other for a moment. Jace walked over to me and asked, "Are you okay?" I nodded. "We need to get out of here in case there are more of them," he said, gesturing toward the lifeless body on the ground a few feet away from us. I flinched. Jace walked back and forth through the tall grass, scrutinizing the area closely. He bent down and picked up a textbook.

I contemplated running back toward the school and screaming for help, but I couldn't seem to propel myself forward. I stood rooted to the spot, my legs trembling, as I fought back a bout of nausea.

"Let's go," Jace said in my direction. When I didn't move, he walked over to me and took my hand. I pulled it away. "Come on, Alisa. You're safe with me. I promise. Let's go back to my house, and I'll explain everything to you when we get there." Through my haze of shock, I felt a brief sense of elation that he even knew my name. He lifted my book bag from the ground and began walking away.

Staring at my book bag dangling from his shoulder, I irrationally wondered whether or not it was a crime weapon and if my limited participation made me an accomplice to a murder. I questioned the wisdom of not having called the police.

"Should I call 911?" I asked stupidly. "I'm sure you won't be in trouble. He attacked you first. I'm a witness."

He turned back to look at me. "Alisa, that thing back there isn't dead. You can't kill a Hunter that easily. He's just stunned. There could be more of them, so we should really get out of here." My choice was follow Jace, this guy I didn't really know, or stay in the field with the dangerous red-eyed man. I followed Jace.

"What's a Hunter?" I stammered, my teeth starting to chatter as shock kicked in. Tears came, but I fought them back. I'd cried enough in front of my classmates. I wouldn't cry in front of this new student.

He seemed reluctant to answer. "Um, it's half Demon and half human…it's hard to explain. You saved my life, though," Jace said, stopping for a moment to readjust my heavy backpack still swinging from his shoulders. "Come on. My mom can explain this much better than I can."

I followed Jace as he left the field and took a short-cut through the woods. When we approached the rear border of one of the newer subdivisions in town, he helped me over the low fence enclosing his backyard. When we stepped through the back door and into his kitchen, he immediately began rummaging through a cabinet. He produced two tall glasses, filled them with water, and bellowed, "Mom! Hey, are you home?" He plunked a glass of water in front of me on the counter and I drank thirstily.

"Jace, you'd better have a good reason for yelling like that in the house," a voice called out. A beautiful woman with caramel skin and curly, ebony hair came into the room. "Oh," she exclaimed, "I didn't realize you'd brought a friend." Her eyes narrowed into a guarded and unwelcoming gaze.

"This is Alisa Cole. She saved me from a Hunter," Jace said. His mother gasped. So much for breaking the news gently, I thought as she swayed on her feet. In a rush, he relayed a garbled version of events, and I wondered how she would be able to make sense of such a confusing recount. When he got to the part about me hitting the Hunter with my bag, his mother put her hand on her heart and flashed me a tearful half-smile.

"Jace, thank God you're safe," she exclaimed. "I couldn't bear to lose another son." She pulled him into an extended embrace. Jace looked guilty and embarrassed by her tearful display.

"Alisa," she cried, releasing Jace and pulling me into a hug. "Thank you."

As I stood in an unfamiliar kitchen locked in the embrace of a woman I'd just met, I felt adrift in a fog of confusion. These people spoke of Hunters and magic as if it were perfectly commonplace. Who were they, and more importantly, *what* were they?

"Jace." A deep, icy voice drifted in from the kitchen doorway. Mrs. Alexander released me and I turned around. I wondered how long this older version of Jace had been standing there listening in on the conversation. His eyes caught mine, and the look he gave me was searching and uncomfortable. I blushed and looked down at my feet. "Dad will be home soon. I think we should wait for him to get here before we tell her anything, don't you?"

I dared another glance at Jace's older brother. He would have been extremely attractive with his tall, muscular frame, and rich, chocolate skin, had it not been for his cold and off-putting demeanor. I shivered as my eyes met his again.

"She saved my life, Bryce," Jace argued. "She knows I'm a Witch; she saw my magic firsthand. We owe her *some* explanation."

"She hit the Hunter with a book bag. Big deal. Why don't we tell her all our family secrets, then?" Bryce crossed his arms in front of him and glared at his younger brother. Thick muscles bulged from his snug-fitting tee-shirt. He looked only slightly less intimidating than the red-eyed man who nearly killed Jace.

"She battled a Hunter, which, for all of your training, you've never done," Jace snapped. Bryce looked murderous.

"Go ahead and mock me if you'd like. At least I've never had to depend on a human to protect me," Bryce spat, advancing on his brother.

"How do you know she isn't the one we've been looking for?" Jace shouted.

"If she was the Innocent, the Hunter would have gone after her instead of you, moron," Bryce said. "She has no magic," he spat out, waving toward me dismissively.

"She has something—" Jace said in my defense.

"Enough," Mrs. Alexander said firmly. "I'll decide who stays and for how long. I'm the adult here, remember? Don't you dare open your mouth to argue, Bryce. At nineteen, you might be considered an adult in the eyes of the law, but in *this* house, you're still under *my* authority."

I finally worked up enough nerve to speak. "Um, Mrs. Alexander? I should probably leave now. I have homework, and…" I trailed off, sounding as stupid as I felt. I didn't do well with new people, especially a whole room full.

THE CLAIMING WORDS

Jace's mother took pity on me. She put her arm around my shoulders maternally and said, "I'm sure this has all been very upsetting and confusing, dear. We'll give you a ride home, but could I ask one favor? Could you come over and have dinner with us tomorrow? I promise we'll explain everything to you then. In the meantime, I would be very grateful if you could keep all of this to yourself."

I nodded in agreement, thankful to be going home at last. My sense of relief was short lived, however, when Bryce grabbed a set of car keys and said, "Toss the human in the truck, and let's go." I felt like a piece of meat.

"Mom," Jace whined.

"Bryce, that's no way to treat our new friend," she said. "If I find out you—"

"Whatever," he mumbled, striding toward the front door. I followed the two brothers outside to a pick-up truck. Smashed in between the two of them, we rode to my house in near silence. Jace tried to fiddle with the radio, but one nasty comment from his older brother had him sitting back in his seat and looking out the passenger side window.

The silence was broken occasionally when I was forced to offer directions. I prayed Bryce would have other plans the next day; I couldn't imagine sitting across the kitchen table from him. I'd never met a more unpleasant and unlikable man in my life and I hated him instinctively. His darkness permeated the small cab of the pick-up truck and I was almost in tears by the time we pulled into my driveway.

I almost laughed when I remembered the promise I'd made to Mrs. Alexander. It was an easy promise to keep. If I told anyone what I'd witnessed, I would be locked away in a mental institution. My family already thought I was crazy.

***

By the time school rolled around the next day, I'd nearly convinced myself I'd dreamt everything from the walk home until I woke up in the morning. When I arrived in first period, I staked out my usual spot in the back of the classroom and tried to finish my homework.

Jace entered the classroom alone and took a seat beside me. "How are you today? Are you alright?"

"I'm fine. How are you, though?" I asked softly.

"Great. I'm looking forward to dinner tonight. You're still coming, right?" He smiled at me, and I fell even more deeply in love with him.

"Absolutely," I said, returning his smile.

"You should give me your phone number," he said. I scribbled my number on a sheet of notebook paper. He hadn't accepted Becky's number when she offered; I wondered why.

Jace spoke to me for a couple of minutes and I struggled to think of witty, semi-coherent replies. I wasn't a very skilled conversationalist, so I was somewhat relieved when he moved to his seat at the front of the room. He probably felt obligated to talk to me, I thought. I decided I wouldn't embarrass myself by trailing after him like a lovesick puppy.

I expected our early morning conversation to be the extent of our interaction at school, but I was wrong. I sat alone at the back of the lunchroom and picked at the unrecognizable food on my lunch tray. A sudden wind lifted the wisps of hair at the nape of my neck, and in an instant, the hottest guy in our school pulled up a chair to sit next to me.

"What are you doing here?" I blurted, gaping at Jace.

"Do you mind if I sit next to you?" he asked, gesturing at the four empty chairs grouped around the table where we sat.

"You don't have to," I said.

"That's good to know. What is this crap?" The fact that he couldn't identify the food before him didn't seem to dampen his appetite. He shoved forkfuls into his mouth, and I cringed as he devoured the mystery meat. Jace chatted in between bites as if it were perfectly normal to be sitting there with me. I felt like I should tell him he was off the hook—that he didn't have to pretend to like me just because he thought I'd saved his life.

"Hey, aren't you eating?" he asked. I shook my head, and he attacked my food with gusto. "My brother and I will pick you up for dinner tonight."

I shivered as I recalled Bryce's penetrating, cold stare. "I can walk. I like walking."

"Yeah, but still. It may not be safe," he insisted, glancing around the cafeteria to make sure no one was watching. They were. Everyone was staring. Jace leaned in closer, and I shivered. "You need protection."

"Your brother said I'm not the one they're looking for. What does that mean?" I asked, shocking myself. Ordinarily, I let others ask the questions, but my curiosity couldn't be contained.

"Shhh. We'll talk about it later. So, do you want to come over right after school?"

"I don't know if I can. I mean, I didn't ask…" I stammered. "My mom's picking me up today…"

"Just make sure she lets you come over tonight." His smile stole my breath away and I nodded in agreement. "Let me know if you need help convincing her, because I can be very persuasive," he claimed. I blushed and glanced away. I imagined he could persuade me to do nearly anything.

Jace continued eating and talking to me as if it were the most natural thing in the world. He didn't act martyred or uncomfortable. I briefly entertained the idea that perhaps Jace actually saw me as a real person. I'd barely said a word to him, and yet he continued an almost one-sided conversation until the bell rang.

As I scurried nervously from the lunchroom, Jace finished up the last couple of morsels of food on my tray. "Hey, Alisa," Jace practically shouted across the still full lunchroom. "I'll see you tonight."

I nodded to indicate I'd heard him, and then made my hasty retreat. I was painfully aware that half the school was watching me as I rushed to my next class. If he continued to associate with me, he'd better be prepared to join me in the cesspool of Cooper High gossip. I hoped he wouldn't choose his budding popularity over our newly established friendship. I was tired of being alone.

CHAPTER TWO
ALISA

Perhaps I should have gone to Jace's house right after school. Going home first just gave me a chance to work up a good case of nerves. My anxiety increased tenfold when I stepped into my driveway and saw Bryce's pickup. Jace tried to talk and joke around during the ride, but Bryce's crabby mood put a damper on any attempt at normal conversation. Jace attempted to turn on the radio to alleviate the tension, but it seemed Bryce preferred the uncomfortable silence.

"Touch my stereo, and I'll set you on fire," Bryce hissed. Jace yanked his hand away from the radio dial. "God, you have horrible taste in music." I stifled a smile; I wasn't a huge fan of pulsating rap music either. The older brother shot me a glance, and I pulled my face back to an expression of solemnity, and tried not to breathe.

When we arrived at the Alexanders' house, Bryce disappeared into another room, and I relaxed immediately. Without the older brother's intensely cold presence, I felt more comfortable. Jace motioned for me to have a seat on the sofa, and the moment I sat down, a fluffy, white cat hopped up into my lap and began to purr.

"That's Whiskers," Jace said sitting down in a recliner across from me. "He's usually shy around new people." I knew just how Whiskers felt. Jace entertained me with ridiculous anecdotes until his mom called us in to dinner.

I didn't know what to expect after everything that had happened the previous day, but the Alexanders were just like a normal family. When we sat down in the dining room, his parents insisted I call them by their first names, Abe and Jerica.

"After all, you saved Jace's life. You're part of the family," Abe said. I caught Bryce's eye roll. In some families, siblings hate each other, so maybe Bryce was being brotherly. Or maybe he was being a jerk.

"Thanks for coming over tonight, Alisa," Jerica began, "And

thank you for giving us a chance to offer you some explanations. Dinner will be ready in a few minutes, but before we eat, is there anything you wanted to say?"

"Um, no." I answered, "I can't think of anything right now."

"Really? You had an encounter with a Hunter yesterday, and you can't think of anything to say?" Bryce commented rudely, "Wow."

"That's enough, Bryce," Abe commanded, throwing a thunderous look at his older son. "Tone it down, or leave the table." He turned his attention to me and said, "I'm going to say some things tonight which may sound unbelievable, but I assure you I will be as straightforward as possible."

Abe looked directly at me as he spoke. "Alisa, there is magic in our world. Not everyone believes in it, but it's there nevertheless. You must understand not everyone you run into in this world is fully human." That part, I could believe. The Hunter was proof of that. "Our family's heritage is based in magic. We are Witches; our bloodline is a mixture of human and an ancient people known as the Fae." Abe paused, waiting for my reaction.

I glanced around the room, looking for the hidden cameras. I wondered if I'd stumbled into some strange, new reality show. I hated to think I was the butt of some elaborate joke. My gaze settled on Bryce, who wore his usual expression of borderline rage. Jace seemed nervous and embarrassed. Jerica and Abe met my searching gaze, and I couldn't help but believe them. No other explanation could make sense of the events from the day before, so I decided to cast aside my skepticism long enough to hear what Abe had to say. He must have seen a look of acceptance, or something like it, pass over my face, because he nodded to Jerica and continued speaking.

"The creature you encountered in the field yesterday was a Hunter, a half-Demon. It was drawn to Jace's magic," Abe explained.

Bryce interrupted with a sneer. "Because Jace is too much of an idiot to mask his powers. If he'd kept using the suppression spells—"

"Last chance, Bryce," Abe snapped.

"I can't freaking believe we're doing this. If Central found out..." Bryce threw a nasty glance my way, and I looked down at the empty plate in front of me.

Abe stood up and motioned for his older son to do the same.

Bryce followed his father into the kitchen. Jerica began to speak, but when the oven alarm buzzed, she excused herself and disappeared.

"Sorry my brother's…" Jace trailed off, shrugging.

I broke in before he could finish. I didn't want his parents to overhear us talking about his family. I didn't want them to think I was sneaky or disloyal. "Don't worry about it."

"Hey, I'll be right back. Let me go get that book before I forget to give it to you," he said, bolting from his seat and shooting down the hallway.

"No…" But it was too late. Alone in a strange dining room in a strange house, I had no choice but to listen to the raised voices on the other side of the door.

"…tell her who we are. But, you're seriously going to tell her why we're here? That's going too far, don't you think?" Bryce's angry words assaulted me through the closed door.

"I have a good feeling, Bryce. I see a good outcome," Jerica said so softly, I had to strain to hear her.

"Perception," her son spat. "Little good that did you when…"

"Don't say it!" Abe shouted.

Jerica interrupted. "Help me with this, Abe. Bryce, go back to the dining room." The door opened, and Bryce stared at me with undisguised disdain. He slammed the door shut, causing me to flinch.

"You hear all that?" he asked, striding toward me. "You don't belong here. You aren't one of us. We're Witches. Does that scare you?" He stood over me, his face so close I could feel his breath on my face, and I cowered away, blinking back tears of confusion and fear.

"I couldn't find it…" When I heard Jace's voice, Bryce shot across the dining room faster than anything I'd ever seen. By the time his brother came into the room, Bryce was in his seat with an innocent expression plastered on his face.

Jace's parents entered the dining-room, casserole dishes in hand, and began to pass the steaming food around. When everyone was served, Jerica smiled and began speaking as if the angry exchange in the kitchen had never occurred.

"The magical community is secretive," Jerica said, "but we believe we can trust you, Alisa. Our family came to Oaktree for a reason, for my job, really. I'm a First Watcher. It is my job to supervise

Warriors, Protectors, and other Witches in my territory and to report Demon and Hunter activity to our Central Headquarters. Abe's job is to serve as my Protector."

She continued, "One of my most sacred duties as a First Watcher is to identify and train Innocents—Witches who are unaware of their heritage."

"It isn't you, so don't get any stupid ideas," Bryce mumbled in my direction. He stuck his finger in his full glass of water, and the liquid began to bubble.

"You're too old to play like that at the table," Jerica said. She turned to me and continued speaking. "I believe the Hunter who attacked Jace was drawn to Oaktree by the presence of an Innocent. Obviously, until we can identify and offer protection, this person is in danger. Jace—"

"—is an idiot," Bryce said.

"—is lucky he wasn't killed. An untrained Witch is no match for a Hunter. It takes a skilled Warrior to...and, then sometimes..." Jerica trailed off, her voice trembling.

Abe gave Jerica a reassuring smile and began speaking. "Our son, Royce, was killed by Hunters five months ago. He was only twenty-two, and had almost completed training."

"I'm so sorry," I whispered. Abe flashed me a grateful, but watery smile.

"Magic is both a gift and a curse, especially for one who is untrained," Abe said.

"Like Jace," Bryce interrupted. Jace glared at him and appeared as if he was about to jump over the table and beat his older brother to death.

"Well, yes." Abe broke in before a fight could ensue. "Jace is like many Witches his age; training takes time. Magic is a tool very few have at their disposal. It can be a remarkable gift, but until it's controlled, it can be a danger as well."

"Dad, can I say something?" Jace asked.

"I don't see why not."

"Oh, great," Bryce said. "We get to hear a lecture from the untrained kid who spends all his time worrying about getting a date to the school dance."

"Like you were dedicated to training when you were in high

school. How many times were you suspended senior year? Weren't so worried about training then, were you?" Jace was livid.

"I did my work. I knew enough to get accepted by the Warrior Training Bureau at eighteen. If you weren't so ..." Bryce stopped when he saw the expression on his dad's face. "Sorry Dad... Mom," he mumbled.

"Jace, please continue," Abe said.

"Alisa, I just don't want you to be freaked out by everything you heard. For the most part, we're just like everyone else." Jace flashed me a crooked smile.

Bryce set out on a mission to undermine his brother's declaration. He stared directly at me as he picked up a fork and dropped it. Before it clattered to the table, he lifted his hand a few inches above it. The charmed utensil spun in the air. Bryce flashed me a wicked smile as I gaped in shock. Jerica slapped his hand and the fork fell to the table. Jace shot his older brother a menacing look, and gave up on his explanation.

I helped Jerica clear the table and prepare desert. As we feasted on chocolate cake, conversation drifted from the supernatural to the mundane. I noticed the Alexanders kept their explanations fairly brief, but that was okay; I'd learned enough thanks to Bryce's scathing comments. I snuck a glance in his direction. He scowled. Bryce watched me the rest of the evening when he thought no one else was looking. I knew he resented my presence and I hated being the object of such animosity.

"Alisa, we're having a barbeque on Saturday if you'd like to come over. Nothing fancy—just family," Jerica said casually. And, so began my relationship with the Alexander family.

***

I woke up too early Saturday morning, and an eternity of waiting stretched out before me. I decided to make some chocolate-chip cookies to take to the Alexanders' barbeque. Jerica didn't ask me to bring anything, but it would have been rude not to. And, baking would help me kill some time and maybe keep me from going crazy with anticipation.

When I saw Bryce's truck pull up in the driveway, I grabbed the platter of cookies, yelled goodbye to my parents, and dashed out the door. I tried to suppress the anxious smile that spread across my face, but it was difficult. My smile dimmed somewhat when I discovered Jace was not in the truck, only Bryce. Oh, great.

"What you got in there?" he asked as I climbed in beside him.

"Cookies. Can you hold this while I put on my seat belt?" I shoved the platter toward him.

"Chocolate chip!" He was already biting into one as he asked, "Can I have one? Oh, these are good." He handed the platter back to me, and backed out of the driveway.

We rode along in silence for about a minute. I concentrated on looking out the passenger side window. I tried to be as still as possible, afraid the slightest movement would remind him of how much he hated me. He finally asked, "So, it's hot out today, isn't it?" I guessed Bryce wasn't any better at small talk than I was. That was probably the only thing we had in common.

"Yes, it is," I replied. "It's always hot this time of year. It doesn't usually cool down until October. Then it's nice."

"I won't be here in October. I'm leaving in a few days and I'll be gone until December," he said.

"So, where are you going? I mean, if you can't tell me, that's okay. I know it's training, so it might be a secret..." Oh, nice. I was babbling.

"I'll be out of the country. It'll be cold there by October. Can I have another cookie?" It seemed like he was changing the subject. He could have told me it was none of my business. The truck swerved a bit when he stretched to reach the platter. I quickly handed him a cookie, and when our hands brushed, a warm rush of energy traveled from my fingertips to my shoulder. I wondered if he deliberately shocked me with his magic. "You don't have to sit so far away from me. I don't bite, you know."

Bryce gave me a sideways glance. "About the other day...I didn't mean to be so harsh, but our family doesn't associate with humans unless we have to. Please don't make us regret trusting you."

"I won't," I replied. It was irritating to be reminded once again that he thought I wasn't good enough for his family; his distrust doubled my determination to prove him wrong. He thought I couldn't keep a secret? He had no idea how closed-mouthed and stubborn I could be.

Bryce pulled his truck into the driveway and turned off the ignition. "Wait. Let me help you," he said as he opened his door. He came around to the passenger side, opened the door, and held the platter until I got out. "The cookies I ate on the ride here will be our little secret, okay? You don't want me to get in trouble with my mom, do you?" I felt a little lurch in my chest. I figured it must be the heat or the excitement about seeing Jace. I knew my heart didn't just skip a beat. Not because of Bryce.

"Hey, sorry I didn't ride over to get you," Jace said as he flung open the front door. "Dad said I had to finish my yard work."

I carried the platter of cookies into the house and asked, "Where can I put these?"

"I can take care of those for you," Bryce offered as he stepped in behind me.

"I'd better hide these," Jace laughed. "Bryce is greedy when it comes to anything with chocolate. You've got to watch him like a hawk." He relieved me of the cookies and started toward the kitchen. "Hey, I'm going to take a quick shower. Sorry, Alisa. Bryce will you get her a drink and take her out to the patio?"

"Sure, Jace. I don't mind entertaining *your* guest." Bryce walked through the kitchen toward the patio door, motioning for me to follow him. He halted in front of a red cooler and rooted around for a drink. "Pick your poison."

"Thanks," I said, selecting a can of Coke. I followed Bryce over to a glass-topped patio table and sat down as far from him as I possibly could; I was at a loss for words. Should I try to make conversation, or wait for the rest of his family to rescue me?

"Mom and Dad should be here in a few minutes. They made a last minute run for supplies. I'm afraid we're not very organized yet." Bryce seemed totally relaxed. He had his feet propped up on the chair next to him. I tried not to stare at his long, muscular legs. "So, Jace tells me you're some kind of genius. You're the only junior in Senior English?"

"Well, I'm not a genius. Actually, my grades are pretty average," I stammered. I hated talking about myself.

Bryce looked intrigued. "So, you're in Senior English for fun?"

"Well, no," I replied.

"So, you're smart?" he asked.

"No...I mean...I don't know." I glanced away from him. "They just advanced me...I don't know why."

"Do you hang out with the seniors?" he asked. His questions came so rapidly, I didn't have time to bolster my defenses. I shook my head. "So, you hang out with the juniors despite the fact they're obviously inferior to you." I shook my head again. "Who do you hang out with?"

"No one," I admitted before I could think.

"You're too good for the people around here?" he asked.

"No. I just..."

"Alisa, you are an enigma," Bryce said clicking his tongue.

I didn't know whether to be insulted or not. "What do you mean?"

"You're afraid to draw the slightest attention to yourself, but brave enough to face a Hunter." Bryce smiled widely in response to my nervous fidgeting. "You're really different from the people in this town. You don't fit in at all, do you?" I couldn't tell if he was asking because he was curious, or because he was a jerk and wanted me to be miserable.

"No, actually, I don't fit in around here. Thanks for mentioning it. You know, in case I forget." I was embarrassed, but angry too. While nearly every other girl in my school was tan with varying shades of long, blond hair, I had short, dark hair which contrasted with my pale skin. I didn't fit in with my peers, or even my own family for that matter. I certainly didn't fit in with this family.

"I'm not saying it's a bad thing. I just don't see how you can get along with the people around here. That's all." If this was an attempt to appease me, he fell far short of success. In fact, he was just digging himself a deeper hole.

"Well, I don't," I admitted reluctantly.

"Do you have a boyfriend?" Bryce asked. "Ex-boyfriend? Friends who are boys?"

"No. I don't really have any friends," I replied quickly, before I could stop myself. I hated admitting this to anyone, especially him. I didn't want the Alexanders to know what a total loser I was. I struggled to fight back tears of humiliation.

"You have Jace," Bryce said. "Hey, I never had a lot of friends in school, either."

"You don't have to try to make me feel better." I was trying to get a hold of myself, to calm down a little.

"Look at you. I bet the girls were all over you." I felt horrified by what I'd just said. I should have stapled my lips shut before I left my house. Or, better yet, I should have stayed home. Oh, God. He would totally think I was flirting with him. As if I'd know how.

"You'd be surprised," Bryce said without acknowledging my slip up. "There were a lot of people who found me difficult to get along with." He shrugged his shoulders. "Hey, do you want another soda?" He pointed his hand toward the cooler several feet away and said, "I can get you one without even getting up."

I remembered the trick he did with the spinning fork, and shook my head. "Your eyes are really blue," he said leaning toward me. What should I say to that? He wasn't complimenting me. He was just making an observation. I hated him for putting me on the spot.

I breathed a sigh of relief when I heard the sliding glass door open. "Hi, sweetie!" Jerica said, stepping onto the back patio. "It's hot out here! Alisa, do you mind helping me in the kitchen for a few minutes?"

"Sure. I wouldn't mind a few minutes of air conditioning," I replied, rising from the patio table, and following Jerica. I also wouldn't mind a few minutes away from Bryce. That conversation had me feeling more uncomfortable than the heat ever could.

***

As afternoon faded into evening, we sat in patio lounge chairs, too stuffed to move. Jace brought up the idea of tossing a football around or setting up the volleyball net, but everyone was too lethargic after all the food we'd consumed over the past couple of hours.

"So, Alisa, how's school?" Jerica asked. I shrugged. "Junior year is a big year. You have to start thinking about what college to go to and what to major in. Have you given college much thought?" No. But I probably should.

"I'll probably go to UGA or Georgia Southern. Somewhere in state," I replied unenthusiastically.

"Botany is a valuable major," Jerica said.

"Mom, nobody cares about that stuff," Jace mumbled. "A bunch of stuffy professors and elderly ladies; they're the only ones I ever see at those conferences you go to."

"Thanks, Jace. You make me feel so young and vibrant." Jerica rolled her eyes and laughed. "Hey, isn't the Homecoming dance coming up soon?"

"Oh, yeah," Jace answered. "That's like a huge deal at our school, at least for the girls. That's all they ever talk about. Hey, Alisa. Who are you going with?"

My face heated when Jerica and Jace turned to look at me. Wonderful. I could sense Bryce listening for my answer. He already knew the truth about me, and I didn't see that as a good thing. "Not sure," I answered, shrugging as if I hadn't given it a second thought. I already knew who I was going to Homecoming with—nobody. I'd probably stay home and avoid the whole thing just like last year and the year before that.

"Hey, we could go together if you want," Jace threw out casually. "I'd rather go with a friend than take some girl who's going to get ideas about us. Girls always take things too seriously. After one date, they're planning our wedding and naming our imaginary children."

"Yeah, cool." I was totally nonchalant, like hot guys asked me out every day. "Sounds like fun." I blushed. I was too embarrassed to admit I'd mentally planned our wedding and picked out baby names the first time I saw him.

"I'll have my driver's license by then, so maybe I can borrow Dad's car. I'm taking my driving test next weekend, so wish me luck. Otherwise, we'll be walking," Jace said.

I was so excited at the idea of going to Homecoming, I hadn't hit panic mode, yet. That would come later. I mean, it's not like it would be a real date. It's not like he was going to be my boyfriend. But it could be the beginning of something, I hoped. I forced myself to stop thinking along those lines. I needed to stay connected with reality and not get my hopes up.

"Does anyone want more food before I put all this away?" Jerica asked, getting up from her lounge chair. We all groaned in response. "Okay. Anyone want to help me take all this into the house?"

"I'll help," I said, hoisting myself up. "Just tell me what to grab."

With my minimal help, Mrs. Alexander stored all the food in plastic containers and stacked them neatly in the refrigerator. She handed me a cold bottle of root-beer and sat down at the kitchen table. She motioned for me to join her.

"I'm not going back out there yet," she said with a sigh. "It's too hot." She took a long drink from her bottle. "You seem a little quiet. I hope you aren't still feeling uncomfortable around us." Jerica smiled reassuringly. "Did you have any questions about what Abe and I told you the other day?"

"Yes, actually, I have a ton of questions, but most of them are stupid. I just don't want you to get in trouble for telling me so much about yourselves." I hated the idea that these people I was coming to care about could get in trouble on my account.

"Don't worry, Alisa. We told you about ourselves because we believe we can trust you. I have a good feeling about you, and in my family, that means something."

"Bryce doesn't trust me," I said before I could stop myself.

"Bryce has a hard time trusting people. He's never had many friends. His heritage means a lot to him, and he finds it very difficult to mix with non-magical people." Jerica looked troubled. "Abe and I worry about him. Are you sure you don't have any questions I can answer?"

Yes, but I didn't want to push my luck. Instead, I said, "No. Thanks for everything today."

"I'm glad you came. I've enjoyed having you." Jerica stood up from the table. "Let's head back outside. The boys will start looking for us soon, and I'm afraid if they come into the kitchen, it will start the feeding frenzy all over again."

Mosquitoes were out in full force as soon as the sun set. That was my cue to leave. I said my goodbyes and hopped into Bryce's truck. I tried to repress a yawn as we pulled out of the driveway. Jace flipped through every channel on the radio, trying to find the perfect song.

"Hey, Bryce? Can you drive me and Alisa into the city next weekend?" Jace asked. It was the first I'd heard of any plans. Wisely, I kept my mouth shut and waited for the older brother to explode.

"I leave Wednesday." Bryce stared straight ahead at the road. "I guess I should start packing soon."

"And you say I'm the procrastinator," Jace chided his brother.

"Yeah, well, I'm just not looking forward to leaving as much as I did last year. This year's going to be tough." Bryce seemed very serious all of a sudden.

"Can I use your truck after I get my license?" Jace asked.

"No. Tell Alisa to get her license. I'd let her drive my truck before I'd let you," he said. It was the first almost-nice thing he'd ever said about me. I thought about his earlier comment—about how my eyes were really blue. That didn't count as a compliment, though.

I felt mildly disappointed when the truck pulled into my driveway. When Jace opened the truck door, I slid over and hopped out. "Bye Jace. I'll see you at school," I said as I stood in my driveway.

"Nah, I'll probably see you before then. I'll call you tomorrow," Jace said. I felt a shiver go through me. He was calling me tomorrow!

"Bryce," I said, leaning through the open door, "If I don't see you before you leave, have a good trip and be safe."

I pulled my head back out of the truck and straightened up. As I turned to head into my house, Bryce called my name. "Alisa." He motioned for me to come around to the driver's side door.

I quickly walked around to his open window. "It was nice meeting you." He must have seen my look of doubt, because he said, "No, I mean that. Take care of my little brother. And take care of yourself."

"I'll do that. Bye, Bryce." I waved goodbye and scurried to my front door. Take care of Jace? I was hoping he would take care of me.

CHAPTER THREE
RACHEL

When I woke up, I felt off-kilter. Dread pushed at my contentment. I pushed back and for a second, contemplated skipping my morning run. It was the middle of football and cheerleading season and no time to give in to laziness. I knocked my covers aside, threw on shorts, a tank top, my ratty tennis shoes, and pulled my long braids into a lopsided knot at the top of my head. I grabbed my I-pod and sprinted out the door.

The sun was just coming up, but it was already muggy and humid—a typical September in southern Georgia. Good Charlotte's *Dance Floor Anthem* assaulted my eardrums as I broke into a steady run. My breath came more rapidly as I gained speed and left my subdivision. I could already feel sweat running down my back, and couldn't wait to get home and take a shower.

As I turned onto the main road, I felt the spine-tingling prickle which usually signaled someone was watching me. I kept running while scanning my surroundings, my anxiety increasing with every step. I ripped the ear-buds from my ears so I could hear if anyone tried to approach. Without my music, it was too quiet. The sound of my own feet as they pounded the pavement freaked me out.

This route was carefully selected. My mother and I drove it in order to get the exact mileage. I never deviated from this path, but that day I did. Somehow, I knew if I continued, I would run headlong into danger. I turned and retraced my route toward home. The dog at the end of my street suddenly began barking, not a friendly bark, or a *hey-you-came-too-close-to-my-territory* bark, but an ears-laid-back, snarling, growling, *I'll-rip-you-apart* bark. The ferocity of his growls made me miss a step, and I staggered, almost falling.

A snarl came from a different direction, and I looked to my right. A figure darted out from behind the house across the street. I broke into a full-out run until I reached my front door and briefly considered waking my mother and telling her what happened, but what *did* happen? Probably nothing. I quickly showered and got ready for school.

The strange experience left me with a lingering feeling of anxiety as I went through my morning routine. Halfway to school, I realized I'd forgotten to put on my necklace. Without it, I felt naked. My necklace had been passed down through my father's family for generations, and I wore it without fail ever since the day he gave it to me. My father told me it was special and to wear it always, so I hardly ever took it off. If I held the bright blue stone close to my heart, I could feel his presence.

I still felt out of sorts when I arrived at school, and my legs shook slightly as I sat down in my first period class. I nodded politely to Jace as I took my seat. As one of the few African-American girls in my small town, I was intrigued by the handsome, dark-skinned new student. I'd considered approaching him, but was reluctant. Our cheerleading captain, Becky, had already made her interest known, and it was social suicide to get on her bad side. Her cousin, Alisa's friendless existence was proof of that.

"Hey, Jace," Becky called as she flounced into the room. It irritated me the way she flirted with him, but I knew my feelings weren't justified—not in the least. After all, I had a boyfriend and Becky did not. And, although the dogs had been circling since the beginning of the school-year, she'd managed to hold them at bay while pursuing Jace relentlessly.

"I wonder how many points Mrs. Hanks deducts for a late assignment?" I heard Jace ask.

"Ten each day," I replied. He turned around and looked at me. I wondered why he seemed so startled that I'd answered his question. A warm shiver ran through me as our eyes met. I felt a spark of connection, which surprised me.

I'd never forged a real bond with anyone and had always felt vastly different from everyone around me. For years, I felt like I was waiting for something, or someone, to come along, for a spark to ignite the flame inside me that had been extinguished when my father died. That quick, brief connection with Jace made me feel more alive than I ever had.

Unfortunately, I'd been fantasizing about Jace since the beginning of the school year, but tried to suppress my desires. Each time I found myself thinking about him, I gave myself a sharp mental slap. Junior year was critical, and I couldn't afford to succumb to the inevitable drama which would result if I dumped my long-time boyfriend to hook-up with this new guy. As far as boyfriends went, Robert was safe—no emotional investment there. Jace was…well, a distraction.

Distraction took on a whole new form the moment the room filled up and Mrs. Hanks passed out our Algebra exams. "This class is stupid," a petulant voice whined. I spun to look at Amber, surprised to hear her speaking out loud in the middle of a test. She looked at me quizzically.

"I wonder if Justin is going to ask me out." Sydney's voice drifted into my brain on a raft of despair. I reluctantly turned to look at her, but she stared resolutely at her paper. I glanced around the classroom and it occurred to me that no one else heard these voices. As waves of depression, joy, confusion, and fear crashed over me, I feared I'd lost my mind.

Becky's voice insinuated itself into my head, and with it, an avalanche of hatred and animosity poured into me. "I can't believe Jace is friends with Alisa. I should totally tell him she's a whore. Everyone will back me up; I practically own the people at this school."

My so-called best-friend's thoughts brought my migraine to a crescendo, and as I felt my emotional pain blend with my physical agony, shards of razor-sharp images slashed through my mind. I felt each act of self-absorbed apathy lash a deeper furrow through my conscience: the time Becky spread a rumor about Amber, effectively ending her relationship with a long-time boyfriend; the time I watched while the football players brutally hazed a weaker player because he made a bad play, resulting in the freshman spending a night in the hospital; the dozens of times Becky tormented her shy, socially inept cousin. Each incident shared a common thread: I did nothing to stop it, said nothing, and helped no one.

By the time first period was over, my nervous system was on overload. As I walked down the hall from one class to another, I tried to avoid looking at anyone. Each time I inadvertently made eye contact with someone, a barrage of feelings assaulted me. Everyone seemed to be surrounded in a haze of color. It was almost as if I could see through to the soul of each person.

THE CLAIMING WORDS

Class changes were agony. I kept brushing up against people in the crowded hallway and these brief episodes of physical contact sent waves of love, pain, fear, and shame through me. I could feel the emotions of others in every cell of my body. As the day progressed, I became increasingly overwhelmed. A thin layer of perspiration covered my face, but my arms were cold and goose-bumped. I was either very ill, or having a complete mental breakdown.

I spent lunch period hiding in the bathroom, begging God to help me get through the day. Tears rolled down my cheeks and fell onto my History book. Wiping at the wetness from my cheeks, I vowed to pull myself together and direct my focus on our upcoming quiz. Neither illness nor insanity were valid excuses for letting my grades go down the tubes.

By the time the bell rang to signal the end of the day, I couldn't take it another minute. My head pounded and my whole body hurt. It felt like every muscle and nerve ending was inflamed.

"Hey, baby. Where have you been hiding? I haven't seen you all day." My boyfriend, Robert, stepped in front of me, blocking my escape.

"I'm too sick to stay for practice." I flinched away from his outstretched arms. "I'll call you later."

"Poor, Rachel. I'll tell the coach you're skipping cheerleading practice. Hey, Vanessa," he called as he led me outside, "Can you give her a ride?"

I managed to endure the agonizing journey home. Being in such close quarters with another human being was a brutal assault on my emotions. I felt weak with relief when I let myself into the house.

I swallowed three of my migraine pills and waited for the agony to subside. Then, noticing my necklace on my dresser, I grabbed it and placed in around my neck. The day's horrific events replayed in my mind; the emotional overload created the most agonizing headache I'd ever experienced. I wanted to feel sorry for myself, but couldn't. Guilt overshadowed my self-pity and discomfort. Maybe I deserved to feel the pain of others as punishment for failing to follow my own moral compass for so many years. Although I'd never initiated gossip or cruelty, there were times I'd encouraged Becky by laughing at her jokes, or gasping with mock surprise at each whispered rumor she started.

Looking back on our days of middle-school and Becky's calculated campaign against her cousin, my headache reached another painful crescendo. Flashbacks of Becky's imagined threats cascaded through my mind. Did I really read her thoughts, or was it a hallucination? It didn't matter. Becky would do anything she could to ruin Alisa's friendship with Jace.

After some painful soul-searching, I finally came to the decision that it was time to draw the line with Becky. Popularity wasn't everything and I was ready to face the consequences if she decided to turn on me. Bolstering my courage, I picked up my phone and dialed Becky's number.

"Hey, girl," she chirped into the phone. "Why didn't you come to practice?"

"If you do anything to Alisa, I'll forward those text messages to your mom, and I'll copy everyone," I said through gritted teeth.

"What the hell is wrong with you? What did *I* do?" she snapped.

"What haven't you done? Seriously, I've stood by for ten years and said nothing while you tormented that girl. It's over," I said.

"It's none of your business," she said.

"It is now. One more word to or against your cousin, and the truth will come out. I can't prove everything, but a picture paints a thousand words," I threatened. I didn't need to read her mind to know what she was thinking. The pictures said it all—a drunken fling with Amber's boyfriend memorialized on her cell phone and sent to me as a joke. Becky knew I never deleted anything. Her reign of terror had come to an end, at least where Alisa was concerned. And that—my first act of kindness based on my newly established Empathy—released the hold on my mind. As the pain subsided, I drifted off to my last dreamless sleep.

***

The following day, I had cheerleading practice after school. Robert was the quarterback on the Varsity team and he usually drove me home afterwards. When practice ended, I changed clothes, sat out on the bleachers to wait, and watched the guys run around in the hot sun. I wondered how they kept from passing out from the weight of all those heavy football pads.

Our football field backed up to the thick trees which bordered the west side of town. The longer I sat on the bleachers with my back to the woods, the more I felt like something was watching me. I told myself I was being silly. I'd never been afraid of the woods before; after all, I'd grown up playing in the wooded area behind our house. During the warm summer days of my childhood, my brother and I used to sit on the bank of the creek all day holding a fishing pole. We used to swing on the kudzu vines overhanging some of the taller trees. I'd never felt weird or uncomfortable in those woods before, so I couldn't think of a reason to feel creeped out now. I remembered the strange incident earlier in the week, but put it out of my mind. I needed to get a grip and stop imagining things.

Football practice ended and my feeling of unease grew exponentially with each passing moment. I had an overwhelming urge to put as much distance as possible between myself and the woods. I couldn't stand it anymore. I got up and jogged over to the football field, just in time for Robert to wrap me in a sweaty hug.

"Let me go inside and shower," he said as I squirmed away from him. "You gonna wait out here?"

I cast a quick glance toward the woods and thought I saw movement. "No. I think I'll wait in the gym." I followed him inside, feeling an instant sense of relief.

When we left the gym several minutes later, I thought I saw something in the trees behind the main school building. "Did you see that?" I asked, gesturing toward the back of the school.

"Yeah," my boyfriend said. "I think it was a deer or something."

"Oh, yeah. You're probably right," I agreed. Robert *was* probably right, but I still felt relieved when we were in the car with the doors locked. I felt even better as we drove away. By the time we'd cleared the parking lot, my fears were almost completely forgotten. I ignored the vibrations in the air which surely signaled changes were coming. After all, nothing exciting, good *or* bad ever happened in our town.

***

Robert picked me up Friday night for a party. Katie's parents were out of town, and everyone was supposed to get together for a night of drunken idiocy. I didn't drink, nor did I approve of others doing so, but it was impossible to change things. I made a lot of noise about not wanting to go, but in the end, I bowed to Robert's wishes and allowed myself to be swept along on a wave of peer-pressure.

He tried to kiss me the moment I hopped into his car, but I pushed him away when his lustful thoughts began to pour into my mind. I couldn't bear for him to touch me again, so I tried to stay out of reach by pressing myself as close to the door as possible. It was going to be tough trying not to brush up against anyone at the party. Anxiety made my palms sweat.

"You okay?" Robert asked, noticing my odd behavior.

"Just a little headache," I said. "Mind if I open the window?" Robert pressed the control to lower my window a few inches.

We rode along in silence for the next few minutes. The party was on the other side of town in one of the newer subdivisions. It seemed that practically everyone in our school was there. Well, at least all the jocks, cheerleaders, and the so-called popular kids. Several people called my name the moment we walked in the door, and some football players shouted to Robert. We went our separate ways for a half hour or so, drifting from one group to another and greeting friends. I still felt a little weird from before, but was starting to relax.

I kept searching for Jace in the crowd, wondering if he'd been invited. Becky had been drooling over him for weeks; surely she would have asked him to come. Why did I care so much about whether or not he was going to be there? It's not like we were friends. We'd never really spoken. Becky had already made it clear that he was her conquest, and therefore off-limits. That in itself should have encouraged me to steer clear of Jace. Becky and I may have had a falling out, but I didn't need to antagonize her deliberately.

Still, I couldn't help thinking about Jace and had to force myself to stop craning my neck scanning the crowd. I didn't want to be obvious by asking about him, either, so, I suffered in silence. There was something about Jace I couldn't put my finger on; he was different. He had traveled to or lived in places I had only dreamed of, but that wasn't the only reason why I was drawn to him. There was something about him. Reluctantly, I admitted that when I saw Jace and Alisa together, I was curious about the nature of their relationship and a little jealous.

I decided not to think about him anymore. Unfortunately, my resolve crumbled after about a minute, when I heard someone speak his name. My hearing zoned in on a small cluster of people standing by the kitchen stairs a few feet away from me. I eavesdropped shamelessly.

"I asked Jace to come with me," Becky said, "but he had other plans."

"What about Homecoming?" Katie asked, "Did he ask you yet?"

"Not yet," Becky admitted. "But he will soon."

"Well, what if he doesn't ask you and everyone already has a date?" This question was from Sydney. Bad move. I turned slightly to see the expression on Becky's face.

Becky glared at Sydney. "Well, if that happens, I guess I'll just go with Justin." Sydney's eyes went wide when Becky threatened to steal her boyfriend. "After all, Justin has been after me for two years. You were just the consolation prize—second choice." Becky and Katie giggled as Sydney walked away.

"Why am I here?" I wondered. These weren't really my friends. A friend is someone who loves and supports you no matter what. These girls couldn't wait to rip someone apart. I turned away from the group I was standing with, and went in search of Robert. I didn't want to be anywhere near Becky any longer.

Robert smiled as I approached. When I reached his side, he grabbed me around the waist and kissed the side of my neck. He knew I didn't like public displays of affection, but I decided to let it go just once. I felt guilty about my waning attraction toward him and didn't want to embarrass him in front of his friends by pushing him away. It only took a couple seconds before I wished I had. His close embrace left nothing to the imagination; I felt his strong desire for me and read his intent to act on it on the ride home. No way was I going to do something I didn't want to out of a feeling of obligation or guilt. I disengaged myself discreetly when he became absorbed in conversation with a couple of the other football players by mumbling something about getting a drink.

Stepping outside on the back patio, I called my mother and asked her to pick me up. I took a deep breath to try to calm my churning emotions. I could tell my mother was curious, but she didn't ask why

I was leaving so soon. We had a deal: if I felt uncomfortable in any situation, especially a date, she would pick me up with no questions asked. I knew we would discuss it later, but I was okay with that. I just wanted to get away from there as quickly as possible.

Robert had obviously tired of waiting for my return. He was engaged in what appeared to be a very intimate conversation with a sophomore I didn't know. She seemed to be pitifully enamored by his attentions. When I interrupted them, the girl blushed and lowered her eyes. Robert seemed irritated to see me, but when I told him I didn't feel well and was leaving, he looked relieved.

***

School on Monday was beyond weird. People kept looking at me strangely, and at first I didn't know why. Shelby came up to me after second period with a look of compassion.

"Are you okay?" she asked, pulling me aside.

"I'm fine," I replied. "Why shouldn't I be?"

"Well, I heard about you and Robert." She lowered her voice to a whisper. "I just wanted to say, I think he's a jerk for replacing you so fast. You were the best thing that ever happened to him. I don't trust that Autumn."

Not wanting to humiliate myself, I decided to pretend I knew what she was talking about. Besides, I already had a pretty good idea.

It was lunchtime before I saw my ex-boyfriend. He and the blond sophomore from the party were sitting together at the far end of the cafeteria. They were so close, it was hard to tell where one ended and the other began. Taking a deep breath and clutching my pendant in my fist, I made a beeline for the table where my ex and his new girlfriend sat.

"Hello," I said. I had been standing over them for a good five seconds before they noticed I was there. Robert seemed startled. I wasn't going to make it easy on him, but I also wasn't going to humiliate myself by making a scene.

I stuck my hand out to the blond. "Hi, you must be Autumn," I said in a very controlled voice. "I'm Rachel, Robert's ex-girlfriend."

Autumn was too embarrassed to shake my hand, and Robert

looked comically uncomfortable. He kept opening and closing his mouth until he looked like that singing fish in the McDonalds commercial. "Um, Rachel," he finally managed to stammer, "This isn't, I mean, I…"

I continued speaking as if Robert hadn't said anything. I looked him straight in eyes and said, "Robert and I broke up under mutual agreement and I'm sure we will remain friends." I smiled with my mouth only. "I hope you two will be very happy together."

I turned and walked away, aware that all eyes were on me. I smiled until my face hurt. After buying a soda from the vending machine, I sat down at an empty table. I was grateful for my brown skin: otherwise everyone would be able to see the dark red blush of rage spreading over my face.

"How can you be so calm?" Shelby asked sitting down across from me.

"It's been coming on for a while. It was only a matter of time. No big deal," I lied.

"Are you going to skip Homecoming this year?" she asked.

"Why should I?" It had never crossed my mind that I would be dateless for the dance. Pretty cocky of me, I thought. "What are you wearing to the dance," I asked just to change the subject. Her eyes lit up in response and she spent the next several minutes describing every intricate detail of her dress and accessories. I nodded occasionally and said "nice" or "wow", but I had checked out from the beginning.

The rest of the day was tough, trying to ignore the looks of pity or scorn. It was also difficult to ignore Becky; I knew she was gloating. *This too shall pass*, I thought.

Cheerleading practice was an exercise in agony. We took our practice outside, so we were practically right on the football field. Autumn watched her new man from the sidelines. Becky, the captain of our squad, found fault in everything I did. At one point she asked me why I was having such a hard time concentrating. I apologized, barely resisting the urge to kill her.

The worst part of the day, however, was watching Jace and Alisa walking together after school. I felt a stabbing pain in my chest when I saw him carrying her book bag. Of all the things I had to worry about, why did that bother me so much?

I wasn't the only one disturbed. Becky noticed too, and as she watched them laughing together, her face said it all. Her vicious thoughts poured into me, and I had to fight back nausea. She would destroy her cousin any way she could, but this time, I couldn't stand by and let it happen. This wasn't middle-school anymore and I wasn't the old, passive Rachel.

"What's the matter Becky?" I asked, breaking into her thoughts, "Having trouble concentrating?" I smiled and stared her down.

Jace captured my attention once again, and I watched while he and Alisa walked toward the field behind our school. A beam of sunlight shot through the cloud cover and illuminated his tall form for a fraction of a second. And, although I hated Becky for her willingness to hurt anyone who got in her way, I couldn't help but wonder if I could do the same. Would I be willing to trample over Alisa to get to Jace? I shivered imagining myself in his arms, and thought I might be willing to do almost anything to make that happen.

***

My extra-sensory abilities, my being able to hear people's thoughts and feel their emotions hung on. I feared I'd never be the same again. I was learning the hard way that the only way I could avoid an avalanche of emotions was to avoid close contact with people. This would not be easy at the Homecoming Dance. I didn't want to go, but I didn't want people to think I was at home crying over Robert.

I met my last-minute pseudo-date, Alex, outside the school. One by one, couples entered the gym until it was noisy and crowded. I glanced at the door just in time to see the last couple enter. I wasn't the only person gaping in surprise; Alisa was nearly unrecognizable. Her pixie-like, black hair was glossy, her blue eyes bright, and she stood straight and confident. She managed to make half the girls in the gym look overdressed and silly, and the other half dreary and boring.

Jace certainly brought out the best in her. I felt a touch of envy. Alisa was completely different with him. I decided to go talk to them. I told myself I just wanted to compliment Alisa on her dress, but in truth, I wanted to be near Jace. I wanted to find out if he was in love with her, or if they were just friends. I wanted to know if I had a chance, and I knew a way to find out.

I left my date with a group of football players and wandered over to the other side of the gym. Jace and Alisa were standing together, deep in conversation. "Alisa, your dress is gorgeous. I love it," I interrupted.

"Thanks, Rachel. You look great." Alisa seemed a little nervous, but she managed to look me in the eye.

"You both look beautiful," Jace said. We watched the few couples who were already out on the dance floor, then Jace said, "I'm going to teach Alisa how to dance." She punched him playfully and he laughed.

"You'd better save me a dance, Rachel." Jace didn't have to say anything at all; he could charm your dress off without ever opening his mouth.

You bet I will, I thought, as they walked away. I danced a few times with Alex and some other guys, but all the while my mind was on Jace. I felt like a conniving witch because of what I had planned—to use my extra-sensory skills to pick through his brain while we danced. I knew it was underhanded and sneaky, but I was desperate. I never would have thought in a million years I would feel desperation toward any man. I had always been a very independent person, and had never suffered the love-sick ailments that had afflicted all of my friends at one time or another.

Each time someone new asked me to dance, I felt impatient and resentful. I didn't want to be stuck with someone else when Jace eventually remembered his promise to dance with me, so I decided to hang out by the refreshment table and skip the next few dances. I almost melted when Jace caught my eye and moved toward me.

I felt anxious. This was probably the first time I'd ever understood what someone meant when they claimed to have butterflies in their stomach. I dragged my eyes away from his and looked down at the ground, trying to compose myself. Suddenly, he was standing in front of me, his hand outstretched.

Hesitating only a fraction of a second, I stepped toward him. He grabbed my hand and pulled me to the center of the gym in one quick motion. A slow song began playing and he pulled me close.

I read those trashy romance novels from time to time. It was my one indulgence, one I'd never admitted to anyone. When the lead female character and the lead male character touch or kiss for the first time, there's always an 'instant connection' or a 'jolt of electricity', or in the really cheesy stories, a feeling of 'coming home.' If I used any of these tired descriptions to explain what happened between the two of us, it would be a gross understatement.

The instant his hand touched the small of my back and I looked into his eyes, his smile faded. Our eyes locked and my breathing stopped. The gym, the music, the laughter, everything was gone in that instant. It was only the two of us and the beating of our hearts. I could feel a sort of rushing in my head, but my awareness stopped there. Unspoken words passed between us on pulsating waves of emotions.

"Who are you?" I asked him in my mind. "What *are* you?"

"You're one of us," he answered, a whisper in my mind. "We've been looking for you."

"I'm here. I've been waiting. This is what I've been waiting for."

Jace's voice moved through me again, a soft caress inside my mind. "Release me, Rachel."

"What?"

"Release me. Pull back before other people notice. We can't let others know what we are." Jace's thoughts were probing and insistent in my brain.

"I don't understand." Suddenly, I felt a jolt. Not an electric jolt of passion like in the romance novels, but a clumsy nudge from a fellow student.

Jace led me to the bleachers and sat down, motioning for me to sit next to him. I could tell he was stunned. His easy smile was gone and his eyes were troubled. He started to speak, but stopped when he saw Alex moving toward us.

"Hey, there you are," Alex said, sitting down on the other side of me. "Me and some other guys are going out after the dance. You wanna come?"

I glanced over my shoulder to look at Jace, but he was already gone, moving through groups of students toward the other side of the gym. Probably looking for Alisa. It seemed my bizarre line of communication had startled both of us. Jace obviously had some power of his own. Instead of getting the answers I desired, I ended up with nothing but questions.

Almost by instinct, my hand reached up to touch my necklace, but stopped before touching my throat. I'd decided to leave it behind that evening. Why did strange things always happen when I forgot to put on my pendant?

Turning my attention back to Alex, I answered, "Sure, why not?" Tonight, I decided, I would go with the crowd one last time. I would pretend to be a regular teenager without worries. Deep in my soul, I now possessed the knowledge things would never be the same because I was not who I thought I was.

CHAPTER FOUR
ALISA

The first part of the evening was like a fairy tale. My mother helped me select my dress weeks before and we paid a small fortune for it. The way Jace looked at me when he picked me up was justification for the expense; my dress was worth every penny. I submitted to my mother's pampering, polishing, and painting, and in the end, I looked just like one of the models in the fashion magazines, only happier and less hungry.

By the time we walked into the gym, I didn't feel like myself at all. Many of my classmates showered me with compliments, and it was the first time I didn't feel like a complete misfit. For some inexplicable reason, Becky had decided to leave me alone as of late. Her lack of open animosity combined with Jace's friendship, pulled me from the abyss of high school hell. I now skipped along the path toward relative social tolerance.

Draped across Jace's arm, I stood taller and possessed a confidence I hadn't felt since I was six years old and learned to ride a bike on my own. I literally couldn't feel my feet touch the ground when Jace and I twirled around the stained and scuffed gym floor. It was magic.

Jace spun me around and asked, "So, why haven't you ever been to one of the Homecoming dances?"

"No one ever asked me. Jace, you know how it is for me," I commented.

"Yes, but I don't see why," he said. "I can't believe none of the guys here ever asked you out."

"Why? Look at me," I said whirling away from him.

He reached out and pulled me back toward him. "I am looking at you. And I see a beautiful girl." I blushed and looked away. "Can I ask you something?" The song ended before I could respond.

When a sophomore came up and asked me to dance, Jace disappeared. The kid I danced with was almost as short as I was. I tried to hide my irritation that he'd distracted Jace before he could ask his question. I craned my neck, searching for my date in the crowd, then finally gave up and enjoyed dancing with the young boy who kept looking at my chest.

I finally spotted Jace with Rachel. She was breathtakingly beautiful with her deep caramel skin and delicate features. Her ebony hair, released from its usual braids, was piled high, revealing her graceful neck. I felt short, squat, and hideous in comparison. The second Jace pulled her close, I knew he was lost to me.

Standing in a daze on one side of the gym, I watched the entire dance. After Jace left Rachel on the bleachers, he joined my side, put his arm around my waist, and led me to the entrance into the school. As soon as we were safe within the privacy of the school hallway, he released his hold on me.

"Rachel is the one we've been looking for. She's strong, so much stronger than she should be. It's dangerous for her," he insisted.

I stood quietly, watching him. I willed myself not to cry because I was afraid of what his next words would be.

"Something happened between us. She was inside my head and I was inside hers." Jace seemed to be searching for the right words.

"I'll have to talk to my parents about it, but I don't want to do it now. I know that sounds irresponsible and selfish, but I just want to have fun tonight. There will be plenty of time later for my parents to give me the third degree," Jace said. "You wanna leave and go get something to eat?"

"Okay." Avoidance was my favorite way to deal with unpleasant topics, so I was thrilled to discover Jace was a hard-core procrastinator as well. Like he said, there would be plenty of time to worry about it later.

After Jace dropped me off at home, my mother brutally forced me to describe in detail everything that happened at the dance. Obviously, I decided to omit mention of the Jace/Rachel incident. I tried to impress upon her the fact that Jace and I were only friends, but she was too busy planning our wedding in her head to actually listen to me. I finally gave up and went to bed.

I fervently prayed things would stay the same between me and Jace. Our friendship was precious to me and I knew once Jace spoke to his parents about Rachel, they would want to meet her. She was the one his family was looking for: the Innocent, the special one, the one who would take my place in their hearts. The agony of knowing I would once again be standing in the shadows alone and ignored was more than I could take.

Prior to our friendship, I never thought about myself as a real person. I was just an extra on the movie set of my own life; I didn't even have a speaking part. Jace made me feel special. I was afraid Rachel would dilute our friendship once she was thrown into the mix.

Jace called me nearly every day; it had been that way for a few weeks. We saw each other after school most days and on weekends. I could talk to him about everything. He knew about my lack of friends, the fact that I had never had a boyfriend, that I'd never been kissed, and that I dreamed of one day becoming a writer. He knew my hopes and dreams and encouraged me to go after what I wanted.

We spent hours talking—at his house, on the phone, or just driving around. He told me about how hard it was when his brother died and about his strained relationship with Bryce. He even told me about his fears and self-doubt. Jace was often afraid he wouldn't live up to his parents' expectations.

When I woke up the morning after the Homecoming Dance, I worried our relationship would change irreparably. Would he call me, or would he talk to his parents first and leave me in the dark? All my fears were scattered when my phone rang. The first words out of Jace's mouth were, "Hey, my family is playing tennis in a couple hours and I need a partner. Can you play?"

I almost fainted with relief. Things were still normal, it seemed. "Yeah, I can come. I'm not doing anything today," I replied.

"That's not what I asked. Can you play? Are you any good?" Jace laughed, "I bet my dad a day of yard work that I could beat him in tennis. He said he wouldn't play without his partner—Mom. That's because she's better than him. He knows he can't beat me alone. So, can you?"

"I'm okay. I haven't played in a while, but I'm pretty good. My backhand sucks, though." I was excited. The weather was cool— only in the seventies. I was anxious to get outside, but more importantly, anxious to nurture my close relationship with Jace.

"I'll pick up the slack," Jace offered. "I'll pick you up at 3:00. Bye."

THE CLAIMING WORDS

After our high-stakes tennis tournament, we headed back to his house for dinner. Jace was flying high on adrenaline. It was his first time beating his parents at tennis, and he was already making complicated workout and training schedules for the two of us. His next goal: beat the dreaded Bryce/Jerica combination.

"We do need to discuss your training schedule, and I'm not talking about tennis," Jerica said with a frown. "Jace, it's time to step it up."

"I know, Mom," Jace agreed. "I realized after last night I have some things to work on. I was waiting for the right time to talk to you."

"What's going on?" Abe asked.

"I'm not inattentive. I swear I honestly never picked up on anything before. But last night at the dance…" Jace paused, thinking. "It was crazy. I danced with her and then…it happened."

"What happened? Tell us everything." Abe leaned forward, and I could tell he was committing everything Jace said to memory.

"I asked Rachel to dance, and as soon as I grabbed a hold of her, she was inside my head." His parents looked expectant, but slightly worried.

"She began sifting through my brain, searching. I tried to protect my magic, but that's not what she was after. I think she was just experimenting. She doesn't even know what I am, or who she is," he explained. "The connection surprised us both. She didn't realize anyone else had the ability she had. She had a very strong link; I couldn't break it on my own. Finally some guy bumped into her and broke her concentration. That's about it. I didn't really talk to her after that."

"What do you mean you didn't talk to her after that?" Abe asked, narrowing his eyes.

"Well, you know. Her date came over and started talking, so I just left her with him," Jace explained.

"Oh, honey," Jerica said, shaking her head. "She is going to need protection now more than ever. You left her alone? And, without explaining anything to her?"

"What was I supposed to do? Drag her away and tell her she's a Witch? She would have thought I was joking or crazy or both," Jace said defensively. "I mean, you can't just tell someone that and expect them to believe you right away."

"Well, I'm worried about her," Jerica said. "She needs our help. We need to invite her over and explain everything to her. She has a gift and she needs to be aware she is vulnerable."

Abe looked at me and asked, "Alisa, how well do you know Rachel?"

"I've known her since kindergarten, but we're not exactly close," I admitted.

"We may need your help in getting her over here. It might even help if you are with us when we talk to her. She's known you longer than Jace, and she will be more likely to believe what we're saying if she sees a familiar face. Do you mind?" Abe asked.

"I'll help anyway I can," I offered. I felt like a fraud. The Alexanders probably thought I was so helpful and kind, but in reality, my motives were completely selfish. I wanted to be there, but not just to help them. The idea of being excluded was worse than anything I could imagine. As strange as it sounds, I felt by being there, I could control what happened—prevent Jace and Rachel from getting too close. Insecurity does horrible things to a person.

I zoned out while the Alexanders continued to talk and make plans. I wallowed in my own worried thoughts. What would happen to Rachel if she didn't accept she was a Witch? What if she refused protection and training? I didn't want anything bad to happen to her. What I told Jerica and Abe was true; we weren't close. She'd never been nice to me, but I didn't want to see something bad happen to her.

"Hey, do want you to watch a movie before I take you home? If we have time, that is." Jace said while we washed dishes. "Why do you always volunteer me for kitchen duty?"

"Because your mom slaved over a hot stove to feed you. The least we can do is wash the dishes. And, no, we don't have time to watch a movie. I have to be home soon," I said, handing him a soapy cup to rinse. "Don't you know any magic spells to speed this up?"

"Do you really want me to try?" He pointed one finger toward the pile of dirty dishes on the counter. A large crack split one dish into two pieces. I tried not to laugh as he tossed it in the garbage can.

"Impressive. You know, I used to think being a Witch would be somewhat glamorous, but that was before you set the patio furniture on fire. If your mom wasn't there to put it out..." I trailed off as Jace splashed me with warm, soapy water. I giggled and tried to duck away from him, but he grabbed my wrist and pulled me close.

"Knock it off, you two," Jerica said, coming into the kitchen. I blushed under her close scrutiny. She didn't seem happy to see us standing so close together, but perhaps it was the huge puddle on the floor which made her frown. Or, maybe she knew about the broken dish. Whatever the case, I stammered an apology and took a couple of steps away from her son.

On the drive home, I kept thinking about the look on Jerica's face. Years of sitting on the sidelines, watching my peers interact from afar, had left me with an ability to interpret emotions fairly accurately. Jerica didn't want to see me and Jace together, at least not in a romantic sense.

"Do Witches always marry Witches?" I blurted before I could help myself.

"No. Well, yes. I think," he replied. "Actually, I don't know any Witches who married a human. But, I don't think there's a law against it. Why?"

I could have kicked myself for asking such a question. I didn't want Jace to think I'd been scamming on him. After all, he'd never shown any interest in me as anything other than a friend. I tried to formulate a careful response. "I don't know. Just wondering. If Rachel has magic, she had to have gotten it from somewhere. What if one parent is a Witch and the other isn't? It's possible, right?"

"Maybe. So, who's gonna ask her to come over for dinner?" he asked as he turned onto my street. Tires squealed as he took the turn a bit too sharply. The bottom of the car scraped against the bump going up into my driveway. I almost laughed remembering his brother's declaration that he'd rather let me drive his truck than to allow Jace to get behind the wheel. The Georgia State driving test apparently wasn't very difficult if Jace had been given a license.

"You. It's your house—you ask," I said.

"But, what if she gets the wrong idea?"

I breathed a sigh of relief. Wrong idea? That must mean he wasn't interested in her. At least, that's what I hoped. "That's a chance you'll have to take. I'll see you tomorrow?" I asked, hopping out of the car.

"Bright and early. Goodnight, Alisa. Sweet dreams," he said, flashing a crooked smile. I knew what I'd be dreaming about that night. I chewed my bottom lip as I thought about the tentative plans for dinner at his house the next day. Hopefully, Rachel would be joining us. Well, the Alexanders were hoping; I was ambivalent.

CHAPTER FIVE
RACHEL

I was completely shocked when Jace asked me to come to his house for dinner. Usually, people go out a few times before parents are thrown into the equation. As soon as I knocked on Jace's door, I realized my mistake. Jace wasn't asking me out. Hooking up with him may not have been on the horizon at all. I barely concealed my shock and confusion when Jace opened the door and I saw Alisa standing behind him. I was still reeling when he introduced me to his parents.

Jace's mother invited me to have a seat in the living room and offered me a cold drink. When she stepped into the kitchen, I looked around the beautifully decorated room with admiration. To my displeasure, I noticed Alisa seemed completely comfortable here. It was obvious she was a frequent visitor.

"Rachel, we're so glad to have you," Mrs. Alexander said as she came back into the living room, a glass of iced tea in hand. I made awkward small talk with Jace while his mother finished making dinner. When they led me into the kitchen, I felt strange and uncomfortable. Conversation was kept light throughout dinner. I appreciated that Mr. and Mrs. Alexander did not ask the obvious questions about school and the dance, although I suspected they had a hidden agenda. I could not image what.

Abe, Jace, and I chatted for a few minutes while Jerica and Alisa cleared the table and prepared dessert. I liked Mr. Alexander—Abe. He was intelligent with a great sense of humor. I could see a lot of him in Jace. After meeting Jace's family and hearing stories about some of their travels, it was hard to imagine them willingly moving to this town. Oaktree was not exactly a bustling hub of culture.

Mrs. Alexander surprised me by sitting down, looking directly at me, and getting right to the point. "Rachel, I'll bet you're curious about why we invited you here for dinner," she said.

Yes, as matter of fact, I was beginning to wonder.

Jerica continued, "I'm not one to beat around the bush, and you seem like a pretty straightforward young woman, so I'm just going to put it out there. Jace told me about what happened at the dance." This declaration kicked off a sharp pounding in my head. Too bad my abilities didn't extend to seeing the future, then I wouldn't have been caught off guard.

"Everyone in our family has special skills of some sort, Jace included. Abe and I try to help people like you who are just beginning to tap into their abilities. Without exception, everyone we've tried to help has been frightened by their newfound talent. You seem to have a handle on your gift, which is rare for someone with a psychic ability so strong, but I suspect you may still benefit from some guidance."

I could have denied it. I could have stormed out and never spoken to them again. But, I took a deep breath and said, "I don't think I really need help with it. At first, it was overwhelming and distracting. Now I can tune it out, sort of like the way you don't notice the sound of crickets or cicadas unless you focus in on it. But it's always there."

"So, the incident at the dance wasn't the first time you'd experienced something like this? Can you tell us about the first time it happened?" Jerica asked.

I gave her a quick summary: my feelings of being watched, my increasing awareness of the thoughts and feelings of others. All eyes were on me as I spoke, and I found myself beginning to fidget under their close scrutiny. I nervously twisted the chain on my necklace, and when my fingertips touched the pendant, a comforting pulse of energy rushed through me. I took a deep breath, sat up straighter, and lowered my hands back to the table in front of me. Jerica's eyes settled on my necklace.

"What a beautiful pendant," she said. "May I see it?" I held it up, but she didn't lean forward to look more closely. I suspected she meant for me to take it off. Everything in me rebelled at the idea of handing it over, but I'd always been told to respect my elders, so I unfastened the chain. I felt a familiar jolt as my hand brushed against hers, followed by her sense of astonishment.

"Lapis lazuli," she murmured. She turned the stone over and peered closely from every angle, even holding it up to the light.

Finally, she held the necklace tightly in her fist and closed her eyes. "This necklace is charmed," she exclaimed with wonder. "I'm very curious about its origin."

"My father gave it to me before he died. He said it had been passed down from generation to generation. He said..." I trailed off, embarrassed. I didn't want to finish my sentence, but four faces peered at me expectantly, waiting for me to finish. "He said it would keep my migraines away. He told me to wear it always. He died shortly after, and I've worn it every day for the past five years. Well, until recently. Actually, the first day I experienced my...problem, I'd accidentally left it behind." I felt stupid saying this to a room full of virtual strangers. I'd never told anyone why my father gave me the necklace.

"Rachel, I'm sorry about your father," Abe said. I gave a little nod. "Can you tell us a little about your family?"

"My mother's family is from around here. I don't know anything about my father's side of the family. His parents were deceased before he met my mother." Recently, I'd begun to regret never pressing him for more information about his family, but I was only eleven when he died, and most kids that age just didn't think about that sort of thing. I had always been surrounded by family, so I'd never felt like anything was missing. Not until now.

"Rachel, I don't want to push, but I'm very interested in the origin of this necklace. I'd like to find out more about your heritage. If you don't feel comfortable asking your mother, would you object to me trying to find out more on my own?" I could tell this was important to him. It was important to me too. Not because of the necklace, but because I wanted to find out if I had any other family.

"What type of research are you suggesting?" I wasn't objecting, just curious about the methods. My father led a pretty boring life; there wouldn't be any dirt to dig up, no skeletons hidden in the closet.

"All I need from you is his full name, date of birth, and the date your parents married. From there, I would check out his birth certificate and those of his parents. It's all public information. Basically, I'll put together a family tree and then go from there," Abe explained. "I'll keep you posted every step of the way, and if at any point you want me to stop looking, I will. Would you like for me to get started on this?"

I was thrilled at the prospect of having a complete family tree of my paternal ancestors. I felt closer to my father already. "Yes, I'd like that."

Jerica handed my necklace back to me and said, "Rachel, I think it's important for you to keep wearing this, at least for the time being. I believe your father gave it to you for protection and to hide your abilities from others. Unfortunately, this type of protection doesn't last forever—just until the person wearing it is old enough to learn to protect themselves. Would you be willing to let me help you with this?" Jerica asked carefully. "I can help you gain greater control over your gift. I can also help you discover if there are more of these surprises in store for you."

"What kind of surprises?" I asked.

"I'm not sure. I think you've learned from experience magical abilities can come out of nowhere with no warning. It's better to be introduced to your newfound powers in a controlled environment." Jerica glanced at Abe as she said this.

"Magic?" I whispered, "Are you sure that's what this is? Is that what you have?"

"Magic has been passed down from generation to generation in our family," Abe explained. "It's nothing bad or shameful. We're born this way, just like some people are natural born athletes or musicians."

"I don't know," I said, backpedaling. "I don't think I have any magic. I'm just extra sensitive to feelings right now. It's just a phase." Anxiety made my chest feel tight. I looked around the room at these seemingly normal people. "Does Alisa have magic too?" I wondered if that was the thread that tied her to this family.

"No, Rachel," Alisa said. "I don't. But I've seen enough to believe in it and to know it's not bad."

"Can I think this over?" I asked, anxious to escape this barrage of insanity.

"Of course," Jerica said, her green eyes holding mine in a penetrating stare. "But I need to warn you. Now that your magic has come to the surface, there are people and other beings who will try to steal it. Wear your necklace always. Never take it off. It's your only protection right now."

THE CLAIMING WORDS

Fear tore through me, raising goose bumps on my arms. I remembered all the times I'd felt like I was being watched. Now, I knew these incidents were not figments of my imagination.

"Rachel," Jerica said, leaning toward me. "We can assign a Protector to keep you safe..."

"What? You mean, like, a guard?" I stammered.

"Something like that. It's the best way to ensure your safety," she said.

"No. That's...no," I said shaking my head. I was finished—done. The conversation was over. I'd never allow someone to follow me around everywhere I went. It didn't matter anyways, because it was all a big mistake.

Jerica reached over and grasped my hand. I didn't know if she was just trying to reassure me, or if she was giving me a chance to read her. I allowed her aura to flow through me, her feelings becoming my own. I could feel her concern and fear, her regret at having to frighten me, and her determination to protect me at all costs. Not only was this something she'd done before, protecting others like myself, it was her life calling. In the instant before I released her hand, I caught one word she passed unintentionally. Witch.

Oh, dear God, I prayed. Is that what I am? What *we* are? I'd always known I was different, but I thought it was a good thing. I believed what set me apart was my drive and determination to leave this town and achieve my goals. I was wrong. I was abnormal, an abomination, a freak. Just the word 'Witch' set off a series of warning bells inside my brain. Not only was I someone I no longer recognized, I was someone I could never like. I murmured my appreciation for dinner, apologized for having to leave so suddenly, and fled.

***

For the first time in my life, I woke up and considered skipping school. That in itself was an indication my life was falling apart, crumbling away. I felt like I had nothing to hold on to or to keep me together. My mother had always tried to instill a sense of confidence and independence in Jeffrey and me. She told me I was a strong, intelligent young woman. I believed her when she told me I could do anything I wanted. And, I believed her when she told me I was good person. Now, I wasn't sure. My family was very religious. Our church believed magic was evil. Did the part of me that was a Witch make me bad? Evil?

I crawled out of bed and got ready for school. I was already seated in first period when Jace and Alisa arrived. Thankfully, some students entered right behind them, so Jace didn't have time to approach me. I could tell he wanted to say something, but I wasn't ready to talk to him yet. My attention kept drifting back to Jace, his family, and how I fit in with them. I couldn't help but feel my life was now intertwined with theirs.

As class progressed, I kept sneaking looks at Jace. How could he seem so focused on the mundane activities of school? School had never been further from my mind. Somehow, I made it through the day. Would every day be like this from now on? Waiting for something to happen? As I drove home after school, I could feel another migraine coming on. So much for the magical protection of my necklace.

When I arrived in first period Algebra the next day, I was surprised to see Jace sitting alone. I hesitated in the doorway, then stepped inside.

"She's sick," Jace said in response to my unasked question.

"How did you know I was going to ask you that?" I placed my books on my desk, and sat down.

"You *did* ask me that," he said, closing the book in front of him and looking at me.

"No I didn't," I argued.

"Maybe I read your mind," he said in a lowered voice. I glanced at the classroom door to make sure there was no one to bear witness to our conversation. "Do you want to try it again?"

"No," I said. "I don't believe in…that stuff."

"That's too bad. Magic can be fun, you know." He winked at me and reached his hand toward the chalkboard. The eraser flew toward him and smacked him in the forehead. He reached up to brush the rectangular patch of white dust from his face.

"You're right, Jace. That was fun," I said, laughing.

"Okay, so that wasn't a good example. Remember yesterday when Mrs. Hanks couldn't find her briefcase, so we got out of taking our tests?" he asked. I nodded. "You have *me* to thank for that. I wonder if Mr. Kendall discovered her briefcase in his refrigerator, or if it's still in there."

"The refrigerator? With the *frogs*? But, how did you get it in there? That cabinet is locked."

"Magic can be fun *and* useful," he said. I couldn't help but feel a bit irritated by his admission. After all, I'd been up late studying for that test.

"Are you supposed to use your magic to play practical jokes?" I asked, lowering my voice. "Isn't that unethical?"

"Only if my parents find out." He chuckled softly, then pulled a sheet of notebook paper from his folder. He scrawled a few quick numbers across the paper and handed it to me. "My mom wanted you to have her phone number just in case."

"Thanks," I said reaching out to take it. My hand brushed against his and I felt a familiar jolt. Our eyes collided, and my breath came in shallow gasps. I wrenched my gaze away. I tore a sheet from my notebook, wrote down my cell phone number, and passed it to him. "Just in case," I said.

I thought about Jace all day—more than I should have. Consequently, I had way more homework than I was accustomed to. After cheerleading practice, I did my chores and went up to my room to study. My phone beeped several times while I finished my homework, but I ignored it. I reached for it as I closed my math book, and scrolled unenthusiastically through my text messages. There was a text from Alex asking me to go to a movie on Friday. We had a decent time at the dance, but I didn't want to lead him on. There would never be anything between us but friendship.

The next message was from a number I didn't recognize. As I read it, my heart began to beat double-time. *Call me. I'd like to see you—Jace.* I read the message three more times, just in case I read it wrong the first time, or in case there was some special hidden meaning I'd missed.

Praying he wasn't inviting me to another family meeting with Alisa, I dialed the number with shaking hands. He answered after the second ring and his deep voice sent chills through my body. "Rachel," he said.

"Jace." I planned to make him do the talking. Not because I was playing games, but because my voice trembled along with the rest of my body. I figured the less I said, the better.

"Hey, I just wanted to go for a ride over to Lakeview later. I heard they have a Dairy Queen and I'm craving bad. You want to come?" Jace sounded casual. I tried to do the same.

"That's kind of far. When do you want to leave?" I wanted to ask if anyone else was going, namely Alisa.

"Any time. The sooner the better. What do you say?" Jace asked.

"My car or yours?" I would find out soon enough if Alisa was coming, I guessed.

"Mine. I'll pick you up in a few."

I hung up the phone and sprinted to my dresser mirror to check out my appearance. My hair definitely needed some work and so did my make-up. My clothes were rumpled from lying on my bed. I raced around the room, trying to throw together an outfit that was cute but casual. I heard a car door slam outside my window just as I was applying a final coat of mascara. I forced myself to take a few deep, calming breaths before grabbing my purse and walking slowly down the stairs.

My mother opened the door and invited Jace inside just as I reached the foyer. I was relieved to see he was alone. My stomach knotted with anxiety as I waited to see how he interacted with her.

"I'm Jace Alexander," he said in a clear, confident voice while looking my mother directly in the eye. She would appreciate the fact that he came to the door and introduced himself. "It's nice to meet you, Mrs. Stevens."

"Well, come on in, Jace," she said, stepping aside to allow him entry. "Have a seat in the living room so we can talk a minute."

"Thank you, ma'am." He followed her inside. Good. It would be the kiss of death to any potential relationship if he tried to rush me out the door. His eyes fell upon me and he smiled.

Jace endured my mother's interrogation for a solid fifteen minutes. If he was anxious to leave, he never let it show. I could tell she was impressed by his obvious intelligence and good breeding. He answered every question she asked, and never resorted to one-word answers or the uncomfortable mumbling which was the calling card of many teenage boys.

Once we escaped her intrusive clutches, he walked me to his car and opened the door for me like a gentleman. Was this a date? I hoped so. If he immediately started in on a lecture about magic or learning to control my powers, I would be so disappointed I would die.

He didn't bring it up once, to my immense relief. The twenty-minute drive was a blur. I was so absorbed in our conversation, I felt slightly disoriented when he pulled the car into the parking lot of Dairy Queen and turned off the ignition.

We sat outside on a picnic bench long after our sundaes were consumed. Before I knew what was happening, he held my hand in his across the table. I felt that familiar jolt of emotion when we touched, but it felt manageable instead of all-encompassing like the night we danced. Either I was able to filter the wave of emotion, or I was becoming used to it. A light buzz of energy connected us and it felt pleasant, comfortable.

"I should get you home," Jace said, brushing his thumb lightly across my knuckles. I was amazed to find the sun had already set. We must have been there for hours. "I want to stay on good terms with your mother if we're going to be dating."

Seriously? We were dating? I tried to maintain my outward composure, but my heart was doing a happy dance. Any doubts I'd harbored earlier in the evening had fled.

Reluctantly, I pulled my hand from his, feeling a sense of overwhelming loss. We walked back to his car in silence. Jace occasionally reached over and touched my hand on the drive home. A feeling of emptiness descended upon me as he pulled the car into my driveway. I felt protected as he placed his hand gently on the small of my back while walking me to my front door. I already loved him. There would be no turning back after that night, whether he felt the same or not.

Sleep was elusive that night. For the first time in my life, I was in love, and that scared me. I didn't like the feeling of falling, of vulnerability. If Jace held my heart in his hands, I wasn't fully in control of my own life. The idea was deeply disturbing. One thing was certain: Jace and I were bound together by magic, by love.

CHAPTER SIX
ALISA

Jace and I needed to have a serious talk. I'd put it off long enough. It was time to discuss what I secretly referred to as The Rachel Issue. I knew something was going on between them. It wasn't like he spent a lot less time with me, just that when we did spend time together, I felt like he wanted to be somewhere else. Or, more to the point, I felt like he wanted to be with someone else.

I saw the way they looked at each other in class. I may not have been a Witch, but I wasn't a complete moron. I could feel their connection. Not just with my senses, either. Their connection was so solid, so strong, you could almost touch it. How could he think I wouldn't notice?

Maybe Jace was a coward. Many teenage boys are. They don't know how to gently break a girl's heart. Perhaps Jace suspected I had feelings for him that were beyond friendship, and he didn't know how to tell me he could never return those feelings.

Every thought, every dream, every fantasy revolved around Jace. Each night, I drifted off to sleep with a picture of his face in my mind. In my favorite fantasy, he would finally discover he had loved me all along. In my vague and disconnected dreams, Jace and I walked together, but I was always a step behind. I could never quite catch up, never quite touch him. It was always another who would reach for me, but his face was hidden in the fog.

With the holidays fast approaching, I knew what I wanted for Christmas. I wanted to know Jace would always be there for me. I didn't want to lose our friendship, and if friendship was all he could offer, I would accept that as long as he would still be a part of my life. It wasn't just Jace I was worried about losing, it was his family. Abe and Jerica meant more to me than I could have ever anticipated. I couldn't imagine not being part of their lives.

Whatever the case, it was time to clear the air. I had already come to terms with the fact that I'd lost Jace. Well, I was willing to work on it, anyways. My anger toward him was beginning to manifest in my increased competitiveness in tennis and my waspish comments every time we spoke. Our sparring sessions with Abe gave me a much-needed outlet for my anger. I almost looked forward to these training sessions, but not quite.

The training sessions had been going on for a few weeks, and came about around the same time Jace started seeing Rachel. "You're part of our family now," Jerica told me. "You're like a daughter to me. I just want to know you're safe. I think you should begin training."

"Why?" I asked Jerica, my heart pounding in my chest. For a brief moment, I felt a spark of hope that perhaps there existed some latent magic in myself. I so wanted to be special, to have a link to this family that was indisputable. "What type of training?"

"Abe teaches Jace a type of mixed martial arts. It's more intense and athletic than anything you would find in a Tae Kwon Do studio. For example, the emphasis is on disabling and killing your opponent using anything you can find, including weapons, magic, or your bare hands." Jerica must have seen the shadow that passed over my expression when she mentioned the words "intense" and "athletic". It wasn't that I was completely opposed to athletic endeavors. I was sort of like a dog; I would chase a ball anywhere. I would run all day long playing tennis, but no way would I exercise just for the sake of exercise.

Jerica smiled, "Come on, Alisa. I've seen you play tennis. You're fast and you're strong. I think you'd be good at this." Her expression turned serious. "Abe and I both agree you need to do this. It's for your own protection. Besides, there may be a time when you're called upon to save someone else. You've already saved Jace's life once. Don't you want to know you have all the skills necessary to jump to someone's defense in the future?"

That was the clincher. If there was a chance, however slim, that I could help anyone in the Alexander family now or in the future, then I would do whatever I had to do. Even if it involved movement or exercise. "Okay, Jerica," I agreed. "Just tell me when to start."

Jerica's hug made it worth it. At least that's what I believed at the time. When it came to the actual training, nothing could have prepared me. It was absolutely brutal. Abe came across as an easy going, joke cracking, black socks with sandals wearing, middle-aged dad, but when I followed him into his basement training studio, he was no-nonsense kick-butt serious. I was ready to collapse and die after an hour. No wonder Jace put off training as long as he could. I almost felt bad for thinking he was a lazy procrastinator.

***

Jace and I were supposed to hang out together while his parents braved the mall on the dreaded Black Friday—the day after Thanksgiving when all the shoppers would be out in full force. Jace was a closet nerd, unlike me, who wore my geekdom with pride. We were going to veg out in his family room in front of the big screen TV and watch the Lord of the Rings trilogy.

I figured I would find a way to bring up the subject of Rachel at some point during the day, but I didn't know how. I didn't want to ruin the day by bringing it up at the very beginning, but I couldn't enjoy the movies with the subject hanging over my head. As it turned out, Jace must have been thinking along the same lines as me, because he saved me the agony of bringing up the topic.

"Alisa, we need to talk." He motioned for me to have a seat in my favorite recliner, and settled down on the chair next to mine. "I don't want to ruin our day, but if we don't talk about this, it's going to drive me crazy." Jace took a deep breath and looked me in the eyes. "Rachel and I have been seeing each other for a few weeks."

"I kind of already know that," I said in a clipped voice.

"You do?" Jace asked, looking confused. "How?"

"I may be stupid, Jace, but I'm not dumb," I said, my anger flowing freely now.

"That doesn't make any sense." He flashed his crooked, charming smile, the smile I used to nearly swoon over. But this time, I was too angry to be charmed.

"Well, what *does* make sense, Jace?" I tried to choke back tears. "Does it make sense to try to hide your girlfriend from your best friend? You know, in a town this small, there's not a lot that goes unnoticed. Maybe you thought you were being smooth and subtle, but you're pretty obvious."

"What do you mean?"

"I've seen you with her. The whole school has seen you with her. Everybody is whispering about it. Are you that oblivious?" I yelled. Jace seemed shocked by my outburst, but looked a little angry too. A good old-fashioned screaming match was imminent.

"You're my best friend, Alisa, not my mother." Jace matched my angry, self-righteous tone. "I have a right to see anyone I want without asking you or the rest of the town for permission. Did it ever occur to you that maybe Rachel and I wanted to sort out our feelings in private? That we might not want to make a public announcement to the world?"

I was fuming now, and embarrassed for feeling that way. "You can do whatever you want, Jace. It's not like I would have stopped you, but I thought I was your best friend. I've told you everything about myself. Why couldn't you have told me this?"

"I'm sorry. I just needed some time." He lowered his voice and took a deep breath. "I wasn't ready to share Rachel with anyone—not you, not my family. She's really important to me. I just wasn't ready to try to explain how I feel about her. It's embarrassing to feel that way about someone. When I'm with her, I just... I don't know."

Jace looked away from me, but I could still see the way his face lit up when he said Rachel's name. My heart ached in a way no words could describe. Everything I feared had come to pass. I couldn't pretend anymore, couldn't tell myself it was just a passing infatuation. He was in love with her. I'd lost.

"Alisa," Jace said, looking at me again. The willpower it took to hold back my tears was more exhausting than any training session Abe could dream up. "You're my best friend and that will never change. I would never let anything or anyone come between us. Please just get to know Rachel. You know she's a good person. My relationship with her doesn't have to change our friendship." I loved him too much to let him down. I didn't want to break his heart the way he just shattered mine.

"You're right, Jace." I tried to control my quivering voice. The lies were flowing like a rain-swollen creek. "I'm sorry I got so upset. I just don't want to lose our friendship. And, I do like Rachel. I just want you to be happy. I don't want to see you get hurt."

"Thanks, Alisa." He stood up and pulled me out of the recliner and into a bear hug. "You'll see. We'll be like the Three Musketeers."

I smiled, remembering the Three Musketeers carried swords. Maybe Rachel would find herself on the wrong end of one, I thought. No, I needed to be nice. Best friends didn't kill the other's girlfriend.

Jace and I finally settled down to watch our movie marathon, but the day was ruined for me. I was grateful for the semi-darkness of the family room and for Jace's absorption in the movie. I was certain my thoughts and feelings were written all over my face.

Rachel was everything I wasn't and could never be. She was intelligent and beautiful, but most importantly, she was a Witch. I wondered if Jerica would be pleased to accept her into the family; after all, she was one of them. And, I was the girl destined to remain on the sidelines of my own life.

***

The first time Rachel, Jace, and I hung out together was the worst. It got easier each time, but not much. Knowing there were many times they were there without me didn't help. They held hands almost constantly. I knew without being told that they communicated almost entirely without words. Magical jerks!

I hated the way Jerica looked at me now. I could read the sympathy and compassion on her face, and it made me feel even more pathetic. If Jerica knew how I felt about her son, then surely everyone must know. I hated myself. I hated the jealously I felt each time I looked at Rachel and Jace, and I hated the fact that everyone knew how envious I was. Too bad Abe's training sessions didn't include lessons on masking emotions.

The Saturday before Christmas brought unseasonably cold temperatures and buckets of icy rain. The three of us (Musketeers, my backside) were hanging out in Abe's training studio. Rachel, still ambivalent about training, watched as Jace and I sparred. Jace was clearly distracted by Rachel's presence, and I'd managed to split his lip and bruise his cheekbone during the half hour we'd been practicing. The more he glanced over at Rachel, the more competitive I became.

I was so intent on taking Jace down, I barely registered the footsteps coming down the stairs. He turned his head to look at the staircase just as I planted my foot in his stomach. The wind knocked out of him, he fell on his backside, grunting.

"And that's my little brother," I heard a voice say, laughing, "getting his butt kicked by a girl." I looked up into Bryce's mocking grin. He was still laughing at Jace, but I noticed a strange look flicker across his face when he looked at me.

"Mikael, this is Alisa. She's a friend of the family," Bryce introduced me to a tall, blond, attractive man in his early twenties. I barely had a chance to nod before they turned toward Rachel.

"This must be Jace's new girlfriend." Bryce reached his hand out to shake hers. "I'm Bryce. This is my training partner, Mikael." I hated Bryce for labeling Rachel as Jace's girlfriend and for seeming to accept her so easily. I wondered if I could kick him in the stomach, or if that would be construed as 'hostile' and 'Grinch-like'.

Smiling at the thought of wiping the floor with Bryce's face, I realized too late that the attractive stranger must have believed I was beaming at him. My face reddened when he winked at me. I mumbled something about helping Jerica in the kitchen and made a hasty retreat upstairs.

"Hi Alisa." Jerica smiled as I entered the kitchen. "Did you beat the mess out of my son?"

"Yes, I thought I'd help you out in here while he recuperates." I quickly washed and dried my hands. No need to get Jace's blood in the supper. "What can I do to help?"

"I've got it under control, I think," Jerica said. "But, if you want to help me make a salad, that would be nice. You're staying for dinner aren't you?"

"Um, I guess." I didn't do well with new people, and Bryce's friend made me nervous. So did Bryce, if truth be told. Jerica and I worked side by side until we heard a ruckus coming our way.

"I wish Jace had half the focus and intensity Alisa has," Abe said as he entered the kitchen, Bryce and Mikael in tow. "This is the third time she's bested him this month. The boy needs to get his head out of the clouds."

"I think I know where his head is," Bryce said.

"All right, boys," Jerica scolded. "Be nice. Bryce, don't talk about your brother in front of his friend and our guest. Abraham, you know better." She waved her knife at him to make her point.

"Yes ma'am." Bryce flashed a wicked grin at his father. I noticed he had the same crooked smile that so endeared me to his younger brother. Funny, the same smile didn't have the same effect coming from Bryce.

The kitchen suddenly seemed very crowded and I felt self-conscious to the extreme. Jerica offered drinks to the three intruders and invited them to sit down at the table. "Mikael, we're so glad to have you for the holidays. Now, where are you from?"

"I'm originally from Southern France. My parents have been based out of Italy the last five years or so," Mikael replied. I adored his accent. What was it about foreign accents that made a man so appealing? I dared to glance up at him, and met his shockingly blue eyes. I blushed and looked away, my eyes landing on Bryce. He looked at me speculatively.

Mikael continued, "They are on assignment at this time, but I know not where. Thank you so much for inviting me to your home." Even Jerica was dazzled by this young man. Maybe Rachel would become so enamored by him, she'd fall in love. They could run away together and…

Dinner that evening was unnerving. It seemed like everyone was communicating on a different wavelength. Even Rachel seemed subdued. If I didn't know better, I would have thought she was shy. She and Jace carried on an almost continuous conversation consisting of brief hand touches and deep, searching gazes. They would nod almost imperceptibly as they came to an agreement on various matters of silent discussion or debate.

I also noticed the same sort of interaction between Abe and Jerica, although I thought their silent communication was based on years of marriage rather than a psychic connection. I intercepted numerous meaningful looks and eye twitches. Bryce was quiet and watchful. Several times, I noticed him watching the interplay between Rachel and Jace. A few times, I caught him watching me. Oh great, I thought. I guess Bryce knows I was in love with Jace too. He must think I'm a total joke. I flashed him a rebellious smile as if to say, "Who cares about Rachel and what's his name? Jace who?" Bryce seemed quite taken aback.

Bryce's guest talked almost constantly about anything and everything with only occasional prompting from Jerica and Abe. He was completely oblivious to the silent communication flying around the room and seemed unaware of the fact that he was pretty much the only one talking. He continued his constant stream of dialogue through dinner and into dessert. It was by far the weirdest meal I'd ever been a part of, and that said a lot considering I regularly dined with a family of Witches and psychics.

When Abe, Rachel, and the boys drifted off to the living room, I gladly stayed behind to help Jerica clean up the supper mess while she finished some baking. I was relieved to be left alone with my own thoughts. Jerica was silent as she measured and mixed ingredients, which was unusual for her. At last, she turned to me and spoke.

"Be patient with my son, Alisa." Her expression was subdued. "I know it's hard, but stick with him. He's worth it."

I was floored. What was she trying to tell me? I had a feeling that sometimes Jerica was able to see into the future, that her intuition was more than it seemed. Did she see that Jace and I would eventually end up together? It didn't make sense. I'd been under the impression she didn't want to see Jace and I together—not in *that* way. "What do you...?" I started to ask.

Jerica cut me off with a wave of her hand. "Honey, I've already said too much. I'm not going to be one of those interfering mothers. Just remember what I said, exactly as I said it. Don't read anything into it because it may not mean what you think." What? Who? Jerica had completely and totally confused me. Since when was she so cryptic? I could tell she wanted to say more, but held back.

With my thoughts in a jumble, I followed Jerica out to the living room. I remembered her plea to remain patient as my gaze fell on Rachel and Jace seated together on the sofa, lost in a world of their own. Irritation bubbled up to the surface as I watched them. I tried to conjure up the spirit of Christmas, but was unsuccessful. The only thing I managed to conjure was the strong desire to drag Jace to the basement and beat him senseless. Abe could call it training; I called it anger management.

Bryce interrupted my bloodthirsty fantasies. "So, Alisa. Dad tells me you and Jace actually beat him and my mom in tennis. Tell me it isn't true." He pulled his face into an expression of fake devastation.

"It *is* true. And, you're next," I said. "We've been training for weeks. It'll be a total annihilation."

Bryce laughed. "What can I do to convince you to join my team? You've already proven yourself superior in the sparring ring. Abandon him, and together we can rule the tennis court."

I spared a quick glance at Jace. He was so wrapped up in Rachel, he didn't even notice the lighthearted bantering between his brother and I, or Bryce's attempt to steal his tennis partner. "Your offer tempts me, I must admit. But what sort of tennis player abandons her partner?"

"A tennis player who wants to win," Bryce replied. "I wonder, though, if you could beat me downstairs. No magic, of course."

My cheeks burned in humiliation. It irked me to be reminded I was not truly an equal in this house. I was the only person here who did not possess magic and I silently cursed Bryce for pointing it out. For some reason, I was embarrassed that my lack of special ability was pointed out so blatantly in front of Mikael. I could see a look of confusion pass across his pale face—the only other pale face in the room besides mine.

"She's not one of us," Bryce said in response to Mikael's unasked question. I heard Jerica's almost inaudible gasp. Even she was shocked by Bryce's rudeness. Before she or Abe could reprimand their son, I spoke up.

Anger ripped through me and it was because of this completely irrational emotion that I agreed to do what I was about to do. "I don't know, Bryce. You may need that magic after all. Let's go." I started toward the stairs. Bryce was right on my heels.

"Stop right there," Jerica called out. "We do not use the training room to settle disputes in this house."

"Your mother's right." Abe didn't *look* as if he agreed at all; he was geared up for some competition. A timer sounded, and Jerica disappeared into the kitchen. "We'll just go downstairs and run a few drills to work off all that energy. Don't let your mother find out," Abe said softly, watching the kitchen door until it closed all the way.

I headed for the stairs again, Bryce right on my heels. "I didn't mean it to come out like that," he whispered. "I was just messing with you. We don't need to do this."

"You meant it, and yes we do," I hissed back. I started down the stairs. Bryce had no choice but to follow. Jace, Rachel, and Mikael followed out of curiosity and a thirst for violence.

"It's getting pretty late, kids," Abe announced, descending the staircase right behind us. Clearly, he was having second thoughts. I imagined Jerica could be pretty scary when crossed. "Maybe we should postpone this. We can do it some other time."

"Don't worry. This shouldn't take long." I sounded false even to my own ears. I removed my sweatshirt and stood before Bryce in a tank top and leggings. I kicked my shoes into the corner. Reading the expression on his face, I hissed, "Don't you dare try to take it easy on me."

"Wouldn't dream of it," Bryce answered. "When I play, I play to win."

We faced each other across the lightly padded mat in the middle of the concrete basement floor. Circling slowly, we didn't take our eyes off each other. I allowed the anger and rage to flow through me, to burn in my veins. Anger at the way I'd been treated my entire life—by my family, my classmates, Becky, Rachel, everyone. Anger at Jace and his blatant disregard for my feelings. Anger toward Bryce for his unyielding refusal to accept me as an equal. All my life, I'd felt as if I wasn't good enough. Well, no more, I decided. The anger had been growing over the last few weeks, maybe longer. It was time to harness that rage and use it as fuel.

Bryce looked deadly with his strong athletic build and formidable height. I remembered he was a Warrior in training, and almost lost my resolve. Then I remembered he was also a jerk. Hoping to catch Bryce off guard, I decided to make the first move. I used my short stature and his ignorance of my abilities to my advantage. Crouching low the way Abe taught me, I used my favorite move, my secret weapon, and launched into a crouching roll, aiming for his ankles. I quickly knocked him off balance and he started to fall to the side in a sloppy, fumbling lurch. The look of surprise on his face was enough to propel me toward my next move. If I didn't make another decent maneuver the rest of the night that goofy look on Bryce's face when he fell was enough to make me happy for the rest of my life.

Using all my strength, I quickly grabbed his ankle and pulled until he was airborne for a split-fraction of a second. He fell on his behind, but sprang to his feet with unnatural speed, and faced me once again. I briefly wondered whether or not he used a little magic, but decided it didn't matter. Bryce smiled at me, nodding once to acknowledge the fact that I'd bested him. He darted forward, and I launched my body to the side, remembering to keep low. I managed to dig my elbow into his side, and was rewarded by his quick intake of breath. Score another point to me.

The battle quickly went downhill from there. Bryce was faster, stronger, and had the advantage of professional training, not to mention magic. Before I knew it, I was lying on the mat flat on my back with Bryce straddling me, his forearm on my throat. He'd managed to disable me without hurting me at all. He hovered over me and I could feel his breath in my ear. Leaning close he said softly, "Well, done, Alisa." He stood quickly and reached down to help me to my feet.

To my extreme embarrassment, Bryce pulled me into a hug and announced loudly, "Well done, my worthy opponent. Jace, I can see why she beat you." Releasing me, he turned his attention to his brother.

Looking around the room, I could see the glow of pride on Abe's face, the look of shame on Jace, and the look of amazement on Rachel. Mikael came up behind me and put his arm around my shoulders. "I am next, no?"

"No." Bryce protectively steered me away from his friend and snapped out a quick reprimand in fluent French. "As victor in this battle, I shall claim my prize, and it is this: the right to Alisa as my tennis partner for the duration of my stay."

"No, no, no. Absolutely not," Jace said angrily. "We've been training forever. She's mine." I glanced in Jace's direction, noticing that Rachel didn't seem very pleased by the two brothers fighting over me. I sighed. Alas, Jace and Bryce only wanted me for my tennis skills. Men never fought over me for the right reasons.

"Break it up, guys," Jerica shouted from the top of the stairs. "It's getting late. Jace, you need to drive Rachel and Alisa home. You guys can continue your smack down tomorrow. Abe, I really need to see you in the kitchen." Now she sounded angry.

"Oh, Dad's in trouble," Jace laughed.

"I drove myself, Mr. Alexander," Rachel said, grabbing her purse and keys. "I'll take Alisa home." Oh great, I thought, locating my sweatshirt and shoes. For all the time Rachel and I spent together, we were always with Jace. I didn't think we'd ever been alone. This should be interesting, I thought.

We said our goodbyes and jogged through the rain out to Rachel's car. "Hey, thanks for the ride," I said as I pulled the seat belt over my baggy sweatshirt.

"Anytime. Hey, you were awesome tonight. I've seen you beat Jace, but Bryce? Unbelievable." She was gushing, genuine in her admiration. "I think I want to learn to do that. Not the magic stuff. I'm still not sure about all that. But I definitely like the idea of kicking some butt."

I felt a stab of anger in response to her announcement that she wanted to start training. Up until now, I felt like it was *my* thing. It was the only thing I was good at. Rachel was good at so many things; I couldn't bear it if she was better than me at this too. "You should learn at least enough to protect yourself, Rachel." I hesitated for a second. "Can I ask you something, though?'

"Yeah, go ahead."

"Why the objection to using magic? I mean, I would kill to have the gifts the rest of you have. I would love to be one of you. As Bryce so rudely pointed out, I'm not like the rest of you and I never will be."

"Bryce really is a jerk," Rachel said. "When Jace told me about his brother, I chalked it up to sibling rivalry, but he was right. His brother has issues. I can't believe what he said to you. I'm so glad you knocked him on his butt and so was Jace. If only someone had thought to grab a video camera."

We were both laughing as we pulled into my driveway. "To answer your question, though," Rachel said turning serious, "I don't know. The idea of magic makes me feel... unclean. Maybe it's my church upbringing. Maybe I'm just in denial. I know the Alexanders are all good, moral people. I don't think the magic in them is bad, but for some reason, I feel like the magic in me is evil." She let out a deep, shaky breath. "Wow. I haven't even admitted that to Jace."

"Can't he, like, read your mind?" I asked.

"No. He only reads what I allow. It's like texting with our brains; he can only read what I send him. I hold part of myself back and I'm sure he does too," Rachel explained.

"Well, thanks again for the ride. Be careful driving home." I jumped out of the car and sprinted through the pouring rain; I was soaked through by the time I reached my front door.

Lying in bed later, I replayed the events of that evening. For the first time in a long time, my heart felt lighter. Some of the pain was gone. I could look at Rachel without the animosity, the rage. I realized much of the anger I felt had nothing to do with Jace; I realized that when I battled Bryce. I had been angry at the world, at circumstances.

Sure, I was still hurt. I still loved Jace, but in fairness to him, he never led me to believe there was more between us. I just wished and hoped. It was time to find a new wish. Searching through my vast catalogue of fantasies, I discarded most. Most of my fantasies involved Jace and I knew I wasn't allowed to love him anymore.

I thought about Mikael. He was cute… and with that accent? Okay, yes. I closed my eyes and tried to think of Mikael, but Bryce's face kept taking front and center in my mind. Yet another reason to be angry with him. I occurred to me I should try to get along with Bryce for the sake of my close relationship with his family, but I couldn't imagine ever liking him. And, he would never be able to tolerate me. Not in a million years.

CHAPTER SEVEN
RACHEL

I told Alisa the truth when I said I felt my magic was evil. It was also the truth that I resisted magical training for that reason. I didn't lie, but I didn't tell her everything. I omitted the fact that the real reason I refused to train was because I didn't want anyone to find out how much I'd achieved on my own. Jace had some idea; he had almost as much to hide as I did.

Mr. and Mrs. Alexander suspected Jace and I had a strong connection. They knew we could speak to each other with our minds while in close proximity, and that worried them. What they had not yet realized was that Jace and I had established a strong long distance link. We were able to continue an ongoing conversation no matter how apart we were. Although this ability would no doubt concern them, it was nothing compared to what Jace and I tapped into recently: Persuasion. Jace and I agreed this skill was playing with fire, but we practiced it nonetheless.

Jace had a few less scruples than I did; at least, that's what I liked to tell myself. "Don't you dare tell me you didn't use Persuasion on Mrs. Hanks," I scolded as we sailed through yet another quiz-free day in Algebra. "You know, it might be a little less obvious if you didn't move your lips while you were working the spell."

"Okay, little Miss I-got-out-of-two-speeding-tickets-in-the-last-week. Are you really gonna give me a lecture on improper uses of magic?" He pulled me into a sideways hug as we walked to our next class. "You could save me the trouble of using Persuasion by sending me the answers across our link." Jace would do anything to get out of doing schoolwork. "Or, just leave your mind wide open, and I'll just pluck the answers from your brain." I shuddered at the mere idea of giving someone unlimited access to my mind. In my opinion, Jace already knew too much about me.

But, even Jace didn't know my biggest secret: I could break into the mind of nearly anyone. Breaking into Alisa's mind was so easy, it wasn't even fair. But, I had to make sure she wasn't scamming on Jace behind my back. I knew she was in love with my boyfriend—everyone did. But would she act on her feelings? A quick skip through her mind told me she resented me for swooping in and taking her place in Jace's heart. Fair enough. I couldn't be mad at her for that. I also learned she would never do anything to hurt Jace no matter what, even if it cost her a lifetime of happiness. I felt guilty for being the cause of such torment.

It took a while to figure out why I couldn't break into his parents' minds, but once Jace explained the concept of magical security, I learned how to break through their barriers. I always felt dirty when I resorted to using my gift in this way. The first time I broke through Jerica's magical fortress was an accident—an experiment. I sent out a delicate fiber of thought into her mind, and expected to find resistance. She didn't seem to know I was in her head, so I continued to probe until I found a hair-width crack in her security.

It was all I needed. Apparently, Jerica suspected my power was stronger than anyone she'd met. She was worried both for me and for those around me. She'd contacted Central and they were keeping close tabs on me. Who were they? I couldn't get an answer to this question without some serious Persuasion, and I didn't want to take a chance on revealing more than I was ready to show. I quickly pulled back, dissipating the tendril of connection.

The experience left a bad taste in my mouth, first because I resorted to such blatant misuse of my power, and second because I realized the Alexanders went behind my back to assign Protectors and Watchers to the area without even telling me. Through Jace, I was able to discover an entire hierarchy of Witches existed and Jerica was a high-ranking member. He'd explained a lot to me, but not nearly enough. Maybe he didn't know about his parents' wheeling and dealing behind the scenes. Perhaps, he didn't realize a legion of Witches was lurking around southwestern Georgia in an attempt to keep the Hunters away.

The weekend before Christmas, I decided to do further 'research' when I met Bryce and Mikael. Mikael's mind was open to the point of being nearly empty. There were no secrets there. Everything he thought was immediately regurgitated into an endless stream of chatter. Bryce was interesting. I couldn't penetrate his mind at all. A swirling black fog of anger served as an impenetrable fortress. I didn't dare push any harder to break through. I gave up after a couple of minutes. Trying to break into his mind gave me a borderline migraine.

Alisa seemed to be possessed of a rage that matched Bryce's own. Her easy defeat of Jace didn't surprise me at all. Her near defeat of Bryce at the beginning of the battle shocked me to the core. I wanted to be like her. I wanted to learn to fight like that, to have the confidence she displayed when facing her attacker.

I made up my mind to begin training at the next available opportunity. I would not turn into the pampered princess, the girlfriend who sat on the sidelines and watched as the boys (and Alisa) kicked butt. I wasn't that kind of girl. And, I didn't want to take a chance of allowing Alisa to upstage me. I'd seen the way Jace looked at her in days leading up to the Homecoming dance, and I was determined to ensure he never looked at her that way again. I wouldn't lose my man to a mere human.

***

It was just a couple of days after Christmas, and I prepared to say my goodbyes to Jace. My mother and I planned to visit my brother in Atlanta until after New Year's. I knew I could keep up an almost constant dialogue with Jace through our link; however, I had already decided we would give it a break while I was out of town. I wondered how Jace would respond to my decision. I was determined to prove to myself that I could live without him for a few days... that my happiness was not entirely wrapped up in my love for him. I couldn't live like that, knowing I was too dependent on a man.

I silently asked Jace to meet me alone in the basement for just a few minutes before I left. I wanted to talk to him—really talk. So much of our conversation was unspoken now, I was almost afraid my vocal chords would atrophy from misuse. This conversation would be conducted in a more traditional way, a way that involved actual speech.

"Wait until you see what I'm going to do to Bryce and Mikael later. I found this spell..."

I interrupted Jace before he hijacked the conversation. "Will you stop plotting against your brother for a moment? I need to talk to you. It's important."

"What's up?" He pushed the question into my mind, frowning at my troubled expression. "Hey, don't worry. We can still talk all the time while you're in Atlanta. It's like we won't even be apart."

"Jace, I think we should stick with one phone call a day while I'm gone." I spoke softly but firmly. "I would like to give my mother and Jeffrey my undivided attention. I think you owe your family the same." I held up my hand to silence the protest already forming on his lips.

"What the hell?" drifted along our silent link. Aloud, Jace replied, "Rachel, don't tell me you've changed your mind about me. Remember, I can read you better than anyone. I know you still love me. I love you. What's the problem?"

The pleading in his voice hurt me and almost shattered my resolve. I tried to hold firm. "Jace, I love you more than anything in this world. Being away from you for seven days is going to be a nightmare. I feel so strongly for you, it terrifies me. I need to know I'm still me, if that makes sense. I need to prove to myself that I'm still independent, that I can live without you even if I don't want to." It killed me to feel the despair radiating from him. "Here," I grabbed his hand and opened my mind, allowing him free reign.

This was the first time I'd allowed him access to my thoughts without putting up some sort of firewall, but I was willing to do whatever I had to do to reassure him. I wanted him to feel what I was feeling, the fear of losing myself, the sadness over our separation, but most of all, the love. I felt his emotions as my own as he discovered the depth of my love for him. Jace pulled me close and kissed me gently on the lips.

"Have a safe trip," he whispered, "Keep your cell phone close by. I'll call you."

"Jace, remember what I said about your family."

"I will. I love you, Rachel." Jace gave me a final squeeze.

"Love you too." I pulled away and moved toward the stairs, wondering how I would possibly survive the next several days.

***

"Rachel, I'm not turning this car around just because you forgot something. What could possibly be so important?" My mother's clipped, irritable tone would normally make me back down instantly, but I couldn't afford to lose this particular argument.

"I *need* to..." I trailed off as I watched the figure draw closer to our car. I could feel his eyes on me and the pull at my magic as it came closer. My heart beat wildly and sweat began to gather on my upper lip. The Alexanders warned me about Hunters, but I'd never really believed them—not until now.

"If you need something, you'll buy it here, or you won't have it. Understood?" She opened the car door and grabbed her purse. I wondered if a Hunter would dare attack me in the crowded Wal-Mart parking lot. Prickles of fear shot up my spine, and I decided I didn't want to find out how persistent a Hunter could be.

"Wait!" I shouted, grabbing the strap of her purse and nearly causing it to break. "I..." The Hunter was so close now; I could make out the ragged outline of his tattered clothing. He slipped in between parked cars and crept closer. I cursed myself for having left my necklace at home. I knew my request to drive twenty miles back home seemed absurd to my mother, but I couldn't afford to travel all the way to Atlanta without it. If the Hunters could find me here, they could find me anywhere.

My mother's furious gaze settled on me, and in times past, I would have stammered an apology. Opening and closing my mouth in helpless desperation, I glanced behind me; the creature was so close, I could see his glowing red eyes. Clutching at my mother's arm, I vowed that if I escaped my present danger unscathed, I would never doubt Jerica's warnings again. Panic emboldened me, and I met my mother's angry stare.

I delved into her mind, felt our connection click into place, and overrode her will with minimal effort. "We must return home. You left the iron on," I lied. Her eyes widened as the implanted notion took root.

She gasped. "Oh, my goodness! Rachel, I think I left the iron on. We'll have to go back home. Call your brother and tell him we'll be a little later than we expected," she urged as she slammed the car door shut. Another mental nudge from my mind had her peeling out of the parking spot, nearly hitting the Hunter as we passed him.

I trembled from head to toe during our drive back home and my shallow breathing made me feel light-headed. Scanning my surroundings, I flew into the house, grabbed my necklace, and fumbled with the clasp as I placed it around my neck. In an instant, my panic subsided, and I took a deep breath.

"Was I right? Did I leave the iron on?" Mama asked as I climbed into the passenger seat.

"Yes. It's a good thing you remembered," I said.

"It certainly was a blessing we decided to stop off at Wal-Mart, wasn't it?" she asked. I nodded in agreement. It was a blessing. Had we made it to Atlanta without my necklace, I'd have been a Hunter magnet for a week. And, had one caught up with me, I never would have made it back to Oaktree. At least not alive.

CHAPTER EIGHT
ALISA

Rachel left two days after Christmas, leaving me alone with Jace. Okay, not exactly alone. His family and Mikael were around as well. It was time to mend my fences with Jace, but having no previous experience with friendship drama, I wasn't sure how to go about doing it. With a belly full of fear, I swallowed my pride and called Jace first thing the morning of Rachel's departure. I almost hung up after the third ring, having convinced myself Jace was avoiding my call. It was absolutely ridiculous that my heart was beating irregularly and my cornflakes were turning into a soggy mass in the bottom of my stomach.

"I was just getting ready to call you," Jace answered. My body sagged with relief. I didn't realize how tense I was until that moment. "The rain finally stopped. I'll be there in an hour to pick you up. I'm worried about all the practices we've missed. If we don't get serious, this weekend will be a massacre."

I struggled to figure out what he was talking about. Then I remembered—tennis. I'd never met anyone so competitive or obsessive when it came to tennis. In a contest between work and laziness, laziness always won where Jace was concerned. Tennis with or against his family was the only exception.

"Um, okay," I stammered, not knowing if it was a good time to bring up any unpleasantness. Things seemed like they were getting back to normal between us. I decided to take the plunge. "Are we still partners? I think your brother may have claimed me as a prize." I felt stupid saying this, but with Bryce, I never knew when he was being serious.

"Yeah. We're still, um, partners. Just get ready and I'll see you soon." Jace sounded very evasive. Why did I feel as if something wasn't quite right?

The second I hopped into his mom's car, Jace grabbed my hand and pulled me into a sideways hug. "I'm sorry," he said.

"Me too," I replied, trying not to get choked up.

"I've been a bad friend." Jace sounded contrite.

"So have I. I'm sorry I've been so hateful lately. I just…"

"No, it's my fault. I haven't paid enough attention to you. I'm really sorry." Jace hesitated for a few seconds before continuing. "I don't want to let anyone or anything mess with our friendship ever again. So, I'm going to tell you something and I want you to promise not to get mad."

"I'm not going to make any promises. Now, tell me," I demanded.

"I made a deal with Bryce that may or may not affect you," he admitted. "You and I are playing doubles against Bryce and my mom on Saturday. If we win, he'll let me use his truck while he's away." Jace's eyes glowed with greed. Only fear of death and/or dismemberment had kept him from messing around with the stereo and sound system inside Bryce's truck while his brother had been away.

"Oh, great. No pressure. I don't feel used or anything," I sighed, exasperated. I noticed Jace was avoiding eye contact. "Wait a minute. What happens if Bryce wins? Does your mother know about all this wheeling and dealing?"

The answer to the last question was obvious. No. Jerica would never participate in the game if she knew the brothers were laying down bets based on the result. Jace said the bet may or may not affect me. What was that supposed to mean?

Jace started the engine and backed out of my driveway. It was an avoidance tactic. He had to stop the car sometime and when he did, I would beat the information out of him with my tennis racket.

Jace was out of the car faster than a bolt of lightning when we pulled into the parking lot in front of the tennis courts. If Jace was the lightning, I was the thunder. I rolled toward him like a storm cloud, my racket clutched tightly in my fist. "What happens if Bryce wins, Jace?"

"It's no big deal, actually. He just wants a rematch in the ring. He felt like you had an unfair advantage the first time." Jace wisely kept the net in between us.

"What exactly is the nature of his complaint? He won. Is he upset he didn't kill me the last time? Needs another chance so he can finish the job?" I was so confused, I forgot about killing Jace. I couldn't understand Bryce's motives for wanting a rematch. Clearly, he was the better fighter. What did he have to prove?

"He claims he was forced to hold back because of Dad being there. Look, I don't know. Mikael is still making fun of him, okay? You knocked him on his butt and made him look like an idiot," he said, bouncing a tennis ball on the web of his racket.

"So you sold me out for stereo equipment and a truck?" I advanced toward him with my tennis racket.

"Relax. The re-match will never happen because we're going to win. So, let's get started, okay?" Jace tossed the ball high into the air and served a straight shot toward me. I didn't have time to think about Bryce after that, because I was too busy sweating and running and trying to catch my breath.

***

Saturday's match was tennis Armageddon, at least to Jace. In his mind, losing the match was the end of the world. I couldn't understand why he was so upset; he may have lost something that was never his to begin with, but I would have to try to avoid Bryce, or be forced to endure the pain and humiliation of being defeated in the ring.

The match started out all right, but after Jace made one simple mistake, Bryce laughed and my partner came unhinged. After that, Jace made miscalculation after overcompensation. He was out of control and there was nothing I could do keep him from unraveling. I'd never seen him play that poorly before, and he was beyond consolation.

To make matters worse, Jerica and Abe went out to dinner after the match that evening and left Bryce, Jace, Mikael, and me to our own devices. Jace was utterly defenseless against the relentless mockery inflicted on him by Bryce. I urged Jace to ignore his brother, but it was like they had both regressed back to early childhood. The evening was a torment of name-calling and tantrums.

Finally, I could take no more. Jace was my best friend, my only real friend in the world, and I couldn't stand by and do nothing. It was only a matter of time before magic reared its ugly head. I had some frightening visions of Jace blowing up the house if he resorted to magic. The more they argued, the angrier Jace became. I had to do something to break it up. Short of killing them both, I couldn't think of a way to get them to quit their bickering.

Out of sheer desperation, I did the only thing I could think of to distract Bryce. "Hey, how about that rematch? Your parents are gone, so they can't interfere. Let's go. You can humiliate me any way you see fit, but I have one condition."

"You're not fighting anyone," Jace said, turning his attention to me.

"What's your condition?" Bryce asked, smiling widely.

"If you say one more word to Jace about the tennis match, I'll tell your mom about the bet," I said.

"What purpose would that serve? Mom and Dad will be mad at both of us. Your buddy, Jace, will be in trouble too." Bryce clearly felt he'd made his point. He winked and started to turn away.

"They'll be way angrier with you, though. You're supposed to be an adult. You know—set the example. Don't they hold you to a higher standard?" I knew I'd won the argument when I saw his smile fade. Mikael laughed appreciatively.

"Take care of Biscuit for me," I said to Jace, wearing my best martyred expression. "And Gem, even though he's mean and will probably claw your eyes out."

"Biscuit and Gem?" Bryce asked.

"My cats," I explained.

"You're being a little melodramatic, aren't you?" Bryce asked, laughing. I wished he would save his laughter for after the match. "Do you think I would really hurt you? Do you think Jace would allow it? Were you actually willing to go up against me based on a bet my brother made? You would sacrifice yourself for a guy who essentially tried to trade you for a truck?"

Okay, I guess it sounds stupid if you phrase it like that, I thought. I could feel a dark blush creep across my face. Bryce spoke again, "I never intended to hurt you, Alisa. I was just messing with Jace and I'm sorry you got caught up in it. When we sparred before, it was just for fun. I would certainly never use our training sessions to hurt someone."

He turned to Jace, speaking a little more sharply, "You're lucky to have such a good friend. Maybe you should consider that the next time you try to trade her for the rights to my truck. You know what?

Go ahead and use it if you want, but if you wreck it, you'll need Alisa's help more than ever. Help walking, help seeing, help drinking through a straw because your jaw will be wired shut. Stuff like that."

It was like someone had flipped a switch and Bryce's multiple personalities decided to play musical chairs. Or maybe, there was some sort of mood stabilizing medication he kept forgetting to take. He caught me off guard with his constant shifts in temperament. I'd always dreamed of having an older brother, but after spending time with Bryce, I was sincerely glad I was an only child.

"You Americans are strange. Are all of your people this way?" Mikael's awkwardly phrased, but accurate analysis broke the tension and enabled us all to have a laugh.

"No, just us," Bryce admitted. He said something in French and Mikael threw back his head and laughed.

An obnoxious rap tune accompanied by a vibrating jolt signaled the end to our evening of fun. Jace fumbled in his pocket for the source of the noise, and upon retrieving his cell phone, dropped it twice before finally depressing the correct button. "Rachel," he nearly wept with relief upon hearing her voice. It was embarrassing to witness.

The rest of us were practically dead to him; he wandered from the room, speaking rapidly into his phone. Bryce rolled his eyes. The three of us watched a boring reality show on television for a few minutes until Mikael yawned and announced he was ready to go to bed.

When we were alone, Bryce asked, "What time do you need to be home?"

"Around ten, I guess," I said, wondering if he was trying to get rid of me. A silly high school student must seem pretty boring to a nineteen-year-old man of the world.

"I'm not trying to get rid of you, Alisa," he explained, as if reading my mind. "I was going to offer to give you a ride if you needed one. Jace and Rachel might be on the phone for an eternity."

"Do you like Rachel?" I asked, cautiously.

Bryce seemed surprised by my question. "Yes, I do. I don't know her very well, yet, but from what I do know, I like her a lot." My cheeks burned with jealousy and rage. What a slap in the face! Bryce made it obvious on more than one occasion that he felt I wasn't good enough for his family, but Rachel was accepted instantly. I remembered what Jerica told me about heritage meaning a lot to Bryce. Clearly, my lack of magical blood meant I was less than nothing in his eyes.

"Rachel is good for my brother. Some men need an anchor—a person to stand by them and help them make the right decisions. Jace isn't very bright, so apparently he needs two people to help keep his feet on the ground." Bryce laughed at his own joke. I was startled. Did he mean that I was good for Jace too? That I was his anchor?

"What about you, Bryce? Who's your anchor?" I regretted the question as soon as it left my mouth and I saw the expression on his face.

"My brother, Royce, was my anchor. I looked up to him. I worshipped him. I thought our family would fall apart when he died. I thought I would die too." Bryce paused, and from his ragged and irregular breathing, I could tell he was barely hanging on to his emotions.

"A Warrior is supposed to be his own anchor. Before our training is complete, we have to learn to be alone, to depend only on ourselves for survival. A Warrior isn't supposed to depend on another person. That's why they give up the job if they get married. They can't have conflicting loyalties. Like my dad. He gave it all up when he married my mom. My mom always felt Royce would have done the same—meet the right girl, get married, and get into a safer line of work. I think that's one of the hardest parts of losing someone so young. You miss the things they never got to do. Like get married, have children, travel to a faraway place they'd always talked about visiting. My heart feels like it's going to split open from the pain, but the anger is there too. I feel like he was cheated like we all were."

Bryce's rage made sense to me now. I could understand the pain of losing someone you love, but never considered the anger that would fill in all the holes left by despair.

"Bryce, I'm really sorry about your brother." I tried to hold back tears. 'Sorry' seemed so inadequate. It was probably the most overused word in the English language. Without thinking, I reached out and held his hand. We sat that way for several minutes, each lost in our own thoughts.

Jace often spoke about his oldest brother. Six years his junior, he didn't spend a lot of time with Royce. The eldest Alexander left home when Jace was only twelve. Bryce was closer in age to Royce. They'd attended Central together for seven months. The nature of their relationship would have been different. I tried to picture Bryce as a little boy who looked up to his big brother, who wanted to be like him more than anything in the whole world. My heart broke for Bryce, a boy who lost his hero. For Jerica and Abe, parents who lost the grown son who would always be their baby.

Bryce gave my hand a squeeze and released it. He moved closer to me, and looked serious when he said, "I meant it when I told Jace he's lucky to have you as a friend. You're a good person, Alisa." Bryce must have sensed my shock and embarrassment, because his next words were clearly intended to lighten the mood. "I wouldn't have tried to trade you for a truck." He smiled and I felt slightly disoriented.

"That's high praise coming from you," I said, trying to sound lighthearted.

"What do you mean?" he asked.

"Well, you never seem very happy to see me. I've always assumed you don't like me," I answered before I could think.

"Why?" Bryce seemed genuinely confused.

"Well, from the second I met you, you've made it clear I'm not welcome. I mean, just the other day, you pointed out once again that I'm not one of you. Right in front of Mikael!" My words were tumbling out, one over the other. I wasn't saying what I wanted to say the way I wanted to say it.

"Okay, first of all, I was pretty shocked the first time we met. My brother had just been attacked. Trust me—I'm grateful you saved his life—more than you could ever know. By saving him, you saved the whole family. My parents wouldn't have survived the death of another child. But, you were a witness to our family's secrets. Do you know how many non-Witches our family has trusted with our secrets? None. At the time, I couldn't understand why my mother insisted on telling you about us," Bryce explained.

"Second, I truly did not mean what I said the other day. At least, I didn't mean it the way it sounded. You *aren't* one of us. You *aren't* a Witch. That's a fact. But, I *can* accept you as part of this family. I know you don't believe that, but it's true." Bryce took a deep breath.

"Third—and don't think I don't listen to every single word you say—why do you care so much that I said what I said in front of Mikael? Why do you care what Mikael thinks?" Bryce sounded annoyed when he asked this.

I felt the heat creeping up my neck and spreading across my face. How could I have known Bryce would be so perceptive? Why, oh, why did I have to mention Mikael? Now Bryce would think I was not only a loser who couldn't get Jace to fall in love with me, but that I was a loser with a very short attention span. I didn't want him to think I had a crush on his friend.

"Well, it's just that…I don't know Mikael and I…uh, don't want him to think…" Smooth. So much for damage control. Every time I opened my mouth, I dug myself a deeper hole. I should have asked for a muzzle for Christmas.

"Well, it doesn't matter to him or any of the rest of us whether or not you're a Witch. Mikael likes you, or at least he did. He was asking all kinds of questions about you, but stopped when I pointed out that it's illegal in our country for a man of twenty to pursue a fourteen year-old girl." I noticed the wicked gleam in his eyes as Bryce said this, and almost choked when everything he said finally sunk in.

"Fourteen?" I sputtered, "I just turned seventeen! You didn't really think…"

"Of course not." Bryce was laughing.

"Then why did you tell him that?" I asked.

It took a moment for Bryce to answer. "I have my reasons." Bryce stood up, checked the time on his cell phone, and announced, "Come on. I'll drive you home. No telling how long that boy's going to be on the phone. Probably forever."

I followed him out to the living room and waited by the door while he told Jace we were leaving. I wondered if Jace cared. I decided on the spot that I would definitely begin harassing my parents about getting my driver's license. Up until that moment, I'd been pretty content to bum rides or walk to get where I wanted to go. Standing alone, waiting for my best friend's brother to drive me home, I decided I was tired of always depending on others. Besides, if I'd been driving myself back and forth, Mikael wouldn't have believed I was only fourteen.

I smiled, thinking about what Bryce said about Mikael asking about me. If only that were true. Bryce certainly had a sick sense of humor. Bryce came down the hallway with Jace in pursuit.

"You sure it's okay for Bryce to drive you? I can call Rachel later if you want me to take you home." I appreciated Jace's efforts to prioritize our friendship.

"It's fine, Jace. Call me tomorrow. And, tell Rachel I said hi." We hugged briefly. Bryce looked impatient. He must be in a hurry, I thought, walking toward the front door.

Bryce led me out to his truck, his hand resting gently on the small of my back. He opened the door for me and helped me in. The spot on my back where his hand previously rested tingled with warmth.

We rode in silence. I felt just as nervous and uncomfortable as I did the first time Bryce drove me home. When Bryce pulled into my driveway, he told me to wait while he opened the passenger side door. He walked me to my front door and grabbed my hand before I went inside. "Hey, I enjoyed talking to you tonight."

"Yeah, me too." I couldn't seem to make eye contact.

"Alisa," Bryce said. I could feel him willing me to look at him. When I met his eyes, it seemed like he changed his mind about something he'd been about to say. "Good night." He turned and walked to his truck. I stood in the chilly night air and watched as he drove away.

CHAPTER NINE
ALISA

I spent just about every day of Winter Break with the Alexanders. My mother made a few half-hearted protests about my frequent absences, but gave in when I reminded her that most people my age spent a lot of time either alone or out with friends. I hinted that she should be grateful that I had friends to hang out with. Sometimes she asked why Jace and Rachel didn't come over to our house. I told her they were both allergic to cats. One time, she even asked me why I never spent time with Becky.

"Becky hates me and always has," I said irritably. Seriously, how could she not know that?

"That isn't true," my mother replied in avid defense of her favorite niece. "Becky loves you. One of these days, you're going to wish you'd spent more time getting to know your cousin." I sincerely doubted that, but didn't bother to correct her. It hurt that my mother knew so little about me.

By the time the holidays rolled around, my parents had pretty much accepted the fact that I preferred to socialize away from home. Their complaints were fewer and farther between, and as long as I came home before curfew, they let me come and go as I pleased.

I didn't quite know what to expect when Jace said "New Year's Eve party," as I'd never been to one. On television, a typical celebration involved excessive drinking and a kiss at the stroke of midnight. I felt certain Jerica and Abe were not going to offer alcoholic beverages to a house full of people under the age of twenty-one. I was equally certain there would be no one for me to kiss at the stroke of midnight. Regardless, I looked forward to the evening.

In previous years, I spent New Year's Eve alone and friendless, usually retiring to bed early with a good book. I assumed it was for this reason that I'd never really liked the holiday. I mean, what was the point in celebrating the end of one lonely and depressing year or the beginning of a new year destined to closely resemble the previous one? I expected this year to be different, seeing as how I actually had friends to celebrate with.

I decided to pay extra attention to my appearance, so I lost track of time and didn't hear the car pulling into my driveway until it was too late. My hair was beginning to grow out a little, and therefore required extensive work. I felt drained. Some girls weren't cut out for the rigors of hair care. I heard the doorbell, so I threw my brush down on the dresser and bolted toward the stairs.

Jace was already inside, exchanging pleasantries with the parents. To my horror, my mother invited him to come over to our house for dinner on New Year's Day and he agreed! It would be a fiasco, I thought, cringing at idea of sitting down at the kitchen table while my mom passed around my naked baby pictures. Now, this had never actually happened to me, but I'd heard stories from other people, and they weren't pleasant.

I tried to practice some deep breathing exercises I'd discovered on the internet. I wondered if it were too late to obtain anti-anxiety meds. Maybe my appendix would burst and I'd spend the next few days in the hospital instead…one could only dream. After several uncomfortable minutes of conversation, we managed to disentangle ourselves from my mother's evil clutches. I tore into Jace as soon as we pulled out of the driveway.

"I can't believe you agreed to have dinner with her!" I tried to control my rising panic.

"What's the big deal? You hang out at my house all the time. Don't you want me to get to know your family?" Jace stared straight ahead at the road, so I couldn't read the expression on his face. I strongly suspected he enjoyed my discomfort.

"My mother is nice and all, but she can come on pretty strong. I just don't think I can handle a whole evening where she tells you about all my embarrassing moments. And when she asks you how many guests we should have at our wedding, don't say I didn't warn you." I was too worked up to control what came out of my mouth.

"Are we getting married?" Jace asked innocently.

"My mother can't wait to get me married off to someone," I complained. "You just happened to be the first guy to step foot across the threshold."

"Oh, well. Don't worry about it. I think my mom had some of

those same ideas when we first starting hanging out. I overheard something she said to my dad once, and it made me feel reluctant to bring Rachel home after we started going out. That's why I waited so long before telling my parents she was my girlfriend. I thought my mom would be shocked and act all weird, but she was fine." This was the first I'd heard about any of this.

"Wait. What did you overhear?" I asked.

"Right after the first night we had Rachel over for dinner, my mom told my dad he should start training you. He told her he didn't think it was necessary. He said any Hunters who came sniffing around would probably ignore you and go after those with magic to steal. She got upset and told him he had to do it. I'm trying to remember how she phrased it. Something like, 'I see far, Abe. She's the only one who can pull my son out of darkness, and I'm determined to do anything within my power to protect her. How do you know she won't need training in order to save him?' She must have had one of her visions about you—something that made her think you would end up saving my life again."

I felt hope rise up from the pit of my stomach and fill my heart. Jerica's visions obviously meant something. Everyone believed in her intuition and scrambled to follow in any direction she might lead. Could this mean Jace and I would eventually end up together? But if that were true, why did she seem so unhappy the time she caught Jace holding my hand? And why would she so easily accept and embrace Rachel as Jace's girlfriend?

I gave myself a mental kick to stop myself from going down the slippery slope of fantasizing about Jace. For the sake of my friendship with Jace and the Alexanders, and for the sake of my own sanity, it was time to let go.

Jace's house was empty when we arrived. "Mom and Dad went to the store to shop for tonight. Bryce and Mikael went to Albany to pick up a buddy from the bus station," Jace explained, rummaging in the refrigerator. He must have figured he had a good half-hour of uninterrupted feeding time before Jerica came home and kicked him out of the kitchen. He spent a great deal of time either eating or trying to snatch food from under his mom's nose. Everyone needed a hobby, I supposed.

The house filled up quickly, and if Jerica noticed a ton of food was missing from the refrigerator, she didn't mention it. After all the crap he ate, I was slightly disgusted by the fact that Jace was able to eat not only the dinner that was placed in front of him, but begged for seconds as well. Sure, Jace's six-foot tall, athletic frame would require a certain number of calories, but where did all that food go? I wondered how much money the Alexander family spent on feeding their youngest son.

I looked around the crowded kitchen table, speculating about the newest, temporary addition to the household. Mordecai, silent and brooding, was the polar opposite of Mikael. Golden hair, sky-blue eyes, fair skin, easy smile, friendly personality: Mikael was a like a magnet that drew light and energy. Mordecai, however, was the darkness to Mikael's illumination. His deep-black dreadlocks hung about his shoulders, and his demeanor was off-putting and cold. Mordecai's ebony skin seemed to swallow the light, and his black eyes were cunning and sharp. When he smiled, it made me shudder. There was something malevolent in the baring of his teeth.

Jerica must have been aware of my covert examination of her newest guest. She interpreted my reaction to Mordecai correctly, I believed, because she nodded her head once and looked toward him with suspicion. I noticed earlier in the evening that Jerica did not insist on him calling her by any name other than Mrs. Alexander. I wondered if this was significant; she'd asked me to call her by her first name right away. "Mordecai, how long has your family lived in the states?" she asked.

"Nearly five years. They shall be moving back to Nigeria in two months time. I believe you know my mother's people, Mr. Alexander." He turned his attention to Abe. "My mother is descended from the family of Nkaribo." Mordecai's smile widened as Abe's dimmed.

"Yes, I knew your uncle Jabron. How is he?" Abe frowned and shot a worried look toward his wife.

"He is dead." Mordecai delivered this answer without any emotion whatsoever. Goosebumps peppered my arms. When dinner was over, I felt weak with relief when the men left the kitchen. Jerica and I looked at each other, and words were unnecessary. She didn't like Mordecai any more than I did.

***

The party was low-key, not much of a party at all, which was fine with me. The boys congregated in the basement, playing pool and listening to music. I tried to hang out with them for a while, but felt too uncomfortable to stay. Mordecai's presence made me feel slightly ill. Despite Jace and Bryce's protests, I escaped upstairs. Abe and Jerica snuggled in the living room and watched the New Year's Eve special on network television. Scantily clad women huddled in the freezing cold desperate to have their face splashed across the TV if only for a second.

I felt weird hanging out with Jerica and Abe; they seemed very subdued, and I wondered if my presence was a nuisance. I mumbled something about getting some fresh air. Stepping outside, I saw movement at the edge of the driveway. Jace's cat, Whiskers, looked up at me, meowing piteously. I walked down to the edge of the driveway and scooped him up in my arms.

"It's cold outside, baby. What are you doing out here?" I murmured and cooed in baby talk as I scratched Whiskers' snowy white chin. "Let's go inside." I made my way back toward the house, and nearly had a stroke when I heard a deep, heavily accented voice come from out of nowhere.

"Poor human." A tiny orange glow faded in and out, briefly illuminating Mordecai's dark form.

"You scared the life out of me!" I exclaimed.

"If only it were that easy," he chuckled. "Bryce's little brother will never choose you, and if the Alexanders were honest, you would have known that. The male of our species craves the magic of the female—power you do not possess. He will never whisper The Claiming Words in your ear. Perhaps you should run along, now, and find someone of your own kind." He threw his cigarette on the ground, crushed the butt under his boot, and left without another word.

What Mordecai said was true. I'd always known it in my heart. Rachel and Jace were bound together by more than love; magic created a bond of its own. Even before Rachel came along, I knew I wasn't special. I'd never be more than who I was. Maybe Mordecai was right. Maybe I should find others like myself: boring, ordinary, non-magical humans.

There was nothing to do but go back inside. I sat stiffly at the edge of the loveseat and pretended to enjoy the New Year's Eve Special. I stroked Whiskers' soft fur absentmindedly. Mordecai's stinging words reverberated in my ears, and I thought perhaps, he was right. No one would ever claim me. I would be doomed to spend eternity with only two-dozen cats to keep me company. My destiny as the Crazy Cat Lady beckoned, and I felt sorry for myself.

The guys made their way back upstairs right before the countdown to midnight. Jace's phone rang, and he disappeared to talk to Rachel in private. I wondered how soon I could escape the Alexanders' house and return to my own.

"10...9...8..." The announcer on TV was manic with New Year's Eve glee. Jerica and Abe arose from the sofa and stretched.

"7...6...5..." The rustling of a paper bag alerted me to the fact that the boys smuggled in illegal fireworks from Alabama. Soon, they would step outside to blow things up. Typical men.

"4...3...2..." I wondered who would be driving me home. I was ready to go.

"1..." Loud screams erupted on TV. Abe and Jerica kissed softly, and Abe brushed a tear from his wife's cheek. I knew it was hard on them to ring in a new year without their oldest son in it. They both went around the room, giving hugs, wishing each person a Happy New Year, before finally saying goodnight and retiring to bed.

Bryce, Mikael, and Mordecai went outside to shoot off fireworks, and I was left alone in the living room. I curled up on the sofa, remote control in hand, and decided to wait a few minutes before interrupting Jace for a ride home. I heard the front door open, and then slam shut. I sat up and looked over to see Bryce.

"Don't you want to come outside?" he asked.

I felt grateful he'd remembered me, even if it took a while to do so. "No. I'm really tired, so I think I'll wait in here. Thanks, though." I didn't even try to suppress my massive yawn.

Bryce came over and sat down next to me on the sofa. "Well, me and the guys are leaving tomorrow. We thought we'd spend a couple of days in New York before our flight leaves. I probably won't see you again for a while, so take care."

"I will. Be careful, Bryce. I'll miss you," I said, realizing I meant it.

"I'll miss you too. Happy New Year, Alisa." He reached out to give me what I thought would be a brotherly hug. Bryce pulled me close, shocking me with his tenderness. As we disengaged from our embrace, he touched the side of my face with his fingertips. My eyes fluttered closed in nervous anticipation. He lowered his hand to my neck, and the calloused skin on his thumb grazed the hollow of my throat as he lowered his lips to mine.

"Goodbye," he whispered. My eyes flew open, but he was gone. I glanced at the front door just in time to see it close. I thought for a second that I'd fallen asleep and dreamed the whole thing. I had never imagined in all my crazy fantasies that my first kiss would come from the crabby older brother of the boy I once thought I'd marry. I wasn't even sure I liked Bryce. Of course, I reasoned, he may not have even meant anything by it. There was no way I could convince myself that his kiss was brotherly, but perhaps it was meant in friendship. We were starting to get along better, after all.

As soon as my legs were working properly again, I started down the hallway in search of Jace. I was definitely ready to go home and give serious thought to what had just happened. I had a feeling my dreams would be filled with Bryce from now on. As I raised my hand to knock on Jace's door, I realized Bryce was already part of my dreams and had been for some time. He was the one who reached for me in the mists. His face was the one I didn't recognize—not until now.

CHAPTER TEN
RACHEL

My brother, Jeffrey, moved to Atlanta three years ago to attend culinary school. His visits home were regular while he was still in school, but after graduation, he couldn't come home as often. His job as a Chef at the hotel restaurant meant he worked many holidays and weekends. As the newest cook, Jeffrey was required to work on Christmas and New Year's, so we decided to come to him. Since there was no way we could all fit comfortably into his tiny studio apartment, my mother booked a room at the fancy hotel where he worked.

My mother dragged us all around the city, pointing out every place my father had ever taken her to. She sounded so much like a tour guide; I had to stop myself from busting up with laughter. To his credit, Jeffrey refrained from mentioning that he'd lived in the city for three years and probably knew more about it than she did. I enjoyed her walk down memory lane for the most part, but my thoughts kept drifting to Jace.

My mother, Jeffrey, and I had just sat down to dinner after a long and exhausting day, when I felt a familiar tug at my mind. While I was proud of Jace for holding back as long he had, I was also irritated he was interrupting my family time.

"Get out of my head, Jace," I commanded. "We're just sitting down to dinner. I'll call you tonight."

"I can't wait that long. I miss you," Jace pleaded.

"Suck it up." I turned my attention back to my mother. She was in the middle of interrogating my brother, and I desperately tried to find an excuse to interrupt her. She could be very overbearing, and poor Jeffrey was squirming with discomfort.

"Well, who said you could stop taking your pills?" she said a little too loudly. A couple fellow diners turned to stare.

"Calm down, Mama. I've been fine for two years. I stopped seeing the doctor. It was a waste of money," he said, looking apologetically at the waiter who'd approached to take our order. My mother waved the stoic young man away.

"Boy, why didn't you call me if you didn't have the money?" she hissed.

"It wasn't just the money. Those pills had side effects; they made me feel worse," he said.

"I don't want to be getting another late night phone call to drive all the way to Atlanta to bail you out of trouble," she said, referring to an incident during his second year of school.

"You won't," he said in a hushed voice.

"Do you know it felt for me to have to see you in that condition? Paranoid, irrational—you said people were out to get you," she reminded him.

"Can we talk about this later?" he asked.

My mother glanced around the crowded restaurant, and nodded curtly in Jeffrey's direction. I felt sorry for my brother. Mama wasn't easy to get along with; no wonder he had a nervous breakdown a couple of years ago. At the time, I believed my mother's assessment that Jeffrey was unbalanced and in need of medical intervention. Now, I wasn't so sure.

After dinner, we stood outside the restaurant and waited for a cab. Mama started in on him once again. "Maybe you should move back to Oaktree if you aren't going to take care of yourself," she said. Jeffrey squeezed his eyes shut, and I knew he'd had enough. So had I.

"Mama," I said. "Can we see the High Museum while we're in town? Isn't that where you met Daddy?"

"Of course, baby. Did I ever tell you the story about how he proposed to me on top of Stone Mountain?" she asked. "Oh, Rachel, we'll have to go there before we head home." Her eyes went misty, and my brother flashed me a grateful smile.

We headed back to the hotel, and Jeffrey went home to his apartment. My cell phone rang just as my mother was climbing into bed. I ignored the call, and switched off my phone.

"That might have been Jace, honey. Aren't you going to talk to him?" my mother asked.

"No. This is our special family time. I'll talk to him later," I said.

"I'm proud of you, Rachel. And, I'm glad you aren't getting too

THE CLAIMING WORDS

serious about Jace. You're too young."

I smiled at her, then contacted Jace across our link. We talked all night.

***

Jeffrey and I had plans to spend time together the following day. My mother had a lunch date with an old friend from college, so my brother and I would have a little bit of time to ourselves. Jeffrey took me shopping at Little Five Points and after that, we headed back to his apartment to hang out. Something had been weighing on my mind for weeks, and I decided to get it off my chest. There were some things I had to know, and it was now or never, I thought.

"Jeffrey, did Daddy give you anything before he died? A family heirloom or jewelry or anything?" I hesitated, afraid once I brought the subject up, there would be no turning back. I wanted information, but not at the expense of revealing any of my own secrets.

"Why do you want to know?" Jeffrey seemed anxious. I could tell he was hiding something. I decided to give him a chance to fill me in before invading his mind.

"Daddy gave me a necklace before he died." I pulled the necklace out from underneath my sweater. Jeffrey glanced at it without expression.

"He gave me something, but it was stolen a couple years ago. Whoever broke into my apartment tore the place apart, but my gift from Daddy was the only thing missing. Before the break-in, I often had the feeling that I was being followed. Afterwards, I thought the people who were out to get me might have been after my family heirloom instead. Mama told me I was imagining things and made me see a psychiatrist. It sounds crazy, doesn't it?" he asked, glancing away from me. He stood up and walked to the window overlooking the busy street below.

"I don't think you're crazy," I said. "What did Daddy give you?"

"It was an engraved piece of marble I carried with me everywhere."

"Why didn't you have it with you that day?" I asked, trying to keep the accusation out of my voice.

"I was afraid I'd lose it," he said. "But, I wrote down the words engraved on it so I could get this. If you tell Mama, I'll kill you." Jeffrey removed his shirt to reveal his secret. Four black lines of unintelligible script were tattooed on the back of his shoulder. "Dad told me it was the language of our ancestors. It must be some kind of tribal language from Africa."

"How long have you had that?" I asked, gaping at a tattoo which was unremarkable, but for the fact that our mother would beat him to death if she saw it. I could already hear her "your body is a temple" lecture.

"I got it done right after...well, after I had my problem," he said. "It made me feel better."

"Can I take a picture of it with my cell phone?" I asked, hopefully. "I have an older friend who's sort of into ancient languages and stuff. She could translate it for you." I almost said "me" instead of "you," but changed it at the last minute. I didn't want Jeffrey to know how important this was to me.

"Um, I guess. I don't know. Dad was really secretive about it." Jeffrey seemed unsure.

"Then why did you tattoo it on your body? You must not have been too concerned with keeping it secret then?" I tried not to push, but I was convinced the meaning of the words were the key to something.

"It was sort of Dad's idea," Jeffrey confessed. "He told me he would have done it himself in his younger years, but never got around to it. That conversation kind of planted the seed in my mind. I'm glad I followed through—that I have something of his always."

Jeffrey's voice trembled and I couldn't blame him. I thought about how I would feel if my necklace were stolen. I couldn't imagine anything worse. "I'm glad you got the tattoo, Jeffrey. Please, can I just take a picture? I've been wondering about Daddy's side of our family and our heritage. It would mean a lot to me."

"Yeah, fine. Go ahead. But, when you find out what it means, shoot me an e-mail. I'm curious too." Cell phone pictures were unpredictable at best, but I tried my hardest to get as clear a shot as possible. That fact that his skin was nearly as dark as the words on the tattoo didn't help, so I made him stand under the light. When I was finished taking pictures, he turned away from me and put his shirt back on.

"Thanks, Jeffrey. If you can think of anything else Daddy might have said about our heritage or his family, let me know, and I'll do the same. Mama doesn't seem to know much about his past. It's weird." Then saying a silent prayer for forgiveness, I pushed my mind toward my brother's. It felt like my skull collided with an iron wall. The nausea and dizziness almost made me lose consciousness.

"Rachel, what's wrong?" Jeffrey asked rushing to my side. Thankfully, he had no idea what had just happened. If he knew what I tried to do, he would never have forgiven me.

"I...I'm okay," I could barely speak. "Migraine...purse... quick." Jeffrey handed me my purse and I fumbled for my bottle of pills. Jeffrey had to open the bottle for me; I had no strength in my hands. He doled out two pills and handed me a can of soda. It was several minutes before the pain began to subside.

"Should I call Mama?" Jeffrey was totally freaked out.

"No...no. She'll just get upset. I don't want to spend the evening in the E.R." I tried to make light of my pain and flash him a reassuring smile, but I couldn't quite do it.

When I was finally able to stand upright, I went to the bathroom to splash some water on my face. I tried to force myself to think about something besides my magic and how it had turned against me. Even in the early days of its appearance, I had never experienced such a violent and painful reaction.

Jeffrey took me back to the hotel after promising me a dozen times he would absolutely not say anything to our mother. I didn't want to worry her, but most of all, I didn't want to ruin her day. I knew how much she'd looked forward to meeting up with her friend, and I wanted her to be able to savor the memory without her concern for me clouding it.

My mother enjoyed the rest of our stay in Atlanta, but I was counting down the hours to our return home. I longed to see Jace with an intensity that both alarmed and embarrassed me. New Year's Eve was probably the most difficult night for me. I tortured myself by conjuring up images of all the fun I was missing at the Alexander home. I promised myself I would wait until after midnight before calling him, but I couldn't do it. Perhaps I wouldn't be able to feel his lips on mine at the stroke of midnight, but I could at least hear his voice. With trembling hands, I dialed his number and waited for him to answer. I carried on a halting conversation with him over the phone for a few minutes under my mother's watchful gaze. Verbally, I kept things light, just glorying in the vibration of his voice coming through the receiver of the phone.

"We're having a great time," I said aloud, while simultaneously sending a private message across our link. "Oh, my God, I miss you so much it hurts. There's so much I need to tell you. I love you so much, Jace."

I ended the cell phone portion of our conversation fairly quickly. I didn't want to incur my mother's disapproval. We continued to communicate across our link. As I lay in bed, the TV's soft light flickering over my skin, I reveled in the fact that our connection was just as strong across the many miles. Only two more days, I told myself. Only two more days until we were together again.

***

The day after I returned from Atlanta, I stopped by to visit my boyfriend. We stood outside in his driveway for an eternity, just holding each other. A fine, misty rain began to fall, and we went inside.

"Hi, sweetie. Did you have a good trip?" Jerica asked, motioning for us to have a seat.

"I wanted to have you all to myself," Jace whined across our link. I ignored him, and sat down next to Jerica. Jace rolled his eyes, and threw himself into one of the high-backed chairs next to his dad.

"We had a great time," I replied. I decided to broach the topic of Jeffrey's tattoo. "Could you have a look at something? I was hoping you could translate it, or at least tell me what language this is."

Everyone in the room fell silent as Jerica peered at the pictures on my cell phone. "Where did you get this?" Jerica asked, casting a quick glance toward Abe.

"I…I took the picture when my mother and I went to Atlanta. I asked Jeffrey if Daddy ever gave him anything, you know, like my necklace." I summarized the conversation between my brother and me. I felt disloyal when I mentioned Jeffrey's breakdown. His problems were a closely guarded family secret, but I suspected his fear of being followed had less to do with a mental breakdown, and more to do with Hunters. I thought the information about the break-in was relevant given the fact that his heirloom was stolen under what I believed were suspicious circumstances.

Jerica's face clouded over in horror as she took another look at the images on my phone. "What is it?" I cried.

"It's a spell," Jerica said. "It's the language of the Fae. I wonder how your father's people came across such a thing and if he knew what it meant. It's similar to a suppression spell—like the one in your necklace. Suppression spells are common; I used to sew them into the boys' clothing to mask their magic when they were younger. But this is different. I'll have to ask an expert to have a look, but I believe it's a Claiming Spell. Those are almost unheard of nowadays."

"What's a Claiming Spell?" I asked.

Abe took my cell phone from Jerica and said, "There are many types of Claiming Words, and not all are bad. Some are used for temporary magic suppression or protection—like the spell in your necklace. Sometimes, a man speaks the Claiming Words to the woman he loves. Demons use them to Mark their followers."

"My brother isn't a Demon follower. What's going to happen to him?" I asked.

Jerica looked at Abe before answering. "Well, the tattoo makes him invisible to Hunters."

"Why is that bad, though? If they can't sense his magic, they can't hurt him, right?" I asked.

"Hunters can't sense him, but Demons can. If a Demon is close enough to sense his magic, he'll believe Jeffrey is a Shifter—a Demon-worshipper," Jerica said.

"How can Demons sense him if Hunters can't?" Jace asked.

"Hunters are mindless; their gifts are strong, but limited. Your brother's magic is suppressed, but not completely hidden. Jeffrey will never be able to tap into his magic, but a Demon can," Abe said. I began to tear up all over again. Jeffrey would never be able to use his magic, not even in his own defense. Abe continued speaking, "Demons are rare in this part of the world. Jerica can increase the number of Watchers, Protectors, and Warriors around the city to enhance your brother's protection."

"I can't understand why my father would have told Jeffrey to get the tattoo," I said. "He didn't know anything about magic or spells."

Abe cleared his throat. "Rachel, I hate to compound your unhappiness, but I've hit a dead end with the research I've been doing in regards to your father's heritage. There's no record of birth for anyone by the name of Darius Franklin Stevens. I have someone I sometimes work with who can look into other possibilities. Do you want me to continue my research?"

"Yes. I want to know everything about my father, now more than ever. I can't believe it. It's like I didn't know him at all." I fought back tears of confusion and rage. How could my father keep so many secrets from his family? Why didn't my mother find out more about him before marrying him?

Jerica told Abe and Jace to brew some coffee while we remained in the living room. Downtrodden and depressed, I examined my fingernails so I wouldn't have to look at Jerica. I knew what she was going to say, and I didn't want to hear it.

"Rachel, it's time to start training. I think you realize that now. Look at me, honey," she spoke in a soft, but commanding voice. I looked into her eyes, hoping she didn't notice my unshed tears. "I know you're worried about Jeffrey, but you won't help him by remaining unprotected. I need you to start training for my own selfish reasons. The more vulnerable you are, the more distracted Jace will become. His concern for your safety will leave him open to attack. If you won't do it for yourself, do it for my son."

Jerica was a truly perceptive woman. I felt guilty that Jeffrey's gift was taken from him before he even had a chance to develop it. He was robbed, pure and simple: robbed of his birthright, his magic, his ability to defend himself.

"Think about it this way," she continued. "Why deny yourself the chance to develop your skills? Your gift may someday save your brother. Punishing yourself will not release his magic. I'm sure your father had good reasons to do what he did. I'm certain his motive was to protect you both. Do not allow any of this to diminish the love you have for him."

"I know, it's just...I'm so angry with him right now. Everything I thought I knew about him was a lie." I couldn't stop the tears from falling.

"Was your father loving? Was he kind? Did he take good care of his family?" I nodded my head yes in response to each of Jerica's questions. "Not everything is about facts and numbers, Rachel.

There is truth in love. He was honest about what mattered: his love for his family. Don't let anything take that away from you."

"You're right." I knew my worry over Jeffrey would be a constant tickle in the back of my mind, probably for the rest of my life. I longed for days past when the only things I had to worry about were grades and college applications. I used to live in a world where magic only existed in my silly little vampire novels; now, magic followed me everywhere, and I couldn't find safety even in my dreams.

***

I'd been to the dream-castle before; it was the site of many nightmares. Familiarity did nothing to decrease my sense of fear, however; terror kicked in the moment I became aware of my surroundings. Shrouded in near darkness, I looked about the castle and marveled at the Gothic architecture. I shivered in response to the desolate evil of the place.

Voices drifted down the far corridor, and I followed the sound against my will. My dream-feet didn't travel in footsteps, but instead floated along on a conveyor belt of compulsion. I stopped abruptly outside a towering mahogany door and hunkered down in the hollow behind the staircase. A disembodied conversation wafted from behind the slightly opened door.

I didn't need to listen; I knew the script by heart—the words of a million identical dreams. Each syllable carried the weight of every fear I'd ever held close to my heart, every icy prickle of dread I ever felt.

"The truce won't last, ancient one, if you continue to interfere in my personal affairs. My vendetta far surpasses any claim you believe you might have," the Cold One hissed.

A deeper voice replied, "Do not threaten me. I walked this earth centuries before you were born, and I'll continue long after your body is rotting under my feet."

A magnetic pull dragged me from my hiding place behind the stairs. I struggled to resist, fought against the urge to reveal myself. I reached the threshold of the high-ceilinged room, and my heartbeat threatened to shatter my ribcage. As the fair-haired man began to turn, I almost breathed a sigh of relief. This was the point where

I woke up. Only, this time, I didn't. His golden hair glinted in the candlelight and his ice blue eyes met mine. He was beautifully, terrifyingly inhuman.

"It appears we have a guest. Perhaps we should let her decide whose Mark to bear," he hissed.

Startled, the dark-haired man turned his head to look at me. His black eyes narrowed and darted toward his adversary. He quickly stepped in front of me to shield me from the other's view. "There is no choice," he said, "only prior claim."

"Jabron had many masters," the other said. "Until she bears a Mark, she is fair game between us."

"This is not a game, Nevare. Not to me. I'll protect her at all costs...and those who guard her," the Dark One insisted.

"So, you insist upon using those pathetic creatures which make up your army? I don't care how well you think you've trained them, Re'Vel, Hunters—"

"Are none of your concern," the Dark One finished. "Unless you choose to encroach upon my territory. Those creatures will rip you apart if come near her."

"Hunters are easily destroyed, you fool. Don't forget, I watched my brother's army of one-hundred fall to a mere five Warriors," Nevare said. "They're mindless—"

"So are you. And remember, those Warriors almost killed you in the desert that day. You nearly met the same fate which took your brother," Re'Vel said.

"Don't speak of that! I'll wipe every Alexander from the face of the earth." Spittle flew from his mouth as he made this threat. I cowered behind Re'Vel, the lesser of the two evils. "I'm warning you. Your claim does not supersede my own. Should you try to take her and use her for your own purposes, it will start a war the world has never seen."

"So, you choose to sever our alliance over such a small matter?" Re'Vel asked, his voice calm.

"If it's so small a matter, why do you fight for her so?" Nevare took another step toward Re'Vel.

"I have my reasons," the Dark One said, turning to me. He lowered his lips within an inch of my own and whispered, "Sleep, my love."

I woke alone in my own bed, my breaths coming in shallow gasps. I lay unmoving until my alarm shrieked a painful "Good Morning." When the unmistakable rumble of the garbage truck became louder, I jolted from my bed, grabbed a book from my bedside table, and ran barefoot down the stairs. I didn't even bother to shut the front door behind me as I sprinted outside. I tossed the book into the trashcan at the end of my driveway just as the garbage truck pulled up.

No more vampire romance novels for me. My life was complicated enough without my questionable choice in reading material intruding upon my usual nightmares. I watched until the garbage—and my book—was gone, then went inside to get ready for school. The disturbing dream stayed with me all day.

CHAPTER ELEVEN
ALISA

I began to panic the day before Winter Break ended. How could it be over? I willed time to slow down, but to no avail. The first day back to school after the long break hit me in the face like a sledgehammer. Actually, I think I would have preferred a blow to the face. Then I could have stayed home, or in the hospital. Anything was preferable to going back to school.

Bleary eyed and depressed, I dragged myself from the warm comfort of my bed and into the shower, ready to begin the second semester of the school year. I tried to count down the days until spring break, but it was early, and my brain power had not yet kicked in. Dead dog tired from lack of sleep, I stumbled through my morning routine.

Jace called my phone at seven to announce his arrival in my driveway. I ran down the steps, yelled goodbye to my mom, and almost tripped over my cat as I ran out the door. "Hey," I mumbled, slumping into the passenger seat.

"Hey, yourself." Jace wasn't any happier about the whole back-to-school thing than I was, but at least he looked better than I did. He always looked good, I thought. So, did Rachel, I reminded myself.

It was hard enough to remember I wasn't allowed to crush on Jace. Having tackled that obstacle in my life (for the most part), I now faced a more difficult challenge: trying to forget about Bryce. Ever since New Year's Eve, I faced the constant torment of thinking about the tall, brooding brother of my best friend. I had finally decided I could let bygones be bygones and try to get along…possibly even be friends, with Bryce. But, then he had to mess everything up with that kiss.

I thought about that kiss long and hard. I obsessed over it to the extreme. I had become irritable and distracted the last part of my beloved Winter Break because of it. After deciding that Bryce was either crazy or drunk, I became angry. I had fantasized about my first kiss ever since I could remember. I'd always suffered from Disney Princess syndrome and had been waiting for my prince to come since potty training. Instead of experiencing my first kiss with my one true love, Prince Charming or the guy from Little Mermaid, I got stuck with the Beast. So, maybe Bryce was cute underneath the fur... okay I was getting lost in princess land again.

I felt cheated. Bryce didn't love me or even want me around. He ruined my first kiss. That's why I was angry. Despite the fact that it was a nice kiss, he ripped a hole in my fantasy: a hole big enough for him to step right in. Now, every time I closed my eyes, I saw his face. When I woke up in the morning, wisps of half remembered dreams dissipating, I saw Bryce floating there for just a moment.

I'm not sure if Jace noticed how crabby and jumpy I'd become over the last few days, but I doubted it. Men were oblivious, and besides, he was happy to have Rachel back from her trip. For once, I was pleased he didn't pay attention to me, grateful to be able to fly under the radar.

The day was a total loss. First period math was categorized by my herculean effort to stay awake. In second period, I did fall asleep. I was awakened by an angry history teacher and twenty cackling students. At least I didn't drool or talk in my sleep. I barely made it through the day, only awakening from my stupor when the bell rang and it was time to go home. I made a mental note to thank Bryce for letting Jace use his truck; otherwise I would have had to walk through a cold rain to get home. The ride was a blur.

I decided to check my e-mail and download a few research notes before taking a nap. As was customary, I deleted spam and junk mail before reading anything of value. Singles website ads, Nigerian mail scams, secret shopper job offers: I hit delete as if on auto pilot, until a familiar name caught my eye. For the first time that day, I was fully awake, my heart beating in my chest as if I had just run a marathon. Not that I ever would.

Bryce. Hands shaking, I clicked on his message to open it. Wherever he was, he obviously had access to the internet. I found it incredible that he would choose to write to me. I wondered how he found my e-mail address.

Alisa,

I'm sorry about the way I left you on New Year's Eve, with a quick kiss and no explanation. Believe me, I don't regret kissing you. I'm not sorry for that. What I'm sorry for, is moving so fast. I know I've been cold, even downright rude to you, and I have no excuse. I've tried my hardest not to like you, but I can't help it. I do. I've never felt this way before, so this is very confusing. If you hate me, I understand. Like I said, I'm sorry for not waiting until you felt the same way about me as I feel about you. If you can find it in your heart to e-mail me back, I would appreciate it. It gets lonely here.
Bryce

I read and re-read his e-mail, confusion making my head spin. My first instinct was to wonder if it was really him writing it. My second thought was that it was a joke. Surely, Bryce wouldn't be so cruel, would he? I reviewed every conversation I'd ever had with Bryce, however insignificant. There was nothing there that would indicate that he liked me. Well, there was the kiss. Oh, and the time Mikael supposedly expressed interest in me, so Bryce told him I was only fourteen. That was weird. Oh, and the time where he tried to claim me as his tennis partner. He was just messing around, though. Besides those few little instances, there was nothing. My general opinion over the last few months was that Bryce could barely tolerate me. Not much to build a relationship on, I'd say.

I needed to talk to someone about this, but who? Jace's face popped into my head first, but I immediately discarded that idea. Bryce was his brother: a brother whom he could barely stand. I would feel disloyal talking about it with him. I wouldn't want Jace to think I'd been scamming on his brother the whole time we were friends. And besides, Jace had said some pretty nasty things about Bryce. I didn't want him to think I was some heartless girl playing one brother against the other.

Rachel. I could talk to her, maybe; or maybe not. She and Jace had some creepy mind reading thing going on, and I didn't want him to pick my secret out of her brain. Not Rachel then. I guessed the only thing to do would be to e-mail Bryce. I would keep it casual and not say anything much, just in case it was a joke. Assuming Bryce was not joking, it would be cruel to keep him waiting, so I decided to reply right away.

> Bryce,
>
> I don't hate you, so don't worry about that. Everything is fine here. Jace, Rachel and I started back to school today, which was a nightmare. I nearly succumbed to the boredom and pointlessness that is public education. Unfortunately, I emerged unscathed and am still alive, only to have to face another day of the same torture. You probably attended high school in some exotic, far-off place, where everyone wore bikinis to school and drank fruity drinks out of a coconut at lunchtime. Well, here it is unbearably dull. I'm grateful, however, that no one wears bikinis to school. I shudder just thinking about it. I will continue to keep Jace in line and will look out for your parents as well. I hope you're okay wherever you are. Please stay safe.
> Alisa

Okay. I thought my response was well-written, light-hearted, but caring and concerned for his safety and well-being. I congratulated myself on a job well done. Refocusing on my research assignment, I surfed the internet for facts on Napoleonic France. Maybe Bryce was in France, I thought, my focus wavering just a bit. No, I told myself, I must get something done today, or this assignment would snowball until I was left with a massive project to complete at the last minute. Been there, done that.

I forced myself to continue until I successfully located four good sources, and printed about twenty pages of documents to read later. After completing my math homework and studying a few Spanish vocabulary words, I went downstairs to set the table for dinner. Dinner with my family was always a silent affair, with Dad in front of the television, and Mom and I at the table, our noses stuck in some sort of reading material. Mom worked for my Aunt Leanne's real estate firm, and often brought work home. Dad was just plain obsessed with ESPN. I cleared the table, started the dishwasher, and said a quick goodnight to my parents. After retreating to the comfort of my bedroom, I replied to a couple text messages from Jace, and decided to check my e-mail before getting into bed.

My heart skipped a beat, then jolted back into rhythm upon discovering another message from Bryce. I opened it, and my eyes darted quickly over his words. I read his message more slowly the second time.

> *Alisa,*
>
> *Thanks for writing me back. I was afraid you wouldn't. I'm happy everyone there is doing okay. It's cold here, and I'm exhausted from training. Don't tell my dad, but I'm starting to rethink my career choice. Hanging out in the tropics sounds pretty good right about now, but Georgia sounds even better. About your hatred of high school: I feel your pain. I hated high school and sometimes have nightmares that I'm back there all over again. I can't wait to come home in June. The next few months will be torture. Write me as often as you can. I don't mean to sound desperate, but I kind of am. All this dormitory type living and male camaraderie gets old. When I come home, can you make me some more of those chocolate chip cookies? I should probably sign off and get some sleep; it's pretty late at night here. Take care of yourself, Alisa, and sweet dreams.*
>
> Bryce

I decided I should go ahead and write back. If it was only seven o'clock here, and it was really late there, he must be…somewhere far away. I sighed and thought for a few minutes about what I should say. My cell phone rang, startling me. I looked at the caller ID. Jace. I'll have to call him back, I thought, turning back to my computer screen.

Bryce,

Of course I'll write as often as I can. Fortunately for you, I have no life, so I have ample free time. Even if I were extremely busy, I would make time to e-mail you. I'm sorry you're having such a difficult time. I worry about you. I'm certain your parents would support you in whatever you decide, should you choose to come home. If there is anything I can do to help you, please let me know. On a more positive note, I have an appointment to take my driver's test this Saturday. If I pass, I will have in my possession state issued identification which will enable me to prove my age in the event that someone should decide to mislead others into thinking I am only fourteen. Oh, and I will also be able to legally operate a motor vehicle without an adult present. That's pretty cool too. When you come home, I can take you for a spin, if you dare. See, that gives us both something to look forward to.
Alisa
P.S. Chocolate cookies are a done deal.

Yawning, I shut down my computer, grabbed my phone, and collapsed in bed. I quickly returned Jace's phone call, pleading exhaustion as my excuse for cutting our conversation short. In truth, I had two reasons for not wanting to talk to Jace. The first reason was I didn't trust myself not to let it slip that Bryce and I were communicating. The second reason was I wanted to lay down in the dark and think about this new development in the unpredictability of my life. I fell asleep fairly quickly considering the fact that I had a great deal to agonize about.

The next morning, I actually sprang from my bed the first time my alarm sounded, and turned on my computer. I showered while my computer woke up. As soon as I pulled on sweats and towel dried my hair, I settled down at my desk and opened my e-mail.

Alisa,

Waiting for your messages has been the only bright spot in my life since I've been back at WTB. I look forward to getting into a car with you behind the wheel. It's not that I have a death wish; I just have a thirst for adventure. As for your state issued identification proving your age, I won't let anyone get close enough to you for it to become necessary. Sorry to disappoint you. I'm not quite ready to bail on training and come home. Adversity builds character, my father always says, so I guess when I come home in June I'll be full of it. Character, I mean. There's a lot to live up to here. My dad trained here, then Royce. I'm afraid I'm not living up to my instructors' expectations. I just need to work a little harder. How is your training coming along? Jace isn't much of a sparring partner. He gets distracted too easily. His speed will be something to be reckoned with if he ever learns to control it. I hate to admit it, but at his best, he is faster than I am. One thing I forgot to tell you before I left to come here—you don't need magic to be special. I know you think less of yourself because you don't have magic, but don't. There's something about you that's way beyond average. My mom sees it and so do I. Have a good day at school, Alisa.

Bryce

I shot off a quick e-mail before finishing my morning routine. Since I didn't fix my hair or wear makeup, getting ready wasn't too time consuming. Jace had a dentist appointment that morning, so I had to rely on my mom for a ride. When I finally made my way downstairs, my mother was waiting impatiently. My father, an electrician, was long gone before my alarm even went off. My mother, although she would never admit it, was perpetually running behind. Like me, she messed around until the last minute, and then became irritated when she discovered she was late.

"Alisa, what are you wearing?" she barked at me.

"Um, sweats?" I tugged at the hem of my hoodie. She narrowed her eyes before turning away and heading out the door toward her car. I knew what she was thinking: too bad I'm not more like my cousin Becky. I tripped over the curb, righting myself before dropping all my books. My mom sighed deeply as we drove away.

She saw me as an uncoordinated, unsophisticated lump. If she could see me in Abe's training studio, she wouldn't even recognize me. Around the Alexanders, I was, for the most part, graceful, confident—everything she wanted me to be. When I was with her, however, I reverted back to the old Alisa. The socially inept, clumsy, scatter-brained girl she was accustomed to living with.

Even Jace was shocked by the way I reacted to my mother. When he came to my house for dinner over Winter Break, my mother was ridiculous in the way she overdid things. So anxious to please him, it was as if she wasn't confident in my ability to keep him as a friend. She tried to make up for my shortcomings, as she viewed them, by initiating conversation, complimenting him, and eventually apologizing for my faults. The more she spoke, the more I tripped over my words. The more she tried to act the part of the gracious hostess, the more I faded into the background.

My dad was no better, but at least he made it through dinner without making an idiot out of himself. He tried to carry on a conversation with Jace, but was stumped when he discovered Jace didn't play football, or even know much about it. Poor Daddy, I thought, with my inability to catch a man, he may never have the son-in-law he always wanted.

To make a long and painful story short, the evening was a disaster. I just hoped my mom learned a valuable lesson and would refrain from trying to accelerate my friendships in the future. For sure, Jace learned an important lesson. He would never accept a dinner invitation to my house again unless I was the one initiating it. And that would never happen.

***

The school day threatened to be even more atrocious than the day before. I hated that there were already students milling around in the hallways when I arrived. I despised entering a half-full classroom and having to walk in front of everyone. I felt awkward and hideous in my slovenly sweat suit get-up. I had barely seated myself, when I heard the most horrifying sound known to man.

"Oh my God. Who's the new boy?" Becky shrieked, "Oh, I'm sorry Alisa. With that short hair and your boy clothes I thought…" She giggled maliciously, her fans eager to join in.

"That's okay, Becky. Don't worry about it. Common mistake. I mean, it could happen to anyone, right? The last time I ran into you at Carol's House of Beauty, right before you got your lip waxed, I totally thought you were a man. Actually," I said, squinting, "you may be due for another appointment." Laughter rang out across the classroom, the loudest, of course, coming from Rachel.

"You might want to be careful," she said in a cold, level voice.

"Or what? You'll spread rumors about me? Or, make my life a living hell? Don't you have anything better to do than to mess with me? Maybe you need a hobby."

Becky was livid, and I knew she would never let me live this one down. She would take swift and brutal retaliatory measures. She wouldn't waste her time trying to embarrass me in front of the rest of the school; that was pointless. I feared she would go after the people I cared about, that she would try to ruin my friendship with Jace and Rachel. I spent the entire class mired in apprehension.

Rachel caught me in the hall before second period. "Hey, don't worry about Becky. We'll stay one step ahead of her in whatever she plans. Right now, the only thing she'll do is say something to your Aunt and try to get you in trouble with your mom." I gave her a weird look, not quite understanding how she came by her information, but suspecting. "I have my ways. I won't let her mess with my friend." She patted me on the shoulder, smiled, and then turned and headed down the hall to her second period class.

I stared after Rachel, barely able to speak. Having endured a lonely existence all through middle and high school, I was now fortunate enough to have two very loyal friends: Jace, the guy I'd once hoped to marry, and Rachel, one of most popular girls in school. My eyes followed Rachel as she progressed down the hallway. She paused in front of Becky, and held up her cell-phone. I could hear her saying, "click, click," from down the hallway. I wondered what that was all about.

As the day progressed, I noticed people watched me with new interest. Some looks expressed admiration for my bravery at standing up to Becky. Other people, I suspected, merely looked at me out of curiosity, like one looks at a horrific car crash. Once, in the hall, I thought I heard someone say "you will not be forgotten," but that could have been my imagination running wild. I hummed the tune to Tim McGraw's old song, *Please Remember Me*, on and off the rest of the day.

On the way home, Jace laughed and congratulated me on "taking Becky down. Seriously, Alisa," Jace said in a more serious tone. "I'm proud of you for standing up to her. I know that's huge for you. And, don't worry about her trying to get even with you. Rachel and I will protect you."

I told him I would call him later as I slammed the truck door and ran into my house. Before I could do homework, have a snack, or do anything else, I had to check my e-mail. I was turning into one of those internet junkies you see on talk shows who spend nineteen hours a day logged on to social networking sites, and eat cold ravioli out of a can while sitting in front of their computers. While waiting for the computer to start up, I changed my clothes. With shaking hands, I clicked on the latest message from Bryce.

> *Alisa,*
>
> *It's been another cold, exhausting day. In case you were wondering...yes, Hell really does freeze over. I know because I am there and it is numbingly cold. I'm looking forward to another summer in the hot Georgia sun, and right now that seems eons away. I spend a lot of time fantasizing about less dangerous jobs, like race car driving or firefighting. How about you? What do you dream about doing? I often wonder what Jace will decide to do. To the best of my knowledge, he has no immediate goals for college or any sort of career when he graduates. Maybe you know him better than I do these days. We were never close and any inter-action between us has been confined to arguments. We're both very competitive, in case you hadn't noticed. When I come home, I'll try to be a good boy and get along with him. I thought*

letting him use my truck was a nice gesture, although I hope it is as much to your benefit as it is his. I don't like the idea of you walking home from school. I gotta go. I'll write you later.
Miss you,
Bryce

I sat for a while, trying to come up with a clever and humorous response. It was difficult after the day I'd had. I still felt anxious about Becky, my first cousin and sworn enemy. Family wasn't supposed to be like this. In a perfect world, the two of us would be inseparable, sharing secrets and having sleepovers. I could never understand why she hated me so. I'd spent my whole life comparing myself to her and wondering why I wasn't good enough for her to like me. I think I'd finally come to the realization that she was the problem.

I typed out an extended e-mail to Bryce, hopefully something that would raise his spirits. I couldn't imagine the dangers he faced in Warrior training. Did they track Hunters and Demons, or was the training confined to the classrooms at WTB? I thought about asking him, but I didn't want to bring up unpleasant topics.

It worried me that he sounded so downtrodden. I had the impression he wasn't sharing his thoughts and concerns with his parents. As soon as I hit the send button on my latest e-mail, I heard my dad's truck pull into the driveway. Time to get serious about finishing my homework, I thought.

Around five, I clumped down the stairs, said hi to my dad, and tackled dinner. I tried to help out in the kitchen when I could. After all, I was the only member of the household who didn't work. My life was easy, as my mom constantly pointed out. Apparently, I was supposed to be experiencing the best years of my life. If that were the case, I was surely headed for disappointment and unhappiness going forward.

I could tell my mom was in a foul mood the second she walked in the door. The way she shut the door a little harder than usual, her clipped, brisk walk across the hardwood floor, her brief hello to my dad as she headed toward the kitchen, were bad omens indeed. I knew instinctively that her anger would be directed toward me and longed for days past when I was simply a quiet disappointment. I started shaking when she came into the kitchen.

"I just spoke with your Aunt Leanne," Mom bit out. "Apparently, Becky is inconsolable. Leanne said you insulted and embarrassed your cousin in front of the whole school. Becky is so upset, she won't stop crying. I've never heard Leanne sound so angry. How could you do such a thing to your own cousin?"

To my horror, I started crying before I could even begin to defend myself. Tears of anger spilled down my cheeks, and before I knew it, I was gasping for air. I couldn't believe the unfairness of the whole situation. After everything Becky had done to me, I was the one getting in trouble.

"I told you she hated me," I choked out. "She's lying. She said something to me first, and I just insulted her back...I..." I was almost doubled over from the intensity of my sobs, and my mom just stood there watching me.

"I don't bel..." Her words were cut off abruptly when my dad walked into the kitchen.

Looking thunderous, he declared, "Jan, that's enough. Whose side are you on here? You gonna believe that conniving little niece of yours over your own daughter?" He said this in his usual slow, southern drawl. He would never raise his voice to a lady, but I could tell how angry he was nonetheless.

"Now, everyone needs to calm down. Alisa, you didn't do nothing wrong, so don't worry about it. Becky got what was coming, and if she's upset, then I say that's her problem. Jan, why don't you go upstairs and take a hot bath? You can call Leanne later and straighten things out. But if I find out you apologized to her over any of this, I'm going over there myself." Daddy gave me a big hug and kissed me on the cheek. "This food can wait until tomorrow, Alisa. Cover it and put it in the fridge. You can drive me over to the Dairy Queen. You need to log some more driving hours before Saturday."

I stored the uneaten dinner without even looking at my mom. I was afraid to make eye contact. "Your father's right," she said softly. "I'm sorry Alisa. It wasn't fair for me to attack you without even getting your side of the story. You're my daughter and I'm always on your side." She hugged me as I started crying again. "I'll finish up in here. You'd better go with your dad before he gets involved in one of his games."

***

The remainder of the week was a blur. Each day brought increased stress as Becky increased her efforts to ruin my already tarnished reputation.

Walking down the hallway toward my locker, I tried to sidestep Becky and her crowd of admirers, but she quickly blocked my path.

"Hey, Alisa. Does it bother you that you couldn't close the deal with Jace? Must suck to see him with Rachel day after day. Week after week." Her smile was evil, victorious. And her comment hit me where it hurt.

Quickly recovering and flashing what I hoped was a brilliant smile, I said, "Well, you should know what rejection feels like. You're the one who told everyone it was only a matter of time before Jace asked you to Homecoming. But, unfortunately…Oh, well. There's always next year."

I concentrated on maintaining eye contact. She scowled at me and opened her mouth to speak again, but her binder suddenly split from end to end, sending notebook paper in every direction. With a cry of frustration, Becky crouched down to retrieve her belongings while I carefully navigated a path around her scattered papers. When I reached the end of the hallway, Jace smiled and winked, giving me a fairly good hint that Becky's unfortunate binder incident was not accidental.

Becky continued to hurl insults my way and I managed to take up for myself each time. She seemed surprised by my new sense of self confidence. Of course, so was I. By the end of the week, I'd managed to endure numerous verbal attacks and still walk the hallways with my head held high. And, by the end of the week, Becky's rude comments meant less than nothing to me, because the only thing I could focus on was the lure of my computer and the latest email from Bryce.

When I received my beautiful, laminated driver's license that Saturday, I was ecstatic. For some reason, I couldn't wait to tell Bryce. Even before I called Jace, I ran upstairs to my computer and sent a celebratory e-mail to the guy whose thoughts and opinions now meant more to me than they should.

My mom let me use her car the rest of the day, so I spent my time driving around town and past the farms, feeling independent and invincible. Every moment I was away from home, a little piece of me wished I were in my bedroom in front of the computer, waiting for Bryce's next message.

CHAPTER TWELVE
RACHEL

I spent four weeks listening to the thoughts in Becky's head and it was enough to drive a person straight to the loony bin. The first time I listened in on her thoughts, I actually had to pull back and take one of my pills. Her mind was so full of bitterness and hatred, I couldn't believe I'd never realized before what a horrible person she was. Inside her wholesome, All-American, cheerleading shell, lurked the soul of a sociopath.

Becky only had two types of thoughts: those about herself and those against others. Seventy percent of what I found in her depraved little mind centered on clothes, hair, and self. The other thirty percent involved which girl was getting too full of herself and needed a reality check. Or, which guy was getting too focused on his girlfriend and needed some distraction from Becky. I was shocked to discover how much plotting and scheming went on inside a brain I'd assumed was virtually empty.

As Alisa had been pre-warned about Becky's initial attack, a juvenile attempt to turn her own mother against her, she was able to not only survive, but to come out ahead. Although Becky's plot did not exactly backfire, my nemesis was almost forced to realize the world did not revolve around her. Manipulations are no match for a parent's love of their own child.

Becky, as expected, set out to systematically ruin Alisa's reputation. Alisa didn't really have any friends other than Jace and me, which rendered that plan utterly pointless. She spread rumors that Alisa and Jace were messing around behind my back. Other than giving the haters something to talk about for a few days, this accomplished nothing. Trying to damage the friendship between the three of us may have worked if one of the intended victims didn't read minds. Becky was completely frustrated and enraged by her inability to hurt Alisa. She even considered physically attacking her cousin, assuming that Alisa was weaker and destined to lose. I almost wished she would try it. Alisa's dedication to Abe's training guaranteed she would wipe the floor with her cousin. Becky, of course, didn't consider this idea very long. A master manipulator, she preferred a less direct attack.

When Becky confronted me, I wasn't really surprised, but I was rather amused by her creative approach.

"I'm not mad at you anymore, Rachel," she said. "Do you want to hang out this weekend?"

Not mad at me anymore? As if I cared. She assumed it was all about her. Well, it wasn't up to her to forgive me. I'd severed our friendship because I realized what a shallow, conniving person she was.

"I can't," I replied. "I'm hanging out with Alisa and Jace. Thanks anyways." I closed my locker and turned away from her.

"You actually like Alisa? Even though everyone knows she's scamming on your boyfriend. She's just waiting for the chance to..."

"And, what are you waiting for? You've hit on every guy in this school. I'd trust Alisa over you any day."

I spun on my heel and walked down the hallway. I knew Alisa had feelings for Jace, and it worried me, but I also knew she would never stoop to dishonest measures to win his love. It was at that moment that I realized I *did* like Alisa and wanted to be friends with her. Not just because of Jace, but because she was good person.

I continued to fill Jace and Alisa in on Becky's vengeful thoughts, no longer caring if they knew my secret. If Alisa worried about me reading her mind, she never brought it up. I thought about the pictures of Becky I'd been saving in my cell phone—those could ruin her. But the idea of causing harm to another human being sent shards of pain through my skull. My developing Empathy made it impossible for me to cause physical or emotional harm to another person. Too bad.

Jace wanted to use Becky's mind against her, to pick out her secrets and mastermind a plot to destroy her. Or use Persuasion to get her to do something humiliating and out of character. I forbade him to act against her in that way.

"Look, there has to be rules," I tried to explain to Jace, while Alisa listened silently. "This is all new to me and I'm making them up as I go, but some moral law must govern how I use my abilities. I don't want to start a slippery slide down the path of evil."

"Becky's already evil. You have to fight fire with fire," he argued.

"That's great for Becky, but I don't want to be evil. I don't listen in on someone else's thoughts without their permission." I felt a little guilty saying this in such a sanctimonious manner since I'd done just that on a few occasions. "I made an exception in this case because it's to protect a friend. If it's a choice between protecting someone I care about and sticking to my own made up rules, I'm always going to choose the first option. I will not, however, sift through her brain at will, pulling out her secrets and using them against her. And, I certainly won't try to plant ideas in there, even though I would probably be doing the world a favor."

"How does that work? I mean getting thoughts out of someone's head?" Alisa interrupted before Jace and I could continue our argument. She seemed curious, but fearful as well. Maybe there was something in her mind she didn't want me to see.

"Well, at first when I looked inside someone's head, I picked up random thoughts, stuff I really didn't want to hear. Now I push a question into Becky's head, and that enables me to focus in on what I want to know. I can filter out things I don't want to know about, or things that are none of my business. I guess none of it's my business, but you see what I mean. I basically zero in on any thoughts that have to do with you and try to block out sleazy thoughts about Justin or her incessant worries about clothes."

I asked Jace silently if I could explain to Alisa how our link worked. He gave me the go ahead, so I went ahead with my explanations. I figured it would be good practice, seeing as how I would need to spill my guts to Jerica sometime real soon. She needed to know what she was dealing with before she could train me properly: at least that was what Jace kept telling me.

"It's different with Jace and me. We have a connection between us that allows us to speak back and forth with no effort whatsoever. We have conversations in our minds the same way people speak out loud. We don't just dig through each other's minds at will, although I guess we could. I ask him a question or make a comment, and he responds. It works that way whether we're in the same room or miles apart."

"Yeah, I tried to talk to her like that when she was in Atlanta and she told me to get out of her head," Jace laughed. I was glad he found humor in my sense of independence. I sent him a quick, nasty comment, and he stopped cackling.

"Can you do that with Jerica and Abe?" Alisa asked.

"No. They don't know our link is so strong, although they suspect. I have to come clean with them soon. I'm already starting to feel panicked about putting off my training for so long." That was true. What Jerica said to me hit home; I could be endangering Jace by leaving myself unprotected. I didn't want to put him in the position of having to defend me. "I'm thinking of talking to Jerica on Saturday, and I'd like you and Jace to be there for moral support."

"My mom isn't that scary," Jace said, exasperated.

"Really, Jace? Cause you've been holding out too. I wonder what she'll say about that." A look of panic flickered across his face as he realized for the first time that he would be in deeper trouble than I would.

***

During those long days of mentally stalking Becky, not only had I neglected to begin training with the Alexanders, but I'd also failed to keep myself in shape. I'd gained ten pounds over the holidays and hadn't exercised since cheerleading ended in the fall. I enjoyed hanging out with Jace, watching movies, and holding hands, and it was beginning to show on my backside. I wasn't a vain person, honestly. But softball season was coming up in a few weeks, and I didn't think I'd be able to run the bases without getting out of breath. And besides, training with Abe would require a certain level of physical fitness. It was time to get in shape.

I called Alisa on Friday evening and told her about my plan to wake up at the crack of dawn to go running. I asked her if she would be interested in joining me. To my surprise, she agreed enthusiastically, asking if I thought it would be a good idea for her to try out for softball as well. I wholeheartedly encouraged her to do so. It was high time she put herself out there and started displaying some confidence.

Jace's response wasn't quite so positive. He said he wasn't doing anything that interrupted his sleep in any way. He also reminded me he hadn't gained any weight over the holidays; in contrast, he'd actually hit a growth spurt and seemed to build muscle effortlessly. This was not what I'd wanted to hear. I put up a block, abruptly ending our mental conversation, set my alarm, and went to sleep.

Re'Vel called to me in my dreams, begging me to follow him. Following his voice into forest clearing, I ran to his side the moment I saw him. My heart leapt with joy to be near him again.

"Rachel, we are so alike. If you come with me, you can live forever. I'll make you my Queen."

My laughter floated along the breeze, teasing him as I spun away, just beyond his reach. "We'll always be together in my dreams. Every time I fall asleep, I'll be waiting for you to find me."

"But, it isn't enough. I want you all the time," he insisted.

"Then come and get me," I taunted, flittering so close to him, the silken hem of my nightgown grazed his long legs.

"I can't, or Nevare will discover your whereabouts. You must come to me. Tell the Witches to teach you Transport," he said.

"I don't know what that is." I frowned and stopped my joyful spinning.

"The ability to disappear and reappear somewhere else. You have the power. The Witches are holding you back," he claimed. "Only I can help you. It is I who protects your home; my spells keep you safe."

"But Jerica's been trying to..."

"You see how they lie to you? They aren't protecting you. I don't trust the older boy. He is unstable. He isn't far from following the dark path. He's brought a known Shifter into his home," Re'Vel said, placing his arm around my waist.

"But, the Alexanders are my friends. They wouldn't put me in danger; they've been trying to protect me."

"I'm your only friend," he said, holding me tenderly.

A burst of discordant music ripped me from his arms.

I sat up in bed and turned off my alarm clock, feeling disoriented at finding myself in my bedroom instead of in the forest. Although I'd considered going back to sleep and searching for Re'Vel in my dreams, I stumbled out of bed. Alisa and I had plans and I didn't want to disappoint her.

Alisa's eyes were puffy and her short hair stood straight up on one side when I picked her up on Saturday morning. Alisa was clearly not a morning person, and had just rolled out of bed. She looked like a bag lady in her saggy sweats, rumpled t-shirt, and grass stained tennis shoes. She seemed way less excited that morning than she did the night before. We planned to drive over to the school and run the track—that way we could record exactly how many miles we ran and could build from there.

The mid-February morning was cold and damp from a light drizzle the night before. Our tennis shoes were already soaked from our ill-considered short cut through the grass. We stretched for several minutes before walking once around the track. As we started around the second time, we jogged lightly, then finally began running on the third pass. Alisa was just slightly ahead of me as we passed the section of track that bordered the thick, dark woods.

Without warning, a man shot out from the thick trees, knocking Alisa sideways. She stumbled and fell hard on one knee. The attacker started towards me and I swerved to avoid his grasp. "Don't let him touch you, Rachel, whatever you do!" Alisa screamed.

The Hunter and I faced each other. Alisa came up from behind him and launched her body full force into the back of his knees, startling him, and knocking him to the ground. "Run, Rachel!" Alisa screamed again. "Listen to my thoughts."

I immediately focused in on her pleading message. "The Hunter won't hurt me, but he *will* hurt you. He can kill you just by touching you. Let me try to distract him long enough for you to make it to your car. As soon as he realizes you're running, he'll come after you, so don't look back to see if I'm okay. Now, go!"

I hesitated just long enough for the Hunter to get back on his feet. Alisa was right. She was like an annoying fly buzzing around his head for all the attention he paid her. His red eyes focused on me, and me only. "Jace!" I screamed through our link. "We're being attacked! Help us!"

"Where?" Jace demanded.

"The school!" I shouted back, once again focused on Alisa. She leaped onto the Hunter's back, her fingernails clawing at his eyes. He howled, less in pain than in anger. I started to run toward the parking lot. If I could just get to the car, I thought, I would run him over. I ran in a full out sprint toward the pavement, Jace screaming in my head the whole time. He and Abe were on their way. "Try to keep running! Don't let him touch you no matter what."

I refocused on Alisa's thoughts, "Rachel, keep going. Don't stop. I'm fine." As I reached the car, I turned to face the track. I threw myself into the car and pushed the button to lock all the doors. The Hunter wasn't on the track anymore. He was just a few feet away from the car as I turned the key. Alisa was running after him, still trying to keep him from me. As the Hunter reached the driver's side door, I threw the car into reverse, knocking him over with the side mirror. I couldn't risk hitting Alisa by putting the car in drive, so I decided to lure him away from her. I reversed slowly, speeding up as he reached the car, then slowing down just long enough to keep him in pursuit.

The Hunter's angry howls rattled the car windows. No horror movie character ever conceived made such a monstrous and bloodcurdling sound.

"We're almost there!" Jace shouted in my head.

"Hurry!" The Hunter turned away from me and starting walking back toward Alisa. Too late, I realized this seemingly mindless creature was smarter than I'd thought; ruled by hunger perhaps, but not too stupid to try to get me to follow him in order to save my friend. Smart enough to know that's exactly what I would do to help the person who had tried so hard to protect me. I stopped the car and opened the door.

"Rachel? What the hell are you doing?" Alisa yelled.

"Hey, over here!" I shouted at the Hunter. He looked at me and continued toward Alisa. Clearly, he meant to lure me away from my car. Alisa crouched down low, and waited for the attack. The Hunter started toward her, running now. There was no way she could survive a collision with the huge monster. He was at least a foot taller than her, and had to outweigh her by two-hundred pounds.

The sound of a car engine and squealing tires made the Hunter slow down and turn back toward the parking lot. Abe drove across the pavement and through the grass. Jace flew out of the car before it even stopped. I watched in horror as the Hunter slumped to the ground, a dagger protruding from its chest. Jace ran to me, scooping me up in his arms as I cried against his chest.

I heard Abe shout, "Alisa, are you okay?" I heard her response,

THE CLAIMING WORDS

"I'm fine. He barely touched me."

"Take the girls to the car," Abe shouted to Jace. "Your mom will be here in a minute."

"Is it dead?" I whispered.

"Only if Dad got him in the heart," Jace answered. He kept stroking my hair and whispering in my ear. He gently placed me in the passenger side of my car. When Alisa reached us, Jace grabbed her in a hug that seemed to go on forever. "Are you okay? Did he hurt you?"

"Just a bruise on my knee, maybe. Jace, I'm fine. Go help your dad." Alisa seemed embarrassed by Jace's tearful display.

I watched through the slightly tinted passenger side window as Abe inspected the body of the Hunter. Abe lifted it by its feet and dragged it into the woods with one hand. The expression on his face was grim. Jerica's car pulled up as Abe returned to the parking lot. She was near hysteria.

"We need to leave, Jerica," Abe announced hastily. "I'll drive Rachel and Jace in her car. Alisa can drive mine. We'll talk at the house."

Jerica cooked breakfast while the rest of us cleaned ourselves up. Alisa was covered in mud and had to borrow a jogging suit from Jerica. We gathered at the kitchen table for breakfast, all of us speaking as little as possible. Abe seemed angry, cold. He was the first to break the silence.

"What the hell happened?" he asked, turning to me. "Why weren't you wearing your necklace?" Abe's voice was loud and intimidating.

"Abe," Jerica cautioned.

"Dad, don't yell at them," Jace broke in protectively. "They were just jogging. People should be able to go for a run without being attacked."

"Rachel isn't like everyone else. She needs protection, and the necklace she wears is only part of that." Abe's voice was softer, but still firm. "I'm not mad at you, dear. You're not used to living the way we are. You're not used to having to worry about Hunters. You two girls could have been killed. It's as simple as that. If you're not going to train, if you're not going to wear your pendant, we can't protect you."

"Fortunately, you were able to get in touch with Jace and I was there to help. If Jace had come alone, he could have been killed too. With his lack of training combined with yours, you and Jace are a tragedy waiting to happen." Abe wasn't mincing words, and I'd noticed Jerica was letting him have his say.

"Sorry, Dad," Jace mumbled. "I'm gonna take it seriously now. I swear."

"Yes, you will." Abe snapped. "You know me; I'm all for having fun and enjoying life. But, now it's time to get serious. How long has this communication between the two of you been going on?"

May as well put it all out there, I thought. No more secrets. "Since November. We were able to communicate even while I was in Atlanta. Jace's ability is limited to reading my thoughts. I, however, can get into nearly anyone's. We are both able to use Persuasion."

"In what way?" Abe asked, sounding concerned.

"We can persuade people to alter their course. It isn't something we've tried very often and I'm not sure how effective it is. I got out of a speeding ticket a couple times, and Jace got out of taking a quiz." I felt so petty and shameful admitting that I'd used God-given talents in such a way. I was scared to look at Jerica. I didn't want to have to see the disappointment I was sure would be in her eyes.

"That's a very dangerous thing to do." Abe's eyes bore into mine. "Not only for the people whom you are trying to influence, but dangerous for yourselves as well. Any time you mess around inside someone else's head, you are taking a serious risk."

Jerica broke in with a question of her own, and I was once again impressed by her perception. "You said you could get into nearly anyone's head? Who is the exception?"

"My brother, Jeffrey. In fact, the block on his thoughts was so powerful, it almost knocked me out. Literally. It took every ounce of will I possessed just to keep myself from passing out," I said.

"That's because of the Claiming Words in the tattoo. His magic is blocked, and therefore, inaccessible to all but the one whose Mark he bears," Jerica explained. I thought about mentioning Bryce. I'd tried to get into his head back in December, but most of his thoughts were clouded by anger and unhappiness. He wasn't Demon Marked, but I couldn't penetrate his mind. I couldn't very well ask his parents to explain this.

"Look, I didn't mean to get so upset, but if we are going to keep everyone safe, we need to agree there can be no more secrets. That goes for Jerica and me as well. There are some things you need to know, Rachel. Maybe if we'd been a little more forthcoming, you would have been more careful." Abe had calmed down.

Everyone looked visibly relieved over our agreement to be totally open and honest with each other—everyone except Alisa. I could tell she had a secret, one which she was unwilling to reveal. I decided to talk to her later, and give her a chance to explain what she was holding back. If that didn't work, I vowed I would take matters into my own hands; I would use my gift to find out if what she was withholding could threaten the family in any way. Wasn't it odd that I now felt like I was part of this family?

Abe insisted Alisa and I phone home and make sure it was okay to stay over for a while. He said he had a lot to tell me, and would need a couple of hours of uninterrupted time to do so. My mother was irritated I'd stayed out so long and hadn't yet finished my weekend chores. I begged and promised her the moon. She relented after a couple of minutes, mostly, I think, because she had to leave to go over to the church and didn't want to waste anymore time listening to me whine.

After clearing the table and tidying up the kitchen, Abe and Jerica spent the next two hours explaining everything I'd ever wondered about and more. From the history of magic to the description of magical beings as they existed in today's world, Abe opened up a universe of mystery. It was mind boggling to imagine this whole world within our world. Perhaps it was good Abe and Jerica waited a while to tell me. I don't think I would have believed any of it upon first meeting them.

"If Witches are decedents of the Fae, why aren't we immortal?" I asked.

"Because over time, our race has intermarried with humans," she said. "Would you really want to live forever? Forever is a long time." It made me feel more connected to the world we lived in to know I had an expiration date just like everyone else. I didn't want to be *too* different.

"So, what exactly is the role of a Watcher or Warrior?" I asked trying to grasp the hierarchy of this organization of Witches.

"I am a First Watcher," Jerica explained, her pride evident in the way she sat up just a little straighter. "I supervise other Witches in the area and report any troubling findings to Central Headquarters. My Watchers cover a certain area, looking for Hunters, Shifters, and Innocents."

Jerica continued. "Abe trained as a Warrior- just like Bryce is doing now. A Warrior's job is to eliminate Hunters and Demons. It is a dangerous job, and not for everyone." She paused for a moment, and I knew she was thinking about Royce, her oldest son who died in a training accident. "Not only is it a path you choose with care, but one which is handed down from generation to generation. Abe gave it up when he married me, and became my Protector."

"Is that how he killed that Hunter so easily?" I asked, trembling at the memory of the attack that happened just a few hours before.

"Yes," Abe replied. "Jerica contacted Central, and a group of Warriors are headed into town to dispose of the body."

"Are they staying here, Dad?" Jace asked. His excitement revealed a deep fascination with those who shared his birthright.

"No. If something goes wrong, their trail would lead back to this family, and we can't risk that happening." Abe's confidence was reassuring. I imagined that he had a lot of experience in such matters before marrying Jerica.

We had been talking, or listening, so long, that my muscles ached from lack of use. I was grateful when Abe and Jerica came to a stopping point and allowed us to get up and stretch. Jace begged me to stay, but I declined. I'd made a promise to my mother, and I intended to keep my bargain.

Abe insisted on following me home, just to make sure I made it safely. He watched as I let myself inside before pulling out of the driveway. I quickly completed all of my weekend chores, but not so quickly that I did not do a thorough job. Those domestic tasks completed, I headed upstairs to shower. As I rinsed off the residue of my crazy day, I began shaking uncontrollably.

Shock from the attack finally wore off, and terror took over. I exited the shower and dried quickly. With trembling hands, I fastened my protective necklace around my neck. After dressing in multiple layers of clothes, I snuggled under the covers of my bed, shuddering until I finally fell asleep.

CHAPTER THIRTEEN
ALISA

After Rachel left, I lingered at Jace's house, too keyed up to go home to my silent family. The Alexanders were so full of life, and even in the midst of a crisis such as the one we had just experienced, they still enjoyed each other's company. I appreciated the way they included me in almost everything.

Jace was being extra nice, fawning over me in his gratitude for saving his girlfriend's life. Abe asked me for a play-by-play account of my battle with the Hunter. He chuckled with pride when I described how I'd landed the first blow. Jerica raised her eyes to heaven, hand on her heart, as she realized just how close Rachel had come to being killed.

"Thank heavens you were there, Alisa. If she'd been alone..." Jerica trailed off.

"You're an amazing young woman," Abe said. "You single-handedly took on a Hunter. I don't know how you distracted him long enough for us to get there."

"I didn't," I said, eager to explain how Rachel had been willing to sacrifice herself for me. I gave the Alexanders a quick recap of the attack. "I never would have made it if it hadn't been for Rachel. I mean, you saw how gigantic he was. I couldn't have held him off for long on my own."

"You're a real hero," Abe insisted. "Don't downplay what you did."

"But I..." I stammered, blushing.

"Can't you just take a compliment?" Jace asked. "I feel like a complete ass. Rachel asked me to come along and I laughed at her. I chose to sleep in instead, and my selfishness could have killed you both."

"You had no way of knowing what would happen," Jerica said. "From now on, we need to watch out for each other. The link between you and Rachel was invaluable, Jace. You helped save her life."

"Wait until Bryce hears about this," Abe said. "There he is, training for the second year in a row, and he hasn't faced a Hunter yet. You've faced two and lived to tell about it. I ought to send him an e-mail tonight and tell him what happened. I wonder how long it will take for news of the attack to make its way to the training quarters. He may have already heard."

"They hear about every attack?" Jace asked.

"No. Just the ones where Warriors are called. Your mom had to call in for help, remember?" Abe said.

Sensing an opening, I asked, "How often do you talk to Bryce? Does he call or e-mail often?" I hoped I sounded ultra-casual.

"I try to send an e-mail about once a week. He responds, but his messages are short and sweet. He never initiates contact. He's never been one to communicate. Abe," Jerica redirected her attention, "send the boy an e-mail. If he's already heard about the request for reinforcements to our area, he'll be worried sick."

Abe rushed to do Jerica's bidding, pausing to kiss his wife on the cheek. Jerica smiled at me and said, "Alisa, I'm so glad you weren't hurt." She blinked back tears and reached out to pat my hand. Her emotions seemed very close to the surface.

I was overcome with emotion as well, but of a different sort. I hadn't decided whether or not to mention the attack when I e-mailed Bryce later. As much as I wanted to tell him about it, I didn't want to worry him when he was so far away from home. It never occurred to me that he would hear about it from other sources. I suddenly felt very anxious; I didn't send an e-mail that morning before I left. Over the last several weeks, our correspondence had escalated to the point where we sent a dozen e-mails a day. If he'd already heard about the attack, he would be beside himself with worry, especially since he hadn't heard from me all day.

The other emotion that threatened to overcome me was confusion. Bryce never initiated contact with his own parents, yet he deliberately sought me out and sent me increasingly long and detailed messages. Could it be, perhaps, that he'd meant what he said in his first e-mail? That he wished he would have waited to kiss me until I felt the same way about him? I knew he saw me as a friend—he told me, even going as far as to say he hoped I had room in my heart for more than one best friend. I trembled, just thinking about the idea that Bryce and I could be more than that.

Ever since the night Bryce kissed me, my fantasy life had come to an abrupt and life-changing halt. At first, I resented the way his image kept haunting my waking fantasies, and stopped them before they could ripen. As my feelings toward Bryce began to change, I resisted day dreaming for a different reason. My fantasies had always resulted in the same outcome—nothing. One hard and fast rule applied to everything I dreamed of during my waking moments: nothing I fantasized about ever came true.

So, as my feelings toward Bryce blossomed into longing and desire, I didn't want to tempt fate by concocting ridiculous fantasies about him. I didn't want to jinx it. My dreams, however, were beyond my control. I drifted off to sleep thinking benign thoughts about Bryce combined with prayers for his safety. My dreams were not so benign, and I started to blush just thinking about it.

"Are you okay, Alisa?" Jerica asked, brow creasing. "You look a little flushed. Are you sure you didn't get hurt?"

"I'm fine," I stammered, my blush deepening. How could I sit here with this remarkable woman and think such thoughts about her son? I felt quite ashamed of myself. Remembering her reaction the time she walked into the kitchen and saw Jace holding my wrist, I shuddered to think what she would say if she found out Bryce and I were...what? What was the nature of our relationship, exactly? I considered asking Jace to take me home, but I wanted to wait for Abe. I didn't want to miss anything, any news at all, about Bryce.

Abe came back in the room, smiling and shaking his head. "Well, he'd heard about it. As soon as I turned on my computer, about twenty e-mails popped up in my inbox. 'Dad, why is a crew being dispatched. What the hell happened?' I sent a reply and waited about two minutes before I got a response. He was so relieved to hear from me. He hadn't been so shaken since..." Abe trailed off. We all knew what he stopped himself from saying.

"Maybe I should head home," I announced, trying to keep the urgency from my voice. "I didn't get much sleep last night, and after this morning, I'm pretty tired." Jace stood up and offered to drive me. I followed meekly, trying to look tired and pathetic. Inside, I was screaming for him to hurry. I was desperate to get home to my computer.

I said hi to my mom and gave Daddy a hug when I got home. They were as inattentive and oblivious as usual, and for once I was glad. I rushed upstairs, locked my door, and switched on my computer with shaking hands. Never had it seemed so slow, so outdated. I changed clothes and brushed my teeth while I waited for the sloth of a machine to come to life.

There were a total of six e-mails from Bryce waiting for me. I read the last one first, vowing to go back and read them all in order as soon as I finished sending Bryce a reassuring message. I sent him a quick e-mail to tell him I was okay, and asked him to write me back as soon as he could.

His first e-mail was the usual morning greeting. Subsequent e-mails were increasingly frantic. The final message was sent after he'd heard from his dad:

Dear Alisa,

Thank God you're okay. When Dad told me you were safe and at our house, I nearly cried with relief. Thankfully, I didn't. The guys here never would have let me live it down, and I would have been forced to leave here in disgrace. After the trauma you've been through today, leaving here doesn't sound bad at all. Part of our training involves an internship in Central Dispatch. When Mom's call came through, I almost died from fear. The only thing I knew was that a Hunter had been killed. I alternated between haunting the halls of Central and sending e-mails from my laptop back at the dorm. The fact that I hadn't heard from you at all today had me worried sick. I can't tell you what it means to me, what you *mean to me. I live for your e-mails. You asked me one time about my anchor. Well, Alisa, you are my anchor. You are my lifeline. I told you in that first e-mail that I didn't regret kissing you. Do you regret it? I'll wait here until you reply. No matter how long it takes.*

Love,
Bryce

I wiped the wetness from my eyes and smiled through tears yet unshed. My reply was immediate and from the heart:

Dear Bryce,
> *Do I regret that kiss? If I'd answered that question after it happened, my answer might have been different. No, I don't regret anything that's happened between us, good or bad. Every argument, every hurt feeling, every second we've spent together led up to this moment. I am grateful beyond anything you can imagine to be here, at this moment, at this computer (slow as it is), writing to you. The only thing that could make this moment sweeter would be to have you here with me. I am closer to you than anyone I've ever known, Jace and Rachel included. So, to answer your question, no. I don't regret that kiss.*

Love,
Alisa

When had I ever been as bold as I was at the moment I pressed the send button? Battles with Hunters, taking up for myself with Becky, walking into the dance with Jace: each scenario would have been impossible for me just a few months ago. I felt a gradual shift in my perspective and my attitude towards myself. With that e-mail to Bryce there was an element of risk, of putting myself out there, of opening up in a way I never had.

Instead of feeling anxious about what I'd just done, I felt at peace. For the first time in my life, I was in love. Those childish fantasies of just a few months ago were a diversion. My survival was tied to those daydreams because I'd never truly lived. My dreams were the only thing that kept me hanging on from one day to the next.

Over the past couple of months, I didn't need to drift off into a fantasy world in order to keep myself afloat. With Bryce, I was able to live in the moment. He kept me tied to this world in a way nothing ever had. I didn't need to dream of being someone else or doing something else. I was happy to be me.

***

Over the next few weeks, I was able to transform my life in ways I could never have imagined. I tried out for the softball team and made it. I deliberately exercised. I began researching different colleges and making plans for my future. The apathy I'd lived with nearly all my life was gone, and in its place was a new determination.

I awoke one sunny day in March, and switched on my computer. I hummed along with the Dixie Chicks' Wide Open Spaces while I waited for everything to power up. The subject line of Bryce's morning e-mail was 'Good Morning…or is it?' I laughed out loud.

> *Dear Alisa,*
>
> *I would love to tell you good morning, but I won't. After all, the word 'good' is a matter of opinion. I have good news and bad news. Okay—bad news first: my unit is leaving for offsite training and I won't be able to contact you for several days. The good news is, hopefully, I'll be able to get cell phone reception when we stop off in town, and I'll be able to call you. Oh, God, Alisa! How am I going to survive the next few days without being able to write to you? Please keep your phone close by on Saturday. The idea of hearing your voice is the only thing that will get me through. Be safe, Alisa, and keep me in your thoughts.*
>
> *Love,*
> *Bryce*

I felt desolate thinking about the next few days without contact. I typed out a reply, not sure whether or not he'd even be able to read it before he left. I went through my normal morning routine, but the light had already gone out of the beautiful spring day.

Jace picked me up as usual, and I felt a shot of heartache at seeing Bryce's truck. I had a feeling everything would remind me of him until Saturday when we could at last speak. "What's wrong?" Jace asked as I climbed in next to him.

"Nothing," I said, "just tired." I leaned my head against the window and pretended it was Bryce I was with. I thought about all the times I'd been a passenger in the truck, but could only count on one hand the times I'd ridden with Bryce. And, I reflected on how drastically my feelings toward him had changed since the first time he drove me home.

"...Bryce..."

I jolted back to reality when I heard Jace speak his brother's name. Oh, my God, I thought. What if he knew about us? What if *everyone* knew? "What?" I asked.

"I was just saying, the brakes are going out on this piece of crap and Dad said I have to have them fixed. I have to pay for it out of my savings, just cause I've been driving it. I swear that's why my brother let me borrow it in the first place—because he knew the brakes were shot and he didn't want to pay for repairs," Jace complained.

"He's so sneaky," he continued. "And, dishonest. Don't you think?"

"I...um..." How could I possibly answer that question? I could agree with Jace in order to cover my own hide, but then I'd feel like a traitor. Or, I could tell Jace the truth and face his certain wrath. Thankfully, it was a rhetorical question, and didn't require a response. Jace continued his tirade until we pulled into the school parking lot.

School was its usual nightmarish hell. Softball practice was better because I was able to run off some frustration. After practice, Rachel drove me home, and commented on my unusual silence.

"Okay, spill," she demanded. "You've been keeping something from the rest of us. I've known that for a while, but out of respect for your privacy, I didn't want to say anything. But lately, you've changed. Jace told me you hardly talk to him on the phone anymore. Now, you're moody and distant."

Rachel waited only a split second for me to explain myself. When I didn't, she continued, "Look, after the attack, the family agreed to a 'No More Secrets' policy. You seemed uncomfortable that day, so I know this secret has been bothering you at least as long as that, probably longer. If you tell me what's going on, I promise you it goes no further. My mind is not an open book when it comes to Jace, remember? He only gets what I give him."

There was a hint of threat in her voice. Ever since the day of the attack, Rachel had been true to her word about pursuing her training.

She met with Jerica at least three times a week. I sparred with her about once a week. I knew she would do whatever she had to do to protect the family. If she felt I was withholding a secret that could put the rest of them in jeopardy, she would read my mind without feeling a shred of guilt.

I decided my best option was to spill my guts. I needed to share my feelings with another person. I was desperate to tell someone, and I finally had a chance. "I'm in love," I announced simply.

This was clearly not what Rachel expected. "With whom?" she asked. I almost laughed at the look of suspicion on her face. She was probably still afraid I harbored feelings for Jace.

"I'm in love with Bryce," I admitted, feeling the burden of carrying the secret drop from my shoulders.

"Bryce, who?" Rachel asked. I could tell she was racking her brains trying to figure out if there was a Bryce who went to our school, or who had graduated in recent years.

"The brother of your boyfriend?" If I hadn't been so nervous about admitting this, I would have enjoyed the play of emotions on her face as the truth slowly dawned.

"Bryce? That Bryce? Why?" she blurted.

"He's been e-mailing me ever since he went back to Central to train. Well, let me backtrack," I said, blushing furiously. "On New Year's Eve, he kissed me. Nothing epic, just a light…kiss." I couldn't bear for Rachel to look at me. I was too embarrassed to continue.

"So, he kissed you, and now he's been sending you e-mails," Rachel summarized.

"Several messages a day. They started out a little flirtatious, but now… I don't know how it happened; I've totally fallen in love." I tried to hide the longing in my voice. "I don't know, maybe to him it's just a close friendship. It's hard to tell. I don't exactly have a lot of experience with guys."

"Look, Alisa. I hope it works out. I really do. But, I want you to be careful. I'd never say this to Abe and Jerica, but I got a peek in his mind over the holidays. I know what you're thinking; I've been holding out on a couple secrets too. Anyways, I took a quick look. Or, rather, I tried to look. His mind is surrounded by a layer of rage. There's some darkness there, Alisa. I don't want to see you get hurt,"

Rachel said in a firm, but sympathetic manner.

"I know about the rage, Rachel," I explained. "It's because of his older brother. He's starting to get past it. He's better, now." I felt defensive toward Bryce. I understood him, and I wanted Rachel to know he wasn't bad, just hurt.

"He's talked to you about Royce?" Rachel seemed surprised. "Jace told me he's never spoken of him, not since his death. If anyone speaks his name, Bryce leaves the room. Jace said he never even cried."

"Yes, he has. He almost cried in front of me when he talked about him. Bryce has talked about Royce several times over the last couple of months. He said Royce was his hero." I hoped I hadn't crossed a line in admitting all of this to Rachel. I figured I could tell her anything because she could pluck it from my brain if she wanted to.

"Wow. That's a side of him no one else has ever seen. Of course, Jace is biased; he's never said anything good about Bryce. They've always had a tense relationship from what I've heard. I wondered why Bryce let him use the truck, though. It seemed out of character for him to do something like that." Rachel was silent the rest of the drive home.

When she pulled into the driveway, she said thoughtfully, "You know I won't say anything unless I have to. For now, it's our secret. But, I really think you should tell Abe and Jerica. Not about the kiss or any of the personal stuff, but about the e-mails. If anything, it might make them feel better that he's got a friend."

CHAPTER FOURTEEN
ALISA

On Friday night, I slept with my phone close by in case Bryce called while I was still asleep. When my eyes popped open at a quarter to eight on Saturday morning, I anxiously checked my phone for missed calls. Nothing. I sure wished he would have been a little more specific about the time. A long day stretched before me with nothing to look forward to but that phone call. I hesitated to take a shower for fear he may call and I wouldn't hear it ring over the rushing water. Or, that I wouldn't be able to get to my phone quickly enough. For the sake of personal hygiene, I finally put my phone in a waterproof zip-lock bag and took a bath.

Hours passed, and still no phone call. I waited for Rachel to pick me up and take me to Jace's house for lunch. "Why are you so jumpy?" Rachel asked as we pulled out of my driveway.

"Bryce is on an off-site training excursion and he might be able to call me today," I explained in a rush. "But, I don't know what time he's going to call. It's driving me crazy."

"It's driving me crazy too," Rachel said, "and I've only been with you for two minutes. You better get a grip on yourself, or you'll worry Abe and Jerica."

I felt too hyper and overanxious to be able to enjoy myself. I tried to put on a good show for the Alexanders. When my phone rang halfway through lunch, I jumped out of my seat so fast I nearly overturned it.

"I'm sorry," I stammered. "I'll be right back. It could be…" I looked at Rachel, willing her to cover for me. She rolled her eyes in response. Rushing from the room and out to the back patio, I pushed the talk button.

"Hello." My lungs felt constricted, and I could hardly get the words out.

"God, it's good to hear your voice," Bryce spoke into the phone. He was practically yelling, so I guessed the reception wasn't as good as he'd hoped. It was good enough, though.

"You too," I said. After several months and hundreds of e-mails, I couldn't think of anything to say.

"Alisa, I miss you so much. I can't wait to see you again. I thought talking to you would make me feel better, but it just makes me want to see you even more." Bryce spoke so rapidly, I could barely keep up.

"I miss you too. These past few days have been horrible. I've probably sent you ten e-mails just out of habit." My voice shook with emotion. After waiting for this moment for days, it was overwhelming.

"We'll be back at the dorm late tonight and I'll read every message you sent. June seems so far away. I can't wait to see you. Did you tell Mom and Dad I might be calling today?" Bryce and I had never discussed how our correspondence might be viewed by others. Did he assume I discussed our long-distance friendship with his family? Maybe Bryce saw us as nothing more than friends and figured it would be natural for me to mention our e-mails. Maybe I'd been reading too much into it.

"No, I didn't. Bryce, have you told them how often we write to each other?" I asked.

"No. It never felt like the right time. I wanted to wait until you were sure about us." Bryce sounded uncertain. He couldn't have been any more uncertain than I was. Tell them what? I didn't know there was an "us." How exactly did he view our relationship?

"Alisa, I want to see you when I come home. Well, I want to do more than see you. I want us to be together. I'm no good at this. Am I making sense?" Bryce sounded very nervous and unsure of himself.

I decided to take the plunge. "So, you want me to wait for you? You want us to be, like, a couple?" I began blushing as soon as the words were out of my mouth. If I'd misinterpreted what Bryce was trying to say, I would certainly seem like an idiot.

"Yes. I can't imagine being with anyone but you, and I can't stand the idea of you being with anyone but me," Bryce pleaded, his voice sending shivers over every inch of my body.

"I'm already waiting for you, Bryce. I couldn't imagine being with anyone else," I admitted, joy making my heart leap in my chest.

"I should call Mom and Dad. Are you there now?" he asked.

"Yes, I'm in your backyard. They're probably wondering why I rushed out to take this phone call. Maybe they think I have a secret lover, or a drug dealer."

"If they try to guess, I would put my money on 'secret lover' as their first choice. The way you blush, you won't be able to keep me a secret for long," Bryce laughed. God, it was good to hear him laugh without a trace of mockery or darkness. He was like a new person.

"We're heading out in a few minutes, and I still need to stop in one of the shops before we leave, so I guess I'd better call my parents. I'll send you an e-mail as soon as we get back to Central. I love you," he said.

"I love you too," I replied. "Bye." The line disconnected. I had to stand outside for a few minutes to compose myself. It was funny how easily those words, 'I love you', flowed from my lips. It was a life changing moment.

I let myself back inside and joined the family in the dining room. "Bryce is on the phone," Jace mouthed to me, pointing at a glowing Jerica. She held her cell phone lovingly, as if she was holding a little piece of the son she missed so badly. I knew she worried about Bryce, not just because of his dangerous calling, but also because of inability to show his emotions.

I began to worry when Jerica started to cry. Abe looked alarmed at first, but relaxed visibly when he realized she was still smiling. "Baby, let me put your dad on the phone. I love you too." She handed the phone to Abe, and mopped at her eyes with a napkin. Jerica waved away Jace's attempt to ask her why she was crying. "Later," she whispered.

I watched Abe as the expression on his face went from confusion, to sadness, to joy. "I'm so proud of you son," he exclaimed, his voice almost breaking, "I love you. Goodbye, Bryce."

It took a few seconds for Abe to get a hold on his emotions. He looked at Jerica, then over at me. He winked and smiled. I couldn't imagine what that was about.

"What's going on?" Jace asked. "Why are you two crying? Is Bryce okay?"

"I'm not crying," Abe said. "Your mom is. Bryce is fine. We just cleared the air a little, that's all. He said he's thinking about exploring a different career. He said he only joined WTB because of

Royce. He stayed out a thirst for revenge, even though he knew he wasn't cut out for the job."

"He actually talked about Royce?" Jace asked in amazement.

"He's looking into making a transfer to the Watcher Academy next year. Or, he may not go back to Central at all." Abe caught Jerica's eye and they both smiled through their tears. "He said he'll send us an e-mail when he gets back to the dorm. Apparently, his unit has been out on a training mission, and he was able to get phone reception on his way back. Man, it was good to hear his voice. I haven't heard him sound so happy in... wow."

The room fell silent. I held my breath, praying no one would think to ask me who called my phone and why I'd been so desperate to answer it. "Well, everyone," Jerica said. I almost jumped out of my seat. "Let me go get the dessert." Thank you, thank you, thank you. I was so relieved she didn't ask me about that phone call.

But I wasn't out of the woods yet. "Hey, who called you?" Jace asked as Jerica left the dining room.

"Jace," Rachel interrupted, "can you do me a favor? I think I left my cell phone in the car. Can you go get it for me?" Rachel saved the day again. I owed her big.

"Oh, yeah. I can't wait to see your new phone." Jace's ADD kicked in, his previous question to me completely forgotten. He got up and bolted out the front door. I hoped he would become so absorbed in Rachel's new technological devise, he would forget all about that phone call. Then, I felt guilty for being such a bad friend. I remembered there was a time not too long along ago that I'd jumped him for keeping Rachel a secret, and now I was doing the same thing. With his own brother!

Jace reappeared after a few minutes, with a look of regret on his face. "I can't find it."

"Oh, I forgot. It's right here in my pocket," Rachel said, thrusting the shiny, new phone toward him. His eyes lit up with glee as he snatched it from her. By the time his mother came back into the room with the cake, he'd forgotten everything but the possibilities presented by a new piece of communication technology.

Silently thanking Rachel—and Sprint— I allowed my mind to drift a little, thinking about the e-mail I hoped would be waiting for me when I arrived home that evening.

"So, Alisa," Jace interrupted my thoughts. "You never answered my question. Who called you earlier?" Damn Jace to the pit of Hell. I could feel everyone watching me as they waited for my answer.

Basically, I had three options. Option one: I could answer the question right then and there and endure the questioning that would be sure to follow. Everyone would know I'd been holding out. Jace, and possibly his parents, would be hurt and angry by my deception. Option two: I could lie and then face all the bad consequences previously stated in option one at a later date, only it would be worse. Option three: I could say "Look, a grizzly bear!" and run out of the house while everyone was distracted, never to return again.

Option three sounded good. Four people waited for my response. I dared a quick glance at Rachel, and she nodded in encouragement. I could feel my face heating and undoubtedly turning fire-engine red, like it always did when I was nervous, embarrassed, or stressed.

"It was some guy, wasn't it?" Jace blurted. "Who is it? Ooh, Alisa's been holding out." Jace smiled, enjoying my embarrassment. Time to wipe the smile off his face. I took a deep breath.

"Yes, it was a guy." I willed myself to continue, and tried not to look anyone in the eye. "It was Bryce. He's been e-mailing me ever since Winter Break and…" I broke off, unable to continue. The silence was so thick, I couldn't breathe. I waited for someone to say something.

"No, Rachel, it's not okay," Jace said loudly, in response to some internal message from his girlfriend. "This sucks. I may have kept Rachel secret for a few weeks, but this is different. Bryce is my brother, and you know how I feel about him. You know he's just doing this to piss me off. He doesn't even like humans, Alisa."

Jace got up from the table and stormed out of the room. I was too shocked to start crying—yet. I knew the tears would come, and most likely at the worst possible time. What if what Jace was saying was true? What if Bryce didn't like me? What if it was just one big practical joke from one brother to the other? I tried to convince myself otherwise, but I couldn't think of one single reason why Bryce would want to be with me in the first place.

All my self-doubts came crashing down, and the tears came at last. Rachel, the good-hearted person that she was, left Jace to pout and rage in his bedroom. She reached over and took my hand. "He's just mad. He'll get over it. Jace didn't mean what he said. You know how he is," she murmured sympathetically.

The thing was, I didn't know. I'd never seen him that angry before. I felt like I didn't really know my best friend at all. Or, maybe ex-best friend.

"Don't cry, Alisa," Jerica said soothingly. "Rachel is right. Jace will get over this in no time. I'm glad you and Bryce are friends. Or, is it more?" I could feel her willing me to look at her. Unable to resist, I looked into her eyes.

"I see that it is. I thought as much. Bryce told me on the phone that you two had become close. Alisa, do you remember what I told you at Christmas time? I said 'Be patient with my son. I know it's hard, but stick with him. He's worth it.' I wasn't talking about Jace." Jerica gave my hand a squeeze and left the room in pursuit of her youngest son.

"Jerica sees things others don't." Abe said. "Have faith in Bryce. And, Jace. Things will work out. I promise." I smiled at him, trying to look reassured. Abe and Jerica sounded like fortunetellers with their vague predictions which could mean anything or nothing.

Abe began clearing the table, waving away Rachel's attempt to help. "You two girls go on out to the living room. I'm sure Jace will be out in a few minutes." I followed Rachel and slumped onto the couch feeling like my life was over. I had totally screwed up things with Jace. After everything he'd done for me, bringing me into his home and into his family, I chose to repay him by hooking up with his older brother and then trying to hide it from him.

"Stop chewing on your fingernails," Rachel scolded. "You worry too much. Jace will out here any second. He feels like an idiot and is trying to find a way to apologize for what he said to you."

"How do you...oh, never mind." For some reason, it hadn't occurred to me that Rachel and Jace would be communicating the whole time. Jerica came into the living room, followed by her shame-faced son.

"Alisa, I'm sorry. I didn't mean what I said." He stopped talking and looked at his mother. She got the hint, and left the room. "Look, you know how I feel about Bryce. We've never been able to get along for more than thirty seconds at a time. I always think the worst of him, so my first instinct was to accuse him of using you to mess with me."

Jace had trouble making eye contact, but at least he was sitting next to me. Rachel sat silently, probably feeding him things to say through their mental connection. "You're my best friend, and I guess I'm jealous. I don't want to share you with my idiot brother. I just don't get it. How did this happen?"

I shrugged. "Nothing has really happened, other than we send e-mails back and forth. I don't like him better than you, just in a different way." I quit that line of explanation when I saw the look on Jace's face.

"Yeah, I can imagine how. Please don't go into details. It'll make me sick. I just wish you had better taste. I mean, Bryce? Really?" Jace was starting to get himself worked up. "I should have known something was up when he let me use his truck. He'd never been nice to me before. And I couldn't understand at the time why he tried so hard to keep Mikael away from you. He told him you were only fourteen."

"You knew about that?" I asked. "I thought Bryce was joking when he told me that."

"I'm not going to say I approve," Jace continued. He looked at Rachel and said, "I can speak for myself. I'm not going to say something I don't mean just because you're here." Looking back at me, he said, "But, I will try to accept it. For now. This isn't making me like Bryce more, you know?"

"I'm sorry, Jace," I pleaded. "It just happened. Nothing has to change between us, right?"

"Fine. Everything's the same until he comes home in a couple of months. Will you two stick to an e-mail only relationship then?" Jace frowned when he saw the tell-tale look on my face. I couldn't help myself; I remembered that New Year's kiss. "Eww. I'm glad I can't read your mind."

Rachel put an end to our conversation. "Let's go to the tennis courts and practice, otherwise team Abe and Jerica will kick your butts again next weekend." Jace sprinted down the hallway in search of his lucky racket. I felt weird around Jace the rest of the afternoon, and was relieved to return to my own house after our tennis practice.

***

I had to wait until almost ten o'clock that evening before finally receiving that much-anticipated e-mail from Bryce. I checked and re-checked my e-mail so obsessively, I was surprised I didn't crash my computer. My heart lurched when I saw his e-mail address pop up on the screen.

Dear Alisa,

Today has been the best day I've had since New Year's Eve. I'm so exhausted, I can hardly move, but just thinking about you keeps me going. Being able to hear your voice, hearing you say that you love me, I can't believe how lucky I am. I told my mom about us. Well, kind of. I told her we've been in contact and that our relationship has helped me get past some issues I've struggled with. I hope you don't mind. She didn't seem surprised. I was even able to tell my dad that I'd only joined the Warriors because of Royce. I think I've decided to finish out this year of training and then transfer. I think I might be more suited to being a Watcher. I don't think I'm cut out for the solitary life. I might even go to college for a couple of years before I make a decision. All I know is that I love you and I can't wait to see you again. I don't know how Jace will feel about us being together. If you don't mind, I think I'll send him an e-mail sometime. Not to ask his permission, but to let him know that things may be a little different when I come home. Or, at least I hope things will be different. I plan to monopolize most of your time, leaving you very little opportunity to hang out with my brother. I desperately need to get some rest, but I'll wait up for a few minutes, hoping you will e-mail me back.
Love you and miss you,
Bryce

I didn't hesitate a second before responding, hoping he would still be awake to read my message.

Dear Bryce,

It was wonderful hearing your voice too. The only problem is, now I miss you more than ever. Your parents were happy to hear from you as well. Your mother was literally crying with joy. Something unprecedented happened today, however. Your brother, for the first time since I've known him, was actually able to concentrate on a single thought and remain undistracted by food. I know. It's like the world suddenly started spinning in the opposite direction. The source of his obsession: who called me right before you called your mom. I admitted it was you, and that caused a bit of a stir. He didn't take it well, to say the least, but by the time I left your house, he had almost fully recovered from the shock. Your parents seemed okay, so that was a relief. I hope you're not angry by the way I've handled things. Please don't be mad. I just couldn't outright lie to any of them. Please take care of yourself until you can come home to me. I miss you more than I'd ever thought possible, but tonight, as always, I'll see you in my dreams.
Love always,
Alisa

I waited a few minutes for a response, and received this in reply:

Dear Alisa,

Why would I be angry? I'm glad it's out in the open, now. I'm sorry you had to do it alone. I wish I would have been there. If Jace gives you any crap, he'll have to answer to me. That goes for anyone who messes with you. I've got an early day tomorrow, so I'd better get to sleep. Rest assured, I'll be dreaming of you too.
Love you,
Bryce

I smiled as I read his message, shivering when I reached the part about taking care of anyone who messes with me. I fell asleep that night with Bryce on my mind, secure in the knowledge that the worst was behind me.

***

Time accelerated, it seemed, the day of our first softball game. Between schoolwork, ball games, practice, and training with Abe, I hardly had time to breathe. Every available moment I could spare was spent e-mailing Bryce or thinking about him and how much I missed him. It was surprising to me how easily I kept up with my busy life.

One amazing thing that happened was I actually got a date to the Prom. A shy senior from my English class asked me to accompany him, and I graciously accepted. He almost fell over himself with gratitude when I said yes, almost to the point that I was embarrassed. He said it was the first time he'd actually attended a school dance, and he was afraid he would never have the chance. Looking back at my life at the beginning of the school year, I knew just how he felt.

I cautiously mentioned my Prom date to Bryce, and he became very jealous and possessive, threatening to use his magic in immoral and illegal ways should my date put a finger on me. I smiled when I read his e-mail; it was the happiest I'd ever been.

CHAPTER FIFTEEN
RACHEL

Training with Abe was grueling. I'd always tried to keep myself in shape and considered myself to be in fairly good physical condition. I was accustomed to jumping and dancing in humid ninety-degree temperatures during pre-season football, and running laps in the warm spring weather during softball season. Abe's idea of training was twice as brutal as anything my high school coaches could devise.

Jerica's idea of training, however, was a million times worse. You would think that meditation and brain exercises would be a piece of cake compared to being thrown around on lightly padded concrete, but this was not so. I found it exceedingly difficult to relinquish enough control to allow Jerica access to my mind.

Although Jerica was surprised and impressed by how far I'd come on my own, she stressed that I still had much farther to go. "Without your pendant, a Hunter could sense your magic from a hundred miles away. You need to learn how to mask your power. Ideally, your magic should be kept under lock and key in the most hidden section of your mind, only to be released at your will."

I didn't understand what she was trying to tell me. One minute Jerica said she needed me to loosen up a bit, to allow her entrance. The next, she told me my security wasn't tight enough. She must have sensed my confusion, because she smiled and reached across the kitchen table to grab a notebook.

"I'm going to draw a picture for you. Hopefully, it will make sense. My artistic abilities are elementary school level at best." She drew a pyramid with five levels. She pointed to the largest section on the bottom. "This section represents your ability to communicate with Jace. This involves a certain amount of give and take. Your security is at its lowest when you communicate with him. Unless you learn to block the rest of your magic, anyone with similar powers could listen in." I felt very uncomfortable at hearing this. I would certainly be interested in learning to block some of our more intimate conversations from others.

"Second level from the bottom is your ability to connect with others. Since this is primarily a one-way flow of magic, your security level is a little higher. This means your magic is better protected. The third level of magic would be your ability to sense feelings—your Empathy. This was, I suppose, the first way your power chose to manifest itself. Again, the flow of magic is one way, and not nearly as strong." Jerica filled in the middle level on the pyramid.

"The top level, the small triangle at the top, is the source of your magic. This is the core of your being from which all of your magic forms. It is also the place where your magic returns and is stored until you are ready to use it again. This is where security should be at its highest. No one should be able to access this. If a Hunter came upon you right now and was able to kill you, it could drain every bit of magic from you before you could even take a breath. You have no block, no filter even. It is very dangerous." Jerica looked me directly in the eye, willing me to understand the seriousness of my situation.

"What is on the fourth level, the one underneath the top triangle?" I asked.

"This is where you will keep readily accessible magic," Jerica explained, smiling at my confusion. "These are the skills you haven't developed yet. The ability to create and execute spells, to move objects, to see and hear at an advanced level; these are gifts you may or may not develop. I have very high hopes for you, Rachel. I think you'll fill that level up nicely."

"Theoretically, your security should be as strong at the lower levels as it is at the highest. Right now, you have none. We will try to start at the top, and work our way down. Learning to put a block on the highest level is the easy part. It gets difficult when you start learning how to open and shut the iron door on the lower levels. I want you to keep this chart. I'm also going to give you some exercises to do at home, and you're going to have to practice at least thirty minutes every night, without fail."

I felt utterly panicked when Jerica told me that. Already, in the last few weeks since I'd been training with Jerica and Abe, my grades had begun to slip. I got a 'B' on my last math test. My first 'B' in my high school history. I couldn't keep up with everything:

school, softball, chores, and now this frustrating and difficult training. No wonder Jace's grades were mediocre.

Jerica and Abe had already determined that my physical training should be conducted without Jace present; it was too distracting for both of us. Alisa made a good sparring partner. She instinctively knew to take it easy on me, but not enough to allow me to win. I noticed her skills seemed to increase as mine did. I assumed this because she upped the ante each time I improved.

Abe was a machine. That was the only way to describe the way he fought. His motions were fluid and elegant, like a dancer. Jace, I noticed, was quickly catching on, at least when it came to the martial arts lessons. The first time I'd observed Abe and Jace in the ring, I was speechless. And, not just because Jace looked absolutely amazing without a shirt.

Abe and Jace were blessed with the gift of Speed. Paired with its twin, Strength, their skill was deadly. They went at each other with shocking ferocity, appearing as if they were sworn enemies. It was sometimes impossible to even follow the match, such was their Speed. The reinforced concrete floor often shook with the force of their collisions. Given the intensity of the training Jace was forced to undergo in the basement studio, I could only imagine what Bryce must experience training at a more professional level. Intense would have to be an understatement, I imagined.

The first time Jace bested his dad in the ring, both men were incredibly proud. Jace could talk of almost nothing else for a week. Even I was impressed, and it usually took a lot to impress me. I certainly admired the effect the rigorous training had on Jace's physique. He was a six-foot tall killing machine. The guys at school looked at him with increasing envy, and the girls looked at him with renewed lust.

The training gave me a new confidence and I didn't even acknowledge the looks or comments I'd intercepted from the other girls. After all, he was still my boyfriend. They could look all they wanted, as long as they didn't touch. I was too busy trying to keep up with my hectic life to even care that girls try to hit on Jace on a regular basis.

Added to the constant stress of everyday living and the new demands brought on by training to be a Witch (I still didn't care for that word), I had an additional, and in some ways, greater concern. I couldn't find comfort even in sleep, for my dreams had become my greatest worry. My mind turned against me as soon as I closed my eyes to go to sleep, and I couldn't figure out what to do about it. Talking to Jerica was out of the question.

When I first hooked up with Jace, I loved sleeping. I dreamed of him each and every night. It's like we were never really apart. Lately, though, I found myself dreaming of another man. This was both disturbing and slightly embarrassing on many levels. I loved Jace more than anything in the world, and these dreams made me feel as if I had betrayed him in some way. For some odd reason, I felt as if I were disappointing the entire family.

Gone were the days of my recurring nightmare, and in its place was a series of dreams, one building upon the next, but always centering around one specific person—Re'Vel. I knew in my soul that he was timeless, immortal. Maybe he wasn't even human. It was hard to tell, because the moment I entered his vast, ancient forest, my mind went as hazy as the mists swirling around my bare ankles.

Re'Vel's whisper caressed my ear. His breath caused the tendrils of hair at the nape of my neck to tease my sensitive skin. "They aren't trying to help you reach your full potential, my love. They're trying to stifle you. Only I can help you."

"That's not true." *My speech sounded slurred and unclear even to my own ears.* "They're doing everything they can to train me."

"When Nevare comes for you, they'll hand you over to save themselves," *he insisted.*

My mind latched onto the name, and for a moment, my thoughts were almost clear. "The blond? I haven't dreamed of him in..."

"Because I drove him away. I won't let anyone harm you, Rachel. You're mine." *I felt so safe in his arms.*

Each morning when I awoke, I yearned for my dream-lover in a way I'd once yearned for Jace.

Re'Vel planted a tiny seedling of doubt into my mind, and once it took root, it choked out every blossom of hope I'd ever felt in regards to the Alexander family. In my dreams, I wallowed in suspicion and fear, but during my waking hours, logic took hold and I knew I shouldn't take my silly dreams so seriously. I couldn't help but scrutinize them a little closer, though. I began to question their motives, and to pull away from Jace ever so slightly.

I felt disloyal for doubting him and for comparing him to my nocturnal visitor. And, although the dreams weren't necessarily romantic in nature, there was an element of physical attraction. Perhaps that was the reason I felt such an overpowering sense of guilt each time I looked at my boyfriend. Or maybe it was because I'd begun to fantasize about Re'Vel while I was awake. I was drawn to him, attracted to him in a way that only an older, more experienced man can inspire.

Despite the fact that he was a Witch, Jace was your typical teenage boy. He liked video games, music, television, cars, eating, and sleeping. I felt connected to him both spiritually and emotionally, but at the end of the day, Jace was just a teenager. I hated to say that I was becoming bored with him, because I wasn't. But, Jace was a known entity; Re'Vel was not.

As the days grew longer and the weather became hotter, my guilt increased exponentially. I found myself thinking about Re'Vel more and more. I tried my hardest not to pull away from my boyfriend, but it had already begun to happen, and what was worse: Jace could feel it too. I knew he was starting to confide in Alisa more and more. It bothered me that our relationship was starting to crumble.

"Rachel, I don't understand why you never want to hang out anymore. You come over, train with my mom, and then leave without saying two words to me. What's happening between us?" Jace's message was sad and pleading. My heart broke just hearing him.

I latched onto his thread of connection, and tried to respond in the most kind and loving manner I could. "Jace, I love you. You know that. I'm just completely overwhelmed right now. For the first time ever, I'm starting to struggle in school. I'm a relief pitcher this year, not even a starter anymore. Mama's on my case for falling behind on my chores. And on top of everything else, I have to train to be something I don't even want to be."

"I'm sorry, Rachel. I don't mean to make things worse by being just another thing you feel like to have to do. I'll back off and give you some space, at least until school is out. Just three or four more weeks, and then you can relax." Jace was so understanding. I felt guilty all over again.

"Thank you, Jace. Things will be different soon. If I could just get my head above water with my schoolwork, I'll be fine. I'm just in panic mode all the time now. It makes me wonder how I'll ever survive senior year, much less college." I was starting to sound panicked and stressed, even to myself. Wisely, Jace didn't point out that the world wouldn't end if I didn't get straight A's. He didn't suggest quitting softball. He'd actually made these suggestions a couple of weeks ago, and I wasn't very nice about it. Yet another thing to feel guilty about.

We broke our link after saying a lengthy goodnight. I finished my math homework and studied for a quiz in History. I almost envied Jace's lack of concern for schoolwork and grades. It was nearly midnight when I finally turned off my light and hopped into bed. Compounding my intense feelings of guilt about the way I'd been treating Jace, was my anticipation of once again meeting Re'Vel in my dreams.

***

Two weeks before finals, I had a run in with a Hunter, but this time I was prepared. On my way home from softball practice, I stopped at the gas station to fill up. I decided to go inside to grab a soda. On my way back out to my car, I caught a glimpse of a large man peeking out from behind a parked tractor-trailer. I was closer to my car than he was, but I wasn't sure if I should risk making a run for it.

I started to panic, but remembered what Jerica taught me. I slowed my breathing to normal and walked back inside the building. I told the cashier that a man had been following me, and asked if I could wait inside while I called someone. I calmly dialed Jerica's number on my cell phone, and explained as cryptically as possible that 'someone' was stalking me, and was waiting outside. Five minutes later, Abe pulled up in front of the gas station. The man fled immediately when Abe got out of the car.

After reassuring the cashier that it was just an old boyfriend, and the police didn't need to be called, I got back in my car and allowed Abe to follow me back to his house. I needed to talk to Jerica. I was fairly certain the magical spell in my necklace was no longer working. I needed different protection.

Jace and Jerica were nervous and pacing when Abe and I arrived. Jace was forced to stay behind, much to his extremely loud, verbal dissatisfaction. Jerica decided until Jace was able to put a stronger block on his magic, he should not be used to protect me. She felt that his sometimes-sporadic leakage of magic would send Hunters into a frenzy of hunger, adding fuel to the fire. He hugged me tightly as soon as I walked in the door. I felt safe and protected in his arms, just like old times.

As soon as Jace released me, I blurted, "My necklace isn't working anymore, is it? The Hunter found me and I was wearing it the whole time." I tried not to freak out, but it was hard. I felt like a moving target.

"Rachel, we knew this would happen, remember?" Jerica's voice was calm and soothing. "The protection in the necklace your father gave you was only meant to last until you were able to protect yourself. In a way, this is a good thing. It means you are exercising a reasonable amount of control over your magic. The downside, of course, is that Hunters can detect you a little easier if you are not careful. If you're worried or distracted, and relinquish just a fraction of the hold you have on your power, they can find you." Oh, great. I was worried and distracted all the time and probably would be for at least two more weeks. Not only that, but until finals were over, the worry would only increase.

"Can't you do something? Just until finals? I feel like I have no control right now. There's too much going on in my life, and my magic is going to be like a beacon for every Hunter in Georgia." I felt bad when I saw the stricken look on Jace's face, but continued anyway. "What's to stop them from getting me at home? What if they come right in while I'm sleeping? I would kill myself if anything happened to my mother because of me."

"Rachel, have you ever seen a Hunter come close to our house?" Jerica asked calmly. I'd never really thought about it, but no. I wondered why. "We have powerful spells of protection in every room of this house. That same protection is built into your home. You are safer there or here in our home, than anywhere else."

I was relieved to know that my home, at least, was a safe haven. But, why, all of a sudden, was Jerica so certain my house was protected? "What did you say? How do you know that?" I asked.

Abe sighed. "Rachel, I can't be certain until my friend completes his research, but I think we can safely assume your father was a powerful Witch. After all, your magic had to have come from somewhere."

"When we have any new information, we'll let you know," Jerica said. "But, right now, I can assure you your home is safe. I can feel the spells of protection surrounding it. Your enemies cannot harm you while you're there."

"But, how can you be sure?" I asked, desperately wanting to believe them.

Jerica smiled and reached out to squeeze my hand. "Sweetie, it's my job. I studied at the Watcher Academy for four years. I've studied spells extensively. Abe studied at WTB—the Warrior Training Bureau. He is my official Protector—and yours for the time being. Do you think we would have sent you home without any protection at all?"

I thought about Re'Vel and his insistence that the Alexanders were holding out on me. "But, why didn't you say anything before? About the spells, I mean."

"We didn't want mention it until we had more information about your father. But, we believe he is responsible for the protection surrounding your home," she explained.

Abe broke in. "Right now, we're just dealing with theories. But we believe the same spell that is tattooed on your brother was engraved inside your necklace." I saw Abe and Jerica exchange a look. "Jerica and I think it might be time to stop wearing the necklace your father gave you. Now that its protection has worn off, the Claiming spell may have a negative effect. Again, this is just a theory. Until we know for sure, you don't have to stop wearing it."

I clutched the necklace in my sweaty hand, looking back and forth between Abe and Jerica, trying to decide what to do. I wondered what Re'Vel would say, but then reminded myself he was a figment of my vivid imagination, and therefore had no bearing on the subject at hand. Jace weighed in with his opinion by sending a short, but definite message across our link. I quickly removed the necklace and handed it to Jerica. The taint of evil on it was evident now that I'd given it up, and I wondered why the Alexanders couldn't feel it too. I shuddered in response to its abhorrent nature.

I felt dirty for having had such a close association to something so wicked. I wondered if I were evil as well. If it took a spell of such horrific proportions to protect me, what did that fact say about me? I felt like I'd contaminated this wonderful, loving family with my dark existence. And, to think, I'd once sensed the darkness in Bryce. Maybe darkness knows darkness, I thought.

Abe followed me home, once again serving as my Protector. I hated that I had become such a burden. I tried to focus on my studies when I got home, but it was nearly impossible. I decided to finish my chores and make dinner. The least I could do was stay on my mother's good side. That would be one part of my life that would be going right.

***

During the week leading up to final exams, I saw a Hunter every day, sometimes more than once. I felt incompetent, my previous sense of independence gone, each time I was forced to call Jerica and Abe for assistance. I began having panic attacks just thinking about the eventual moment when it would be me and the Hunter, with no one to call, and not enough time for anyone to save me. I saw Hunters everywhere it seemed, even when they weren't there at all. For each time Abe showed up and said, "It's okay, he's gone," there was at least one other time he came to rescue me, only to say, "I don't sense anything. He must have left before I got here."

The Alexanders tried so hard to be nice to me, never once insinuating it was my fault for getting myself in that position. I knew my inability to control my magic drew Hunters to me like magnets. The more I stressed about my lapse in security, the less control I had. Only my link with Jace worked on a consistent basis.

"It going to be okay, Rachel," Jerica said one night when I stopped by to drop off some math notes for Jace. "As soon as school is out, you should be able to relax. When the pressure of finals is gone, we can concentrate on your training. Just keep practicing at home. The exercises I gave you should help." I hadn't practiced in over a week. I didn't have time.

"I'm sorry, Jerica. Am I driving you crazy with all the phone calls? I could have sworn I saw a Hunter when I left school today. I'm sorry I made Abe come all the way over there." My voice had become whiney, and I hated the sound of it. It didn't feel good to have to add paranoia to my already long list of character flaws. Paranoia, dependency, irrational fear, irritability: the list went on forever. I had become unrecognizable even to myself.

"Are you sure you don't want a full-time Protector? We can find someone who will be very discreet. You'll hardly even know he's there," Jerica offered. For a moment, I actually considered it. But, when I thought about my mother's reaction should she find out, I declined.

I couldn't understand how Jace managed to tolerate me and my swiftly changing moods. I felt guilty for putting him through it. On the upside, I didn't feel the burden of guilt I'd previously felt over my dreams of Re'Vel. No sleep, no dreams: that was the way things usually worked. Stress and worry over finals prevented me from sleeping for more than an hour at a time, and I hadn't had a good night's sleep in over a week. When I finally did crash, I slept so hard, I didn't dream at all.

***

Our final exams were spread out over three days of pure, scholastic hell. On Monday, I took my finals in Math and History—my two most difficult subjects. I was so ill with anxiety that morning, I was throwing up. My bouts of sickness caused spurts of magic to shoot across my link with Jace.

"I don't care what you say, Rachel. I'm coming over there. There's no way you're driving yourself to school." Jace's concern for me was evident in the strength and clarity of the message he sent over our thread of connection. True to his word, I looked out my front window ten minutes later, and saw his borrowed truck sitting in my driveway. I hurriedly dressed and ran out to meet him.

I was a bundle of nerves up until the very moment the Math final was placed in front of me. The second I picked up my pencil, the real Rachel, the calm, self-assured Rachel, the Rachel who had always excelled at school, took over. She told the imposter who had taken over my mind and body over the last few weeks to take a hike. An ice-cold calm flowed through my veins. I put pencil to paper and rocked it. It felt good and right. It felt like an 'A'.

Walking out of the classroom after the exam, I smiled at Jace and he almost stumbled as he realized who he was with. The old me, the good me, the me he fell in love with—I was back to stay.

"I take it the exam went well." Alisa smiled as she walked over to me. "I'm sure you got every question right just to accentuate my pitiful display of mathematical stupidity. Show-off." Alisa was genuinely happy to see me settle back into my old routine of acing a test and knowing it. I could feel joy radiating from her in waves. I knew she had been almost as worried about me as Jace had been.

My experience during the next exam, History, was the same as the previous test. Every date, every fact came rushing into my head the second the test was placed in front of me. I calmly completed each question, knowing in my heart each answer was correct. I knew the material like the back of my hand. How could I not? I'd studied obsessively for weeks.

At the end of the day, Alisa and I piled into the truck, laughing and talking while Jace drove away from the school. It occurred to me as I hopped out of the cab of the truck and practically skipped to my front door, that I had not seen a Hunter at all that day. Not once. I was giddy with relief.

The next two days were the same. The only difference was my lack of anxiety and extreme illness in the morning. I felt great when I woke up, ready to face the world. The fact that I was able to sleep certainly helped. Each exam was a breeze. The information I'd accumulated over the year seemed to be easily accessible in my brain. I envisioned a file folder in my mind, each clearly labeled with an index and sub-index. Each fact I required was neatly filed and readily available. The exams were almost too easy.

I looked around the classroom after completing my last exam. The English final had been easier than I could have hoped. I usually agonized over five paragraph essays, writing, erasing, and re-writing compulsively. This time, however, the words flowed effortlessly, each sentence forming almost instantaneously.

***

Alisa and I met at Jace's house for a post-school year celebration. Jerica and Abe couldn't believe the change in me as I breezed through their front door and tossed myself into a recliner. I whooped in glee, startling them both. Laughing out loud, I declared, "It's over! Hello summertime!"

I felt relaxed for the first time since I could remember. No school to torment me, no sports to monopolize my time, nothing but three solid months of sleeping in. Oh, yeah. And training. But still, the whole summer stretched before me, a beautiful, magical gift that would restore my soul. I smiled and let out the deep breath I didn't realize I had been holding. With it, all my frustration, anxiety, and unhappiness evaporated into the air.

With my summertime curfew now in effect, I stayed at Jace's house until eleven o'clock, thoroughly enjoying every moment we spent together. Alisa bowed out gracefully around nine, leaving, undoubtedly, to rush home to her beloved computer and the man who breathlessly waited for her next e-mail. Jace and I enjoyed our time alone by vegetating in front of the television, our silence broken only by the occasional comment. "God, I'm glad school is over." Or, "I can't wait to sleep in tomorrow." We felt so exhausted, we were unable to carry on a real conversation.

***

That night, I drifted off into the deepest sleep I'd experienced in a long time. I found Re'Vel on my favorite forest path, his opalescent skin glowing in the moonlight. I ran to him, leaping and bounding, almost flying. "Oh, Re'Vel, you should have seen me. I am myself again. I aced it. I wish you could have been there," my dream-self rhapsodized.

"I was there, my love," he replied in a soft whisper against my skin.

As the dream progressed, my feelings toward Re'Vel began to change. He became too insistent and forceful. His face held a hint of menace, and his dark eyes narrowed as he glared at me. "This isn't a game, my love. I won't wait for you any longer. Once you give yourself to me, Nevare's claim will not matter."

"But, I'm in love with Jace." It was a struggle to remember his name.

"Your father gave you to me, and spoke my Claiming Words when he named you. You're mine, Rachel, even if he changed his

mind and tried to give you to another. Mine," he insisted, grabbing my arm.

He pulled me towards him, and I tried to twist out of his grasp. A cold breeze lifted a strand of his black hair from his pale forehead. Tendrils of his shoulder-length hair brushed against my cheek, igniting my senses.

"You're hurting me," I cried. I jerked away from him, and he grabbed my nightgown. I heard the tearing of fabric. He captured my wrist and twisted it until I stopped moving.

"Say nothing to the Witches. They will cast you away like last week's rubbish," Re'Vel hissed in my ear.

That expression of air continued to tickle my ear even as I jolted up, relieved to find myself alone in my bedroom. I felt sluggish, almost drugged. Images of Re'Vel slipped through my mind, making me feel somewhat violated. I sat at the edge of my bed, letting the memories of my nocturnal travels wash over me. I tried to remember all the details of our conversation, but the memories scattered like the particles of dust illuminated by the ray of sun shining through my bedroom window.

I lurched to my feet, swaying for just a moment. I walked on unsteady legs toward the bathroom, turned on the shower, and lifted my nightgown over my head. Disappointment hit me full force; it was my favorite silk gown, and I'd never be able to wear it again. Somehow, it had become torn beyond repair. I had a brief vision of Re'Vel, face twisted in rage, but the memory disintegrated when I stepped under the steamy hot water. I rinsed away my nightmares, marveling at the way a bad dream could sometimes haunt you even by the comforting light of day.

CHAPTER SIXTEEN
RACHEL

Sometimes Jace seemed like a little boy to me: the way he found joy in blowing things up on a video game, or the way he laughed like a hyena when he got away with one his juvenile practical jokes. Boys will be boys, my mother always said, and that was probably true. I could maybe overlook the video game playing and stupid jokes, but it was difficult to ignore some of his more annoying traits.

Bryce would be home in a week, much to Alisa's delight and Jace's displeasure. Jace used and enjoyed his brother's truck to the point where he was loathe to give it up. I couldn't blame him, really. It would be hard to give up my source of transportation after getting used to having it for so long. As the deadline for giving up the truck approached, Jace began harassing his parents with a vengeance. Even after Jerica carefully explained that his older brothers had to wait until graduation to have their own vehicle, Jace continued to beg, plead, and complain.

Given my strict background, I had a hard time understanding how a child could argue with a parent. It would never have crossed my mind to say 'no' to my mother, or even bring up a topic she had previously closed for discussion. Jace reminded me of a three year old, who in their limited understanding of social interaction, believes a tantrum will yield desired results.

Jace was not a three year old, and as long as he was my boyfriend, he was going to treat his parents with respect. Our 'discussion' over that issue, and I use that term loosely, was our first major fight. I decided to approach him after listening to yet another bout of whining and manipulative pleas over dinner. Thanks to Jace, the meal was ruined, and I felt sorry for Jerica for having to feed such an ungrateful son. After I helped clear the table, I suggested to Jace that we should hang out in the basement and talk.

As soon as we'd cleared the staircase, he immediately pulled me into an embrace and started kissing me. This was my fault. I'd forgotten that 'talk in the basement' was code for 'make out in the basement.' After regaining my senses, I gave him my sternest look and told him to sit down across from me so we could talk.

"Okay, let's talk," Jace offered non-verbally. His crooked, sexy smile almost made me lose my resolve. What was I supposed to talk about again?

I answered out loud. Screaming matches were better conducted using actual words. It was hard to get a lot of volume during a psychic discussion, thus eliminating all the fun. "You'd better stop smiling now, because you won't have anything to smile about after you hear what I've got to say." I thought that was a pretty good beginning to the conversation. It set the tone.

"What do you mean?" Jace seemed confused.

"I'm sick and tired of coming over here and listening to you complain about not having a car. It's getting old. Your parents said no, and that's final. The next time you start up with that crap, I'm gonna call you out on it." I said this as calmly as possible, still using my 'inside voice.'

"You know, that's easy for you to say. You have a car. Besides, it's none of your business. But, I don't expect you to understand. You roll over and do whatever your mother tells you to do." Jace's voice increased in volume, and his tone dripped with venom. It was on.

"It's called respect, Jace. Do I like everything my mother tells me? No. But, I listen to her whether I like it not. Her house—her rules. Same thing applies to you. As long as you're living with your parents, you need to obey them." I matched Jace volume for volume, tone for tone.

"I can't believe how self-righteous and preachy you sound. You remind me of an old woman, or Bryce. Maybe you and Bryce should have hooked up, and I should have hooked up with…" Bryce stopped himself abruptly, but I knew what he'd been about to say.

This was not how the conversation was supposed to go. We were supposed to scream at each other until he came around to my point of view. Then, he was supposed to apologize so we could make up. I thought I had been doing Jace a favor, helping him to see the error of his ways. I had his best interests, and concern for his relationship with his parents, at heart.

I easily filled in the blanks of what he'd been about to say. Alisa. He should have hooked up with Alisa. My heart literally hurt. I had a sharp pain in my chest, but I knew I was too young to have a heart attack. This was my fault. I'd pushed him too far. Did he harbor feelings for his best friend, or was he just trying to hurt me any way he could? It didn't matter. I stood up and walked toward the stairs. My limbs felt numb, and my head was spinning.

"Rachel," Jace called out, using both forms of communication. I slammed the lid shut on the nonverbal messages he tried to send, leaving him no other choice but to shout up the stairs. "Rachel, I'm sorry. Come on. You know I didn't mean it. Please." I knew he was close to tears, but my feet continued to carry me toward the front door, away from his ragged pleas for forgiveness.

I grabbed my purse and keys on the way out the door without even stopping. For once, my manners failed me, and I didn't even say goodbye to Jerica and Abe. I wondered if and when I would see them again. I got in my car and backed out of the driveway without even checking my mirrors.

I was devastated. I couldn't imagine how our relationship could recover from such a blow. We could both apologize, certainly, but I would always wonder if somewhere in the back of his mind, he'd meant what he said. I thought back to the day he found out about Bryce and Alisa, and how strongly he'd reacted. He was vehemently opposed to any relationship between the two of them, and he didn't even know the whole story. I wondered how he would have reacted had he known Bryce kissed her.

Every look, every conversation Jace had ever shared with Alisa, was now suspect. No matter what happened beyond that point, I would always wonder, and things between Jace and I would never be the same. Even if Jace gave me access to his mind, he could still block certain memories. He had become very skilled all of a sudden at putting up security blocks in his mind. Maybe it was because he had something to hide.

I was about halfway home when my front tire blew out, causing me to swerve and slide into a ditch. This was bad. I didn't know how to change a tire, but even if I did, it was too dark to see. Technically, my neighborhood backed up to Jace's subdivision. Cutting through the woods and people's yards, I could walk to his house from mine in about twenty minutes. Driving took about ten minutes because you had to stick to the roads, and it was not a straight shot. The fastest way from his house to mine, was to drive along a dirt road that ran through the middle of the woods. Unfortunately, this was the path I'd chosen.

I fumbled around in my purse for my cell phone, but didn't feel it. I quickly searched my pockets before remembering that I'd left my phone on the end table in Jace's basement. I could easily reach Jace through our link, assuming he hadn't become as enraged as I had and put up a block. I didn't even want to try to reach him. I wasn't ready to talk to him yet.

The car would be fine for a while, I decided. I hadn't become too pampered or spoiled to walk. I pulled the keys out of the ignition, turned on the hazard lights, grabbed my purse, and hit the road. I walked quickly and purposefully along the dirt road toward my neighborhood. I could see lights in the distance, and with every step I took, they looked a little brighter.

My thoughts began to drift toward Jace once again, and my steps slowed. I was so absorbed in my own inner turmoil, I didn't notice I'd been surrounded until a dark form stepped in front of me, blocking my path. As I turned to run, I saw four figures blocking my escape.

"Rachel, don't be afraid. You know me." The voice was familiar. I'd heard it in my dreams. I whipped around and faced the source of that seductive voice. Re'Vel stood before me. I recognized him even in the dark. He took a step forward, and I quickly stepped back, stumbling over a tree-root, and dropping my purse. The moonlight cast an eerie glow along the path, illuminating the Hunter who stood closest to me. He growled, and I wondered why he had not yet attacked.

"Don't touch her unless she tries to run, and even then, only if I command it," Re'Vel snarled in his direction. It seemed he controlled this group of Hunters, but only barely. I suspected he had been behind the recent increase in Hunter activity in the area.

"I just came to check on you. I became worried when I found you'd blocked me from your dreams. You didn't think you could avoid me forever, did you?" My mind felt sluggish and thick, just like it did the morning after he tried to force me to follow him. I couldn't recall why I'd resisted.

THE CLAIMING WORDS

"You're not real," I protested feebly.

He closed the distance between us in one lightning quick stride. "Feel my heart beating against yours. Then tell me I'm not real," he said, pulling me into his arms. "Why aren't you pleased to see me, Rachel? You should be glad I've come. My Hunters can't watch every move you make, and it seems those charged with your protection aren't carrying out their duties."

"It wasn't their fault," I said, feeling honor-bound to defend the Alexanders. "I got angry and I left."

"And, now you're coming with me. Let Nevare try to take you. He'll be dead before he lays one finger on you," he said, running his fingertips along my jaw line.

"I can't go with you, Re'Vel..." I trailed off as he lowered his lips to mine. He nibbled on my lower lip, and my fear flew away. Re'Vel was my friend, my only friend. But the thought wasn't really mine. It came from a source outside of me rather than from within. He just wants to talk, the voice surrounding me insisted. I should listen. I should follow him. Yes, leave the Witches. Witches! That word sparked a memory, but, of whom? Jace's face flickered in my mind, and I became instantly alert.

"Jace!" I removed the block, praying the link would still be open on his side, praying he was not as foolish as I was. "My car broke down on the dirt road. I started walking and now I'm surrounded!" My growing panic was causing leaks. I was trained well enough now to feel it happening, but not competent enough to contain it.

"Rachel," Re'Vel's voice soothed. "Come along, now. It's time for us to be together."

"Rachel!" A different voice shouted in my mind. I latched onto Jace's voice; it was the only thing keeping me from giving into Re'Vel. "We're on our way. Two minutes! Talk to me!" His command swelled in my mind, pushing out some of the fog of confusion. I held on tightly to the sound of his voice, his presence in my mind.

"Jace. Warn your parents. There are four Hunters, maybe more. But, there's someone else. He's keeping the Hunters from me so far, but..." I trailed off, wondering if I should try to keep my thoughts to myself. Jerica told me my link with Jace was the weakest part of my security. Could Re'Vel read my mind? Did he know I'd summoned help?

The last thing I wanted was for Jace or his family to get hurt. I prayed with all my heart there weren't additional Hunters hiding in the woods, ready to ambush the Alexanders. I also wondered if reinforcements were close by, and if Jerica had enough time to summon them.

Re'Vel held my hand in his, and I felt a sizzle of connection. "We're going to take a trip, my love. Hold on tight." He closed his eyes, and I felt him call upon his magic. An upward magnetic pull tugged at the core of my being, but my feet stayed firmly on the ground.

He hissed in frustration. "Aid me with your magic, Rachel. I can't Transport with you while the other holds Claim. But if you help me..." he trailed a line of kisses along the side of my neck. I felt myself go limp in his arms. Just a split second before I released the hold on my magic, I heard Jace's voice in my mind.

"Hold on, baby. We're almost there," he said across our link.

I twisted away from a startled Re'Vel, and took a few staggering steps away from him. I couldn't believe how easily I gave in. If it weren't for Jace, Re'Vel could have taken me anywhere, done anything to me.

As Re'Vel walked toward me, hand outstretched, I heard a sickening thump behind me, followed by a sound similar to that of a tree trunk falling. I turned in time to see a Hunter lying face down on the ground, a dagger protruding from his chest.

"I'll get the girl. Kill the Witches," Re'Vel commanded. The next Hunter went down before the words were out of Re'Vel's mouth. He howled in frustration and rage. He grabbed my arm and pulled me close to his body. I felt the sharp point of a blade against my throat. Re'Vel stood still as the last of his Hunters were ambushed and eliminated. Clearly, his entourage was intended to annihilate, or at least distract anyone who came to help me. Five figures crouched on the dark path in front of me. I assumed the group was comprised of Jerica, Abe, Jace, and whomever they'd managed to summon at such short notice.

"She's mine, Abraham." Re'Vel voice sounded composed, but I could feel his body trembling with rage. What creature was this who commanded Hunters and had no fear of the Warriors before him?

"You have no claim, Demon." Abe's voice was cold and lethal.

"Release her and we'll spare your life. You're too weak to travel with her. Your magic's taken a downward turn lately, hasn't it?" Abe surprised me by laughing, "I can feel it. It's weak. Forget to feed, did you?"

Re'Vel's grip tightened around me, an involuntary reaction to Abe's taunt. "The weakest Demon is stronger by far than the mightiest Warrior, old man. Your bones will be centuries in the ground while I'm still walking this Earth. Keep your loved ones close, else I shall choose to feed on them if you continue to interfere."

Abe laughed again. "What claim do you think you have on Rachel?"

"Her father, Jabron, gave her to me. I've come to take what is mine," Re'Vel hissed.

"If you were able to Transport with her, you'd already be gone," Abe said. "Let her go."

"I could drain her power right now," my captor said. I tried to concentrate on keeping tight control on my magic. His hold on me made it difficult to filter out his rage.

"Try it," Abe threatened, "and it will be the last thing you ever do." The blade pressed more tightly against my throat and I felt a trickle of wetness slide down my neck. Re'Vel removed the blade and caressed my throat right before I slumped to the ground.

For just a fraction of a second, I wondered what had happened. "He's gone," at least two voices shouted.

"He disappeared without her," a strange voice declared.

Jace scooped me into his strong, comforting arms. After everything that had happened between us, he was the only one I wanted. I cried in a mixture of confusion, pain, and relief. What I assumed was a cut at the base of my throat burned with an intensity that surprised me.

"Jerica, how long before the rest arrive?" Abe asked softly, but urgently.

"Any minute. Let me take her back to our house and examine the wound. Jace, carry her to the car. I'll be with you in a moment. Craig, you and Quinn stay with Abe until the others arrive." Jerica barked out commands, and I could hear people moving around me. I was still too weak and frightened to lift my head from Jace's chest. As he carried me down the road to his dad's car, I vaguely wondered who Craig and Quinn were, and how they'd come to be there.

Jace crawled into the back seat beside me, whispering in my mind. "It's okay. Mom will know what to do." I heard a car door close, and Jerica's voice instructing Jace to watch for approaching enemies. I heard the ignition start and gravel crunch. I wondered what would happen with my car and if my mother was worried.

"Calm down, baby," Jace sent the thought into my mind. "My dad will take care of your car and bring it back to the house. You'll be okay. I'll never let anything happen to you again, I promise." For the moment, I believed him. I always felt safe in his arms.

The second Jerica pulled into the driveway and stopped the car, she ran to the front door and unlocked it. Jace carried me inside and placed me on the couch as gently as he could. I squinted a little as my eyes slowly adjusted to the light. "Jace, go get the first aid kit," Jerica instructed calmly. She spent the next several minutes examining my wound and asking me questions while Jace hovered around looking helpless and concerned.

After assuring her that the cut on my neck was the only wound I'd suffered, she examined it at length. It stung when she cleaned it with antiseptic wash. I flinched, sucking in a deep breath when she poured the cold liquid over my wound. Again, I was shocked by the intensity of the pain.

"Jace, what time is it?" Jerica asked. It took him a minute to locate his cell phone and read off the time. It was just a few minutes after ten o'clock. "What time do you need to be home before your mother starts to worry?"

"I have to be home by eleven. I'm never late," I said, remembering how Jace had accused me of doing whatever my mother told me to do. The flashbacks of our argument were more devastating and painful than the memories of Re'Vel's attack. I closed my eyes against the emotional pain.

"I want you stay here a while longer, if that's okay," Jerica said as she packed up her first aid supplies. "I just want to make sure you're not in shock. I think it might be a good idea to let Abe have a look at you as well." I could read the worry in her eyes as she leaned over me, feeling my forehead.

Abe rushed through the front door about fifteen minutes later. "Everyone okay?" he asked. "Rachel, how are you holding up?" His

THE CLAIMING WORDS

tone was light, and he smiled at me as he spoke, but I could tell he was shaken by what had happened. He sat down next to me.

"Let's have a look at that cut," he said. I lifted my chin and he gave my wound a quick visual once-over. "It doesn't look too bad, but I'm a little worried about the blade the Demon used to cut you. I'd bet my life he used a magic-laced dagger."

"How can we know for sure?" Jerica asked.

"We can't," Abe replied.

Jace cut in on the conversation. "But, you said the cut looks fine. What difference does it make if the blade was magical?"

"I don't know for sure, but some blades are infused with properties which enable them to collect blood. If he used the kind of dagger I suspect, it collected her blood like a syringe. Not just a little bit of blood like you would expect to find if the Demon had used an ordinary knife, but a sizable amount, preserved until the time he needs it." Abe glanced at Jerica. I could sense he did not want to go into too much detail until later.

"Is she safe?" Jace asked.

"Rachel is most definitely safe while here or in her own home," Abe replied, looking at each one of us in turn. His eyes landed on mine. "She is safe as long as one of us is with her."

I hated to tell Abe, but I most certainly was not safe in my own home. Re'Vel was able to gain access to my dreams while I slept in the supposed safety of my own bedroom. Sure, I'd found a way to block him for the time being, but I believed wholeheartedly that my refusal to allow him entry led to recent events.

I wanted to tell them about Re'Vel, but I couldn't do it. I knew it would take forever to explain, and I didn't want to be too late getting home. Besides, I didn't want to worry Abe and Jerica. I got myself into the mess I was in, and I would train as hard as I had to until I was safe. The first two reasons, of course, were important and had some bearing on my decision to keep my silence. The main reason I said nothing about Re'Vel was because I didn't want to further damage my chances to mend my relationship with Jace. Admitting my near romantic relationship with a Demon was sure to be the kiss of death to any chance we might have.

Re'Vel was real. He wasn't just a dream, and that put everything that had happened in a different light. We'd shared confidences, embraces, love. Because of him, I'd become bored with Jace and consequently, snappish and irritable. Basically, I'd cheated on my boyfriend with a Demon. I may not have known much about the magical world, but I knew this didn't make me a good person.

"There's one other thing, Rachel," Jerica said. "We need to decide what to say to your mother. Now, Abe put the spare tire on, so you can drive your car home if you want to, but someone will have to follow you home. I don't think it's a good idea for you to go off on your own for a while, either. If you don't feel ready to drive yet, I'd be happy to drive you."

"I think the most important thing to consider, though, is whether or not it's time to talk to your mother about who you are. You can't keep it a secret forever, and I think she should know the danger you could be facing." I shook my head, and Jerica backed off a little. "Rachel, you don't have to explain everything tonight, but you need to tell her something. Do you want to me help you talk to her?"

I appreciated the offer, but there was no way I was going to tell mother anything about magic. I could just see myself marching in and telling her, "Hey, Mama. I've got some crazy news. You see, I'm a Witch and so is my boyfriend. Oh, yeah, and all his family members wield magical powers as well. And before I forget, I had an affair with a Demon, but it's no big deal because it happened in a dream." I almost laughed out loud at the thought.

"Thank you, Jerica, but I think I'd better talk to her alone. I'm not sure what I'll say yet, but you're right; I'll have to say something." I tried to be as kind as possible while rejecting her offer. "I don't think I can drive, but if one of you could maybe drive my car while Jace follows in the truck, I would appreciate it. I don't want to inconvenience anyone, though. I've already been enough of a burden lately." I almost started bawling.

"Oh, sweetie," Jerica soothed, "of course you're not a burden. You're part of this family and you would do the same for us if we needed you to. Come on, let's get you home."

Jace helped me to my feet; I was still a little unsteady. He hugged me gently, caressing my mind with thoughts of love and regret. "I'm so sorry, baby. None of this would have happened if we hadn't argued. And, you were right all along. I've been acting like a kid," Jace said desperately. "I love you, Rachel. Please say you forgive me."

THE CLAIMING WORDS

"I love you too, Jace. I'm not angry with you, but I'm so tired. Can we please talk about this later?" I replied.

***

My mother greeted me the moment I walked in my front door. I knew I wasn't in trouble; I still had five minutes to spare until curfew. I would have some explaining to do about the car, and of course, the tiny cut on my throat. I decided to take the plunge and jump right in.

"Mama," I started to say. "I had some trouble with my car and..."

"What happened? Are you hurt?" Leave it to her to overreact.

"I'm fine. My tire blew out and I went into a ditch. Mr. Alexander came and put the spare on, but I was pretty upset, so he helped me get home." I concentrated on keeping my explanation as simple as possible.

"Oh, Rachel, you should've called. I'll have to thank Mr. Alexander," she said. "What happened to your neck?" She peeled back the band-aid, and frowned. "That cut looks deep. It might need stitches. Maybe we better have someone have a look at it." It was time for me to take control of the situation before the police and paramedics were called. Mentioning Witches, Hunters, and Demons was absolutely out of the question. In my opinion, it was never really an option.

I took a deep breath and felt an icy calm descend upon my mind. "Mama," I said, pushing a thought ever so lightly into her brain. When I felt the connection, felt her succumb, I said aloud, "I scraped my neck when I reached down to pick up my cell phone from the floorboard of the car. When I pulled against the seat belt, there must have been something sharp on the strap. It is just a tiny scratch and will be gone before you know it." It was possibly the most ludicrous story ever told.

"Okay, Rachel," Mama replied, and I exhaled a huge sigh of relief. "We'll take care of the car tomorrow. I'm just glad you weren't hurt."

And so the legacy of lies began. If Re'Vel had set out to lure me to the side of darkness, he had surely succeeded. Rachel the liar, Rachel the cheater, went to bed with a heavy heart. On my way upstairs, I spied an envelope on the table in the foyer. It was from my school—probably my report card. I ripped it open; I was still a straight 'A' student. Strangely, I didn't care.

"Rachel," Jace called across our link. "Is everything okay?"

"Goodnight, Jace," I replied before severing our connection. I fell across my bed, and although I wanted to cry myself to sleep, to drift off into the oblivion of slumber, I couldn't do it. Re'Vel would find me there—my own personal Freddie Krueger. I struggled to stay awake until the early hours of the morning, but at last, my tired eyes could take no more.

I shut off my magic the way Jerica taught me—my link to Jace included. I called upon my church upbringing, mumbled a desperate prayer, and succumbed to my emotional and physical exhaustion. In my dreams, I could see the forest, but I chose to run the other way.

CHAPTER SEVENTEEN
ALISA

I spent the first days of summer vacation in front of my computer alternately waiting for e-mails from Bryce and sending replies. Obsessive perhaps, but it was my summer vacation and I was determined to spend at least the first couple of weeks doing whatever I wanted. I wanted Bryce. Our e-mails as of late had become short, but numerous. He sent me a message every chance he got, often sending out just a sentence or two in between testing sessions.

Bryce faced a grueling week of final exams. These tests were unlike anything I'd ever experienced: less pencil and paper, more exertion and pain. High school seemed pretty tame in comparison. Bryce seemed desperate to come home.

> *Alisa,*
> *I'm still counting the hours until my flight home. I'd like to count the hours until I actually see you, but you know how air travel can be. My actual arrival time is unpredictable at best. My question to you is this: can you survive an entire 24 to 36 hours without e-mailing me? It seems all you do nowadays is sit in front of the computer. Not that I'm complaining.*
> *Love,*
> *Bryce*

My smart-aleck response was as follows:

> *Bryce,*
> *Why do you assume that I sit in front of the computer all day? My cats take turns handling my correspondence so I may lay in the sun all day working on my tan. As for being able to survive a day or two without hearing from you, I've done it before as you*

well know. I plan to use our time apart to bake chocolate cookies by the dozens. If you're mean to me, I won't save any for you.
Love,
Alisa

My e-mails, for the most part, were humorous and fun. I tried to keep things light, tried to keep him feeling upbeat and positive. The messages Bryce sent to me tended to be more serious. Some of his e-mails were so full of love and affection, I blushed just reading them. He was very poetic at times. His elegant words of romance were certainly no match for a lowly high school student. I feared that if we ever broke up, all men thereafter would never match up.

About a week before his anticipated return, I received a very alarming e-mail. It was about ten o'clock at night, and I had just stepped out of the shower and settled back in front of my computer. I had a towel draped around me and my hair dripped down my shoulders; my dedication to my e-mail relationship knew no boundaries. I clicked on his newest message. Bryce's e-mail hit me like an aluminum bat to the chest.

Alisa,

Central just received word of another attack. No casualties have been reported, but additional back up has been requested. I'll send an e-mail to Dad right away. For once, I am praying you're not with my family. Please, please be at home, Alisa. Send me an e-mail to let me know you're okay, then if you can, call Jace and find out what the hell is going on.
Love,
Bryce

I dialed Jace's cell phone and listened to it ring while I typed out a quick e-mail to let Bryce know I was at home, and therefore, safe. Jace's phone rang six times before his voicemail picked up. I hung up and immediately called him back. I tried Rachel's phone and the same thing happened. No one picked up the home telephone either. Panic began to set in.

THE CLAIMING WORDS

I spent the next hour alternately dialing cell phones, burning up the Alexanders' home phone, and typing Bryce reassuring messages. I felt completely worn out and borderline hysterical by the time Jerica called me back a little after eleven.

"Oh, my God, Jerica! Is everything all right?" I cried into the phone, probably bursting Jerica's eardrum.

"Everyone is fine, Alisa. I'm so sorry. I should have known Bryce would have told you about the call for assistance. I'm sorry for not calling you sooner and for making you worry," she apologized. Typical Jerica, she always worried more about others than herself.

I rapidly typed an e-mail to Bryce, letting him know everyone was safe and that his mom was on the phone with me. "I'm just glad everyone is okay. What happened?" Jerica gave me a quick, but detailed account of the Demon's attempt to abduct Rachel. I felt both grateful and amazed that Rachel was able to escape virtually unscathed. I couldn't wait to see Rachel, Jace, and his parents, just to reassure myself they were all okay. Before ending the call, I promised Jerica that I would see her soon.

I typed another e-mail to Bryce, a longer message than usual. I tried to replay Jerica's version of events. After hitting the send button, I realized Abe had most likely sent the same type of message to his son. Oh, well, I thought. I was a little surprised I hadn't heard from Jace yet, but, I reasoned, he was probably too concerned with Rachel to think about calling me.

Bryce and I sent several more e-mails back and forth in fairly rapid succession, each of us speculating about this Demon who showed up in my small Georgia hometown. Not exactly a regular occurrence in this neck of the woods. I finally insisted that Bryce go to sleep. I knew the time there was extremely late, and he had examinations to contend with in the morning. I received one final e-mail from Bryce before he went to sleep.

> *Dear Alisa,*
>
> *Every time I hear about some horrible event back home, I can't breathe out of fear of losing you. The most recent incident has only reinforced what I've known for longer than I care to admit: I love you and I can't stand for us to be apart for months at a time. Since you and Rachel seem to attract trouble, I have*

> *decided I will not continue my training in the fall. My mom may have ordered additional Warriors to cover the area, but I think I'd prefer to protect you myself. I hope you're not disappointed by my decision to abandon my calling as a Warrior only to take up residence in a small town, attending a small college. I'm still counting the hours, Alisa.*
>
> Love,
> Bryce

I realized after reading his message, that Bryce had some deep-seated insecurities: yet another thing we had in common. He feared I would not love him as much without the glamorous sounding title of 'Warrior.' I worried he would become bored with a silly high school girl and seek a sophisticated woman for companionship. I suspected we were perfect for each other; we were both completely unbalanced.

***

I expected to receive a call from Jace the following morning filling me in on the crazy events from the night before. As morning turned into afternoon, I decided to go ahead and call him. Jace sounded completely exhausted when he answered the phone. I could tell he didn't want to talk to me. Something beyond last night's attack was weighing on him, and for some reason, he didn't want to tell me what it was. Jace continued to act evasive and uncommunicative, and eventually succeeded in getting me off the phone.

My attempt to contact Rachel was completely fruitless. She didn't answer my phone call and never returned my text messages. I tried to convince myself she was still upset from the night before, and would respond when she felt better, but in my heart, I knew something was wrong. Just thinking about Jace and Rachel made me feel anxious. I decided to stay home that day. No trips to the Alexander house for me; I would stay by my beloved computer, and focus my attention on the guy who appreciated every word I typed.

Bryce had a rough day of final exams. Even though he'd basically decided to leave for good, he still put forth the effort to finish in good standing and to gain his Protector ranking. I talked him into waiting until fall to make a final decision. Not because I was trying to get rid of him, but because I didn't want him to burn any bridges.

Bryce had quite enough to worry about, so instead of sharing my concerns over Rachel and Jace, I sent him upbeat, happy e-mails. Each time I remembered we would be able to see each other in less than a week, I shivered in anticipation. Unfortunately, I found myself reverting back to my old ways, fantasizing about our reunion and rehearsing in my mind every word I wanted to say to him. In an effort to avoid heading down into the dark abyss of the fantasy world of years past, I devised a cool strategy to occupy my mind in between e-mails from Bryce.

I carried my I-pod everywhere, ear buds plugged into, volume turned up, signing along to each song at the top of my voice. My parents were probably ready to kill me, but my creative and effective solution worked. Each time I lapsed into a daydream, my loud, obnoxious music jolted me back into the present.

After three days of Rachel ignoring my phone calls and Jace rushing me off the phone, I decided I'd had enough. Hopping behind the wheel of my dad's death trap of a truck, I headed over to the Alexander home without even calling first. Jerica answered the door by pulling me into a fierce hug.

"Long time, no see, kid. We've missed you," Abe announced, smiling from ear to ear. "I'll go get Jace. He's been hiding in the basement." Abe disappeared down the steps.

"I've been worried about him," Jerica confided. "He and Rachel had a huge blowout fight. She rushed out of our house and the attack occurred immediately after. I don't think they've really spoken since. He won't talk to us; maybe he'll talk to you."

Heavy footsteps sounded on the steps, followed by a sullen looking Jace. "Hey," he mumbled as he slumped into the room and onto the couch in one seamless, lazy movement. His eyes looked tired and full of despair.

"Hey, yourself." I said, sitting down next to him. "So, it's been a crazy week, right?" I paused, waiting for him to say something. The conversation was going nowhere and someone needed to take charge. I wasn't a take-charge kind of person. I waited in vain for the friendship fairy to come and make everything better, but as always, she failed to show. It was up to me. I had to do everything, apparently.

"I'm not leaving here until you tell me what's wrong, so you better start talking." I thought I was off to a good start—firm, yet friendly. "Now, if I've done something to offend you, tell me. If not, then stop treating me like crap. What's going on?"

"It's too hard to explain. Rachel and I...we almost broke up that night. She left the house because of something I said. She was upset, and I just let her drive away. She could have been killed, or taken, or...I don't know. It was my fault." Jace looked like he was ready to cry, but I wouldn't relent. He needed to get this out in the open.

"What was your fault, Jace? The fight? Okay, maybe. But the attack would have happened regardless. Maybe not that night, but eventually. If it was really a Demon who was after her, then he was going to find her at some point. Stop blaming yourself for the attack. That's just stupid." I hesitated for a second before asking, "What were you guys fighting about that almost caused you to break up?"

Jace couldn't look me in the eye, so I knew it was bad. "We started off fighting about something totally stupid. Rachel was lecturing me about the way I treated my parents. She said I should stop bugging them about getting me a car. She was right, I mean, I have been acting like an ass. I called her preachy and said she reminded me of an old woman. I told her she was just like Bryce and maybe she should have hooked up with my brother instead of me."

Okay, that didn't sound so bad. Yell and scream for a few minutes bad, but definitely not break up bad. I had a sneaking suspicion Jace was holding back some critical information... the missing piece of the puzzle. "What else did you say?" I asked, trying to sound threatening.

He studied his shoes and avoided making eye contact with me. I cleared my throat to remind him I was still waiting for an answer. "I said something stupid that I totally didn't mean. I told her...I... should have, um, hooked up withyouinstead." He said this last part so fast, the words blended together and I had to think for a minute before it dawned on me. Jace was an idiot!

I tried to block out all the thoughts swirling through my head at that moment, and focus on solutions. 'What ifs' and 'what if I'd' wouldn't solve anything, but it was hard not to consider the implications of what Jace admitted. Rachel had obviously considered the deeper meanings of Jace's statement, causing her not only to stop speaking to Jace, but to me as well.

It was the first time my crush on Jace had been openly acknowledged, and I blushed in remembrance of the way I'd felt for him all those months ago. On the flip side of that comment, however, was the possibility that at one time Jace had felt the same way about me. If only I'd known at the time, I may have pushed a little harder, but none of that mattered now. Rachel and Jace were together and they were perfect for each other. They had an undeniable connection, which went beyond ordinary love.

I'd found happiness with Bryce. He was everything I never knew I wanted until I had him. Or, something like that. I knew what I meant. Bryce and I had forged a more traditional bond: a relationship based originally on loathing—at least on my part—that evolved into friendship and love. I didn't regret for a moment that things turned out the way they did.

No wonder Rachel chose to avoid Jace. He'd hit a nerve and played on her insecurities. I punched Jace in the arm as hard as I could. His cry of pain helped me clear my head and enabled me to formulate a plan. "Let's go," I said.

"Where?" The whine in his voice indicated his spirit had been broken. Every second he sat on that couch represented an additional moment I had to spend away from my beloved computer.

"We're going to Rachel's so you two can make up," I said.

"I'm not going anywhere," he replied, recoiling from my outstretched hand. I could understand his fear; I was frightened of Rachel, too. Jace cowered on the couch like a whipped puppy.

"When's the last time you talked to her?" I asked, trying to prove a point.

"I talk to her every day. On the phone, though," he admitted. "Her mind is blocked, so I can't talk to her that way anymore." This was serious. Clearly, there was something going on with Rachel, something more upsetting than Jace's foolish comments.

"Don't you want to talk to her? Don't you miss her?" I pushed. "Jace, you can't just let your relationship fall apart without even trying."

"She's coming over tomorrow night for dinner. Dad's friend has some information about her father. Rachel asked me to leave her alone until then. One phone call a day is all I get. I feel like I'm in jail." Well, this was news to me. I felt excluded for about a second, but reminded myself that news about Rachel's father was none of my business. I couldn't expect to be included in everything, could I? Besides, my computer would be lonely if I was away for too long.

"Jace, I'll give you until tomorrow. Maybe this information about her dad will ease her mind. If you guys can't work things out though, I'm going over there. She's my friend and it hurts to think she has the wrong impression about us. I'm afraid if you leave it too long, you won't be able to mend your relationship. Tick, tock, Jace." I hated to pressure him, but time was critical. The longer they were apart, the less likely it would be that they would solve their differences.

"Okay," Jace agreed reluctantly. "Oh, and thanks, Alisa. I'm glad you came by."

I left Jace with a worried Jerica, and drove back to the relative serenity of my home. I missed my computer. It beckoned. I lied to my parents, telling them I'd already eaten, and rushed upstairs to my room. I had become strange and reclusive since school ended. I spent much of my time alone in the dark with only the eerie blue glow of the computer screen to light my way.

But, I wasn't alone…not really. Bryce was with me, if not in person, then in spirit. Our conversations over the internet were my only link to reality these days, and I often wondered if it would turn out that this was all a dream. I feared I would wake up one day to discover it had all been a product of my rich and vivid imagination. Or, worse, that Bryce would come home and say he'd changed his mind. That a silly, sheltered, high school girl was not what he'd been looking for after all. I pushed all of these negative thoughts out of my head and focused on the e-mail message waiting for me.

***

The doorbell rang, pulling my attention away from my newest e-mail. No one else was home, so it was up to me to answer. I rapidly tapped out another sentence before pressing the *send* button, then bolted down the stairs and threw open the door.

"Oh, hey," I said, blinking at Becky in surprise.

She smirked at me and stuck out her manicured hand. "Here. I'm supposed to drop this off for your mom."

I took the book she offered and set it down on the table next to the door. "Thanks."

When I tried to shut the door, she put her hand out to block it. She glanced over her shoulder and I followed her gaze. A white convertible stuffed full of tanned, blond teenagers sat in my driveway. Everyone seemed to be laughing.

"You look great, Alisa," Becky said. "You must be having a fantastic summer. I *would* invite you to come along with me and my friends, but it looks like you're already super busy." She laughed and looked down at my bare feet.

I refused to feel inferior for my choice in apparel or lack of footwear. Though, my ensemble of faded denim shorts and a baggy Braves shirt might not measure up to her polished appearance, I wouldn't stammer and make excuses. Nor would I try to justify how I chose to spend my time. It was none of her business.

"I *am* busy," I replied with smile. "I appreciate the offer, though. I'm glad you came by."

She seemed taken aback by my refusal to acknowledge her petty insults. I waved at her waiting friends before giving Becky a heartfelt farewell. My inbox had one unread message in it when I ran back upstairs. I shivered when I read the newest e-mail from Bryce. Becky was right; I *was* having a fantastic summer.

CHAPTER EIGHTEEN
RACHEL

The reason I'd been avoiding Jace had nothing to do with my insecurities over his relationship with Alisa. Yes, it was a blow to my ego to hear him openly acknowledge that he liked Alisa as more than a friend, even if it was before Jace and I got together. My female vanity insisted that Jace should have loved me, and only me, from the moment we first met. In reality, of course, it was perfectly acceptable for Jace to have had other love interests before we became an item. After all, I was dating Robert when Jace and I first met. Everyone had a past.

I repeatedly tried to reassure him that I no longer cared about his insensitive comment about choosing Alisa. It was a juvenile attempt to hurt me, nothing more. I had reacted badly at the time, and I felt ashamed for carrying on like a drama queen. Had the incident with the Demon not happened immediately following our argument, Jace and I probably would have made up within a day or two.

When I tried to explain to Jace that my recent silence had nothing to do with him, I meant it. My seclusion was self-inflicted. It was an attempt to punish myself for my evil, by denying myself the only thing that gave me comfort. I spoke to him just often enough to reassure him that I was alive and safe.

I'd severed our link the very night of the attack. Actually, I'd put up a block against all magic, both incoming and outgoing. It was my only way to ensure that Re'Vel could not access my dreams. The fact that I barely slept was another precaution. I couldn't tell Jace why I closed our link, so he just assumed I didn't want to speak with him. I hated that he believed this. The last thing I wanted to do was hurt him.

My entire life had become defined by the secrets I carried inside. My dream relationship with Re'Vel, the lies I'd told my mother, my use of Persuasion on someone I loved: all of these secrets had taken something from me. I could perhaps excuse my interactions with

Re'Vel. I believed at the time, that I was dreaming, and that Re'Vel wasn't real. I didn't know he was a Demon, otherwise, I would not have allowed him access to my mind.

I might have even been able to explain away the use of Persuasion on my mother. The first time I used Persuasion on her, it was to convince her take me home to get my necklace—a matter of life or death. This time, I'd used it to keep her from panicking. As for telling the truth about my magic, I believed it was necessary for my protection and hers. I wasn't ready to tell her the truth about me, and she wasn't ready to hear it. My mother was strict in her practice of religion. She believed anything paranormal or supernatural was evil. She didn't even like the use of magic in fairy tales. How could I ever tell her I was a Witch? How could I expect her to accept that aspect of my life if I couldn't accept it myself? I still hadn't come to terms with who I was. The idea of explaining it to her brought all my doubts about my magic to the surface.

Added to my underlying fears about my magic, was something I'd heard that horrible night. It was dark and frightening, the night I encountered Re'Vel on that dirt road. My confusion and fear made it difficult for me to completely follow everything that had been said after the Alexanders showed up. One thing I kept replaying in my mind was Re'Vel's declaration that I belonged to him, given to him by my father. Perhaps he had me confused with someone else, though; he said my father's name was Jabron. My Daddy's name was Darius. I held onto this discrepancy like a life raft. Maybe Re'Vel targeted me in error. A case of mistaken identity. I prayed that this was so.

I looked forward to my dinner date with the Alexanders and their friend, a man who had been conducting research on my father. I hoped he would be able to clear up some doubts I had about my origin. I hoped once my questions were answered, I would discover my father was the man I'd always thought he was. Until these secrets concerning my father were revealed, my sense of self hung in the balance.

Jace called me a few hours before I was scheduled to come to his house and meet their much-anticipated guest. He gently reminded me that I should try not to be alone and asked if I would mind if he picked me up. He sounded so sad, so unsure of us, I felt even guiltier than before, which I hadn't thought possible. My continued silence and rejection had broken him, and his voice sounded empty and lost.

"I would love for you to pick me up. I can't wait to see you." I hesitated a second before continuing. It wasn't fair for me to lead him on and then break his heart all over again when he found out the truth about me. I couldn't help it though; I had to say what was in my heart before it burst. "I've missed you."

"I've missed you too," he replied, his voice sounding almost normal in its happiness. "You can come over any time, you know. I can pick you up now if you want. Dad's friend won't be there until later, but you can hang out with me." His words gushed forth in his excitement. I thought for a minute before answering.

"Give me about an hour, Jace. I need to get ready. I'll see you then?" As much as I wanted to keep my distance, I couldn't. I just couldn't be without him. Our link, the one I'd severed almost a week ago, was more than just a line of communication. It was a bond, emotionally, spiritually, almost physically. We became one. As much as I hated to admit it, I didn't feel whole without him.

I took my time getting ready. My hair was a hideous mess and needed to be tamed before I could leave the house. I carefully selected an outfit, almost laughing out loud at the stupidity of caring about my appearance when so much was at stake. Girls will be girls, I guess. I deliberately skipped the application of eye makeup because I was fairly certain tears could be expected in my immediate future.

When Jace pulled into the driveway, I began shaking all over. The need to be with him was so strong, it was overpowering. Thank God my mother wasn't home, because I don't think I could have endured the tedious ritual of her small talk with Jace. I was out the door and in his arms before he made it to my front door. His initial shock was quickly replaced by elation. He hugged me with a ferocity that matched my own. Our kisses were desperate, filled with a mixture of love, relief, apology, and joy.

To my surprise, the link I believed had been severed was as strong as ever. The instant we touched, his emotions rushed into me with shocking intensity. I released my pent up magic, letting it flow through him. A week's worth of tension and heartache was alleviated the moment I removed the block.

"We can't ever let this happened again," he whispered against my neck. "Never. We can't be apart, Rachel. We can't."

"I know. Never again," I replied, my tears beginning to flow. Jace drew back gently and led me to the passenger seat of the truck, helping me in. As soon he shut the door, I lay my head against the back of the seat, sighing with relief. Jace was right; we couldn't be apart. We both knew it in our souls.

Jace drove carefully, silently, watching for any signs of Hunters…or worse. I had some serious thinking to do. The way I saw it, I had two choices. I could shut down my link to Jace once again, effectively blocking Re'Vel from my dreams; I could still keep my secret. This option hadn't worked out very well so far. Re'Vel was gone of course, but the separation from each other was killing Jace and me.

Option two involved spilling my guts to Abe and Jerica and asking them for help. This option was risky, to say the least. I risked alienating the entire family, including Jace. How would they react to my admission of evil? How long would they tolerate me if they knew the truth? That my evil was so strong, I attracted Demons, not only while awake, but in my dreams?

I spent the afternoon with Jace, talking very little, but feeling closer to him than I ever had. Despite the secrets I had yet to reveal, I relaxed for the first time in days. It was hard to keep my eyes open now that I'd finally let my guard down. I struggled to stay awake, my fear of seeing Re'Vel in my dreams the only thing that kept me conscious.

"Baby, you're so tired. Why don't you take a nap? I'll wake you up before dinner." Jace offered. It was so, so tempting.

"No matter what, don't let me fall asleep. I'll explain later, I promise. After dinner, I'll tell you everything. There's a reason I blocked you, and it had absolutely nothing to do with you."

His forehead creased with concern. "Rachel, please. You can't say something like that and not tell me what's going on. That's not fair." I wanted so badly to give in.

"I promise I'll tell you later. I only want to say it once, so I want to wait until your mom and dad are around to hear it," I explained.

"You don't have to say anything. Just open your mind." He reached out and caressed my cheek, and I almost gave into him. He made it even more difficult to temper my flow of thoughts when his lips crashed down on mine. His mouth traveled a fiery path down my neck, and I finally pushed him away when I heard a car door slam outside.

"We'll continue this later?" he asked.

I nodded in response, not quite trusting myself to speak. Would we continue our conversation later, or would our relationship be irreparably changed after my heritage was revealed? Only time would tell.

***

If I hadn't been so anxious to hear about my father, I would have enjoyed Albert's stories. He'd certainly led an interesting life, changing careers with a frequency that boggled the mind. I wondered how he and Abe had formed such an enduring friendship; they seemed so different.

Abe and his buddy spent dinner catching up on all the latest gossip in the magical world. Over coffee and dessert, they reminisced about the days of their youth. Abe and Albert met during their first year at the Warrior Training Bureau. Albert looked like a very unlikely candidate for that type of work, but apparently back in the day, young men were automatically expected to follow in their father's footsteps. That first day of training, Abe took him under his wing, but Albert didn't last long. By the end of his first year, he'd already decided to transfer to the Watcher training facility on the other side of Central.

Albert completed his training to become a Watcher, and graduated by the skin of his teeth. He was never able to settle into an assignment, and quit while he was still a Novice. Over the years, he auditioned many careers including research assistant, interpreter, and computer programmer. He finally opened a detective agency in the private sector, taking occasional assignments from those in the magical community. The idea of working with a private detective seemed kind of sleazy, but if Abe trusted him, I decided that was good enough for me.

Some of Albert's stories were so interesting, I got caught up for a brief period of time and almost enjoyed myself. But the majority of that long dinner, I just wanted to tell him to shut up and either destroy my life with his damning information, or grant me a reprieve by telling me that my father was honest and all was right with the world.

Jerica, Abe, Albert, and I gathered in the living room while Jace quickly cleared the table. Jerica flinched a couple of times when Jace made some particularly loud crashing sounds in the kitchen. He didn't want to miss anything, so he was trying to work at lightning speed. Minutes later, he emerged from the kitchen and sat down on the loveseat next to me.

Suddenly, I couldn't breathe. Unsure if I wanted to hear what this man had to say, I considered getting up and leaving, or telling Abe to forget about it. As Albert gathered his notes, I concentrated on remembering to breathe. Jace whispered in my mind, begging me to calm down.

Albert was all business when he began speaking. "Well, Abe, this was an interesting case. When you first approached me, I thought it would be a breeze, but I'll tell you, I had a hard time unraveling this one." Clearly, he relished the idea of dragging it out, increasing the suspense. I barely resisted the urge to rip the notes out of his hand and read the results of his inquiry myself.

"Basically," Albert said, finally cutting to the chase, "the man known as Darius Franklin Stevens is in fact Jabron Nkaribo. He was born in Nigeria on December 21, 1958. He had an older sister, Keira, and a younger brother, Palo. Palo was killed just a couple of years ago. Keira has two children—Mordecai and Samuel Bojang."

"Mordecai? Is that the same dude Bryce brought home for New Years?" Jace asked.

"Yes," Abe replied, frowning.

My head began spinning as I considered the implications of everything I'd heard so far. I had two first cousins I didn't even know, one of whom had visited this very house while I was in Atlanta. Had I stayed behind...

"Jabron attended the Watcher academy from 1975 through 1979." Albert paused, switching from his cold reading of the facts to a more personal tone. "I trained with him. He was just a couple of years ahead of me. Do you remember him, Abe?"

"Yes, I do," Abe answered shortly. I was unable to determine from his tone whether or not he'd liked my father—this Jabron, this man I didn't know.

Albert shuffled through his notes, finding the spot where he'd left off, and continued, "In 1980, he was assigned to the Birmingham area and finally settled in Atlanta in early 1982. In December 1984, he married a young lady named Amelia Jane Stanford. That was actually the first legal record I found where he'd used the name Darius Stevens. A son, Jeffrey Alan, was born October 16, 1985 and a daughter, Rachel Francine, on June 1, 1991. He passed away February 19, 2003 after his car spontaneously burst into flames. The authorities suspected foul play, but gave up on the investigation before they determined exactly what had happened. There was something suspicious about that, if you ask me."

My heart clenched in pain. My father was a liar who hid his true identity from his family. He was a Witch, trained as a Watcher. That he died in a car accident I knew, but I'd never heard anything about suspicious circumstances. "I'm here, Rachel," Jace soothed my mind with his calm assurances. "We'll get through this."

Albert continued, "Now, for the interesting part: Darius worked for a Demon named..."

"Re'Vel," I said, finishing his sentence.

Everyone looked at me. Albert stammered, "Re'Vel. That's right. How did you..."

I cut him off by saying, "We've met."

Abe broke in and shared with Albert the story of my run in with Re'Vel. Albert was visibly shocked. Most Witches went their whole lives without seeing a Demon, or even meeting someone who'd seen one. I decided to lay all my cards on the table. There was no reason to hold anything back now.

"I recognized Re'Vel the moment I saw him out on the road. Even in the dark, I knew it was him. He's had access to my mind for weeks. I thought they were just dreams, but I was wrong. At first, he was like a friend. Then he began tempting me, trying to convince me to follow him. The last time I dreamed of him, he scared me. He told me I belonged to him, just like he said that night." I looked at Jace. "That's why I put a lock on my magic. I've been trying to block him, and I didn't know how to do it without blocking you too. I was afraid he'd come for me. Truthfully, I've hardly slept in days."

Jace whispered in my mind, "You've been through so much, and I haven't been there for you. I'm sorry Rachel. I should have beat down your front door when you refused to talk to me."

"Oh, Rachel. I wish you would have told us. You didn't have to through this alone," Jerica said. I couldn't believe they weren't angry with me for dragging their whole family into all this trouble. Jace wasn't upset that I'd been dreaming about another man. He still loved me. So far.

Albert stammered for a second, trying to get his bearings before picking up the threads of his story. "The Demon Re'Vel convinced Jabron to work for his cause. Jabron fed him information about the inner workings of Central until an investigation was launched sometime in late 1988. He was released from his duties in 1989 pending further investigation. Jabron began using the name Darius exclusively, and settled right here in Oaktree. He worked as a 'traveling salesman' and spent a lot of time away from home." Again, Albert paused. When he said 'traveling salesman', he'd used his fingers to form quotation marks. I hated it when people did that, especially now that it was used to illustrate what a sneaky liar my father was.

"The verifiable portion of my investigation ends here. Rumor has it Jabron had a change of heart a few years ago and tried to contact Central. He died shortly after. The Witches I've talked to believe Re'Vel had Jabron killed. The Demon couldn't risk allowing Jabron to spill his secrets. One interesting fact I forgot to mention, was while Jabron attended the Academy, he took quite an interest in ancient curses and Claiming Spells." Albert paused again, this time to open a portfolio of photographs. I recognized many of them.

Albert extracted a couple of pages and passed them to Abe, who in turn handed them over to Jerica. "These are just a few photos of Jabron at the Academy. As you can see, the graduation photo for Jabron is nearly identical to the wedding announcement for Darius." Jerica wordlessly passed the photos over to Jace and me. My father's face stared back at me when I viewed the photographs. The graduation picture could have been my brother Jeffrey, they looked so much alike.

"This next set of photographs, you will recognize." Albert passed over another page. "Jerica, your translation of the tattoo, of course, was correct. I asked a Spell Master at the Academy to have a look to verify. He made a few notes on the side for your review."

"Claiming Words," Jerica read aloud, "Demon Mark…can be used as a suppression spell. A tattoo, of course, would be permanent as opposed to a written or verbal spell which could be reversed." Jerica offered the page to Jace and me, but I waved it away. I didn't need to see images of the curse my brother would bear for the rest of his life.

"That almost wraps it up. The rest is conjecture. There's not a lot we know about Re'Vel, or any Demon for that matter. I don't think Jabron ever really had a chance to escape Re'Vel; anything the Demon touches is corrupted by pure evil," Albert said.

My eyes stayed fixed on my tightly clasped hands. Tears fell silently and I watched them trickle between my fingers. I was afraid to move or look at anyone. Corrupted by pure evil, that's what I was. Any minute, I suspected, this wonderful family would recoil from me in horror. Abe heard Re'Vel, we all did. My father gave me to the Demon. Re'Vel claimed me as his own: evil knew evil. I felt Jace stand up, and heard his quiet footsteps as he walked away. I didn't blame him; I would have left me too.

I was too absorbed in my own pain to hear Jace's soft footsteps as he returned. He sat on the loveseat next to me, closer than before, and handed me a box of tissues. He put his arm around me and reached up with his other hand to wipe a tear from my cheek. "I love you," Jace said out loud.

"I love you too," I replied using our private form of communication. I couldn't speak at that moment. I loved Jace more than ever before. I felt like an idiot for comparing him to Re'Vel and finding him lacking. I'd once viewed Jace as an irresponsible teenage boy. To me, from this point forward, I saw him as a man—a man who just drew a line in the sand and openly declared his love for me in front of his parents.

I sat in a daze for the duration of the evening. Abe steered the conversation around to lighter topics, chatting with Albert about some things I didn't pay much attention to. Before Albert left, Jerica took down the name of the Spell Master he'd worked with at the Academy. She said she had a couple of questions about the curse. Abe and Jerica thanked their old friend for his help, and before I knew it, he was out the door.

We all breathed a sigh of relief when he was gone. I couldn't remember a more stressful and upsetting evening. Jace sat next to me through it all, holding my hand, whispering in my mind. Abe and Jerica messed around in the kitchen for a few minutes, emerging with a tray of steaming cups of coffee.

"You doing okay, Rachel?" Abe asked, smiling. "You've had a lot to take in. It's been a shock for you hasn't it?"

"I'm okay, I guess. I have a lot to think about. My whole life has been turned upside down. I don't know what to think about my father. How could he appear to be so normal, when he was so evil?" My voice shook with emotion, and I prayed I wouldn't start crying all over again. My eyes already felt puffy and a headache was setting in.

"The word 'evil' has been used entirely too much tonight. We don't know what was in Jabron's heart. Let's not judge him tonight, okay?" Jerica always knew what to say to make me feel better.

"I think before it's all said and done, we'll find out a lot more about your father. As for tonight, I think we should focus on solutions. We need to find a way to keep Re'Vel from attacking you in your dreams," Abe said, lifting a cup of coffee from the tray and taking a sip. "It has become apparent that the protections surrounding your house are not adequate. We'll need to use some different spells to keep the Demon out."

"But, you said Rachel's house already had protective spells surrounding it," Jace said. "Why did the protection stop working? Why wasn't it strong enough to keep Re'Vel away?"

I broke in, "Re'Vel told me in one of my dreams that he was the one responsible for providing protection. He said he put up the spells."

"Well, then that explains it," Abe said, "We'll just have to put up different spells. Jerica and I can use the same spells we used when we moved into this house. It's very simple. We can write down each spell on a piece of paper. All you have to do is bring the papers into the house and hide one in each room in a safe place. I can reinforce the spells later when your mother isn't home."

Abe and Jerica discussed certain spells and their various uses before deciding on the best combination. I zoned out, barely able to stay awake, while Jerica inscribed each spell onto a separate piece of paper. I heard them discuss the merits of hiring a Protector to accompany me when I left my house, but my head hurt too badly to stage a protest. It was a battle I would save for later.

Jerica insisted that Abe drive me home just in case. Since my extreme exhaustion and stress made it impossible for me to control my magic, she feared Hunters would be drawn to me that night like palmetto bugs to a porch-light. I did not find this reassuring. I did, however, find it comforting that Jerica and Abe were putting forth their very best efforts to protect me. Armed with my Words of Protection, I nearly staggered out the front door and into the backseat of Abe's car. Jace sat beside me, his arm wrapped protectively around my shoulders.

I fell into bed, more fatigued than I'd ever been. With our link reestablished, Jace and I talked until I couldn't keep my eyes open any longer. Despite the fact that I'd relaxed tremendously since my admission to allowing Re'Vel access to my dreams, there was still something pulling at the back of my mind, making it difficult to me to fully surrender myself to sleep.

I remembered what had been bothering me as my eyes began to close. "Jace," I whispered across our link, "I forgot to confess one thing, one very bad thing. I lied to my mother about the cut on my neck, and I used Persuasion to make her believe me. Do you think I'm evil?"

"You're a good person, Rachel. I love you." Jace's voice was the last thing I heard before I sank into the oblivion of sleep. I slept safely, soundly, secure in the knowledge we would never be apart. Never again.

CHAPTER NINETEEN
ALISA

I woke up feeling wired. It was way too early to be up and about. Being awake at nine A.M. during summer vacation was unheard of. I couldn't even contemplate falling back to sleep. It was the day I'd been waiting on for months. Barring any flight delays or other travel complications, I would see Bryce by nightfall. I thought I might possibly die if anything happened to extend the time I had to wait to see him. Already, I painfully counted the hours. Any delay would be heartbreaking.

It didn't seem real. Could I even fully remember what he looked like? Was the image in my head accurate after these many months? More importantly, would I live up to his expectations? Just thinking about Bryce's possible rejection brought on a bout of nausea. I couldn't bear it if Bryce's expression of happiness at seeing me faded to disappointment when he realized what he was getting.

It wasn't only Bryce I was worried about seeing that evening. This would be my first time seeing Rachel since her huge fight with Jace. He assured me she was fine now and harbored no ill feelings toward my friendship with him. But still, Rachel and I hadn't spoken in a week, and I felt weird about that. Maybe if she saw how happy Bryce and I were together, she wouldn't worry that I still had feelings for her boyfriend.

Oh, no. I was starting to make assumptions again. I knew I shouldn't expect Bryce and I to be an instant couple the second I saw him. But, we kind of were a couple already. At least I hoped so. He was certainly open about his feelings in his e-mails to me, but all that could change when we talked face to face. I felt dizzy with apprehension and riddled with self-doubt.

My parents had already left for work, so I had the house to myself. I quickly showered, dressed, and headed downstairs to bake the chocolate chip cookies I'd promised Bryce. At first, I figured baking cookies would take up at least a couple of hours including preparation and cleanup. It would be something to do to keep me occupied and help keep my mind off Bryce. The problem was, after the initial mixing of ingredients, there remained a lot of time where I did nothing at all. Once a batch was in the oven, I had to wait ten minutes for the cookies to bake.

Waiting led to thinking. Thinking led to daydreaming. Daydreaming led to trouble. While I paced around waiting for the oven timer to shriek, my thoughts inevitably strayed to Bryce. I kept finding myself skipping down the lanes of Fantasy Land, and I had to yank myself back to reality repeatedly. To distract myself, I blasted twanging country music so loud it nearly burst my ears. I sang so obnoxiously, I feared I would shatter windows for miles around.

At last, the cookies were finished and kitchen spotless once again. I caught a glimpse of my reflection in the hallway mirror and had to double back to take a second look. The tan that I'd worked so hard on during softball season, the first in my life, had begun to fade after sitting for two weeks in a semi-darkened room doing nothing but staring at a computer. My skin looked a little pale and sickly.

Determined not to frighten Bryce when he saw me, I quickly donned my bikini and the necessary supplies for a day in the sun. A tan wasn't the only benefit of playing softball. Between training with Abe and playing ball, I'd finally lost the ten pounds that had plagued my thighs for years. My mother purchased a lime-green bikini to celebrate my weight loss—not that I would ever wear it out in public.

Armed with a towel, sun tan lotion, and my I-pod, I headed outside, draped my towel across my favorite lounge chair, and prepared to bake in the hot afternoon sun. I set the alarm on my I-pod, determined to give myself enough time to make myself presentable before Bryce came home. The first time I turned over and checked the time, I was appalled to discover I'd only been outside for about twenty minutes. After what seemed like a million years, I flipped over on my stomach and drifted off to sleep for a while. When I woke up, my back felt sunburned, making it impossible to go back to sleep. I passed the time by singing along to my tunes, making up my own lyrics when necessary.

"Rock!" I bellowed, shouting out one of the few words I knew. I loved this song; no way could I fall asleep to this one. "Rock!" I shouted out again, at one with the music. I heard something then—

something that was not part of the song I was listening to. I opened one eye, squinting against the bright sun. I pulled the ear buds from my ears.

Bryce stood over me, almost doubled over with laughter. He was home early, and I was embarrassed beyond belief. I jumped to my feet, covering myself with my towel as quickly as I could. "What are you doing here?" I blurted.

"It's good to see you too, Alisa," Bryce said, still laughing. "I was able to take an earlier flight. I tried to call you several times, but you didn't answer."

"I guess I didn't hear it," I said, mortified.

"No wonder," he said, gesturing toward my I-pod. "So, I decided to come over. I couldn't wait another minute to see you. I knocked on your front door and had almost decided you weren't home, until I heard a strange sound coming from the backyard." Bryce started laughing again. It wasn't my fault I couldn't carry a tune.

"Sorry, I..." I didn't know what to say. I had expected to meet Bryce at his house. It was rather disconcerting to see him here, hours ahead of schedule, standing in my backyard. The fact that I was half-naked didn't ease my sense of discomfort. So much for the cute outfit I'd carefully chosen and the hours I planned to devote to looking my best before I saw him. I clutched my towel more tightly around me.

"Why are you so nervous, Alisa?" Bryce asked taking a step toward me. His voice was deep and smooth, sending shivers across my sunburned skin. He looked bigger than the last time I saw him—more muscular and...well, big. I blushed and took a step back.

"God, I've missed you," he said, reaching one hand out to me. That was my undoing. Gone were all my reasons for being nervous, and in their place was pure joy and relief at being near him at last. I stepped into his embrace. We stood there for a long time, my head against his chest, his heart beating against my ear. He stroked my hair and whispered, "I've missed you so much."

After an eternity, we pulled apart. I couldn't quite look Bryce in the eye; my shyness was back in full force. "Um, I should go change," I stammered.

"Why? You look great," he commented, his eyes traveling the length of my still towel-clad body. "I guess you could lose the towel, though."

"Funny. I need to take a shower. Can you give me, like, fifteen minutes?" I asked, wondering what I would do with him while he waited. "Do you mind waiting?"

"If you need some time, I can come back," he offered, but the look on his face made it clear he would like to do no such thing.

"No, no, no, no," I insisted, almost afraid to let him out of my sight. "I'll hurry. You'll have to wait outside, I think. I'm probably not supposed to have guys in the house when my parents aren't home."

"Probably not?" he asked, one eyebrow lifting.

"The subject has never come up. I've never had a boyfriend before, so I'm just guessing," I said. "My dad would probably go ballistic if he came home and saw you inside." I blushed darkly, giving myself a mental kick for using the word boyfriend.

"Should I be afraid of your father?" he asked warily.

"He likes to hunt and he has a lot of guns. You decide." I shrugged, and starting walking toward the sliding glass patio door.

"I'll wait here," he said. Wise choice. "Take your time."

I showered at the speed of light and towel dried my hair. I was ultra-aware of the passage of time. I had an irrational fear Bryce would leave the second my fifteen minutes was up. I dressed, brushed my teeth, and flew downstairs. I grabbed the Tupperware container filled with the cookies I'd baked, and rushed to the back door. As promised, he was still waiting. He'd stolen my lounge chair, though, and looked like he was half-asleep. Hovering in the doorway, I stared open-mouthed at his long, muscled, jean-clad legs; the sleeves of his blue t-shirt stretched tight over his bulging biceps; the spot where his shirt had come untucked, revealing a stretch of taut, ebony skin on his abdomen. I blinked to clear the fog of desire from my brain, then shut the sliding glass door.

"Hey, you're tan enough, show-off," I said. He sat up and looked at me, again giving my appearance a once-over. I hoped he didn't find me lacking.

"What took you so long?" Bryce smiled and stood up, stretching. Spotting the container of cookies, he asked, "Is that what I think it is?"

"Maybe. Are you ready to go?" I was getting anxious to leave before one of my parents got home. I didn't think I could endure the painful introductions which would lead to the inevitable questions later about what I was doing hanging out with a grown man. In reality, our age difference was only a little more than two years, but Bryce looked...well, old. Not like an old man, but he didn't look like a teenager either.

Bryce, it seemed, could not keep his hands off me. Not in a sleazy way, or anything; he just kept touching me. He hugged me again before we left my backyard. He held my hand on the way to his truck, and again after he backed out of the driveway. He actually paid more attention to me than the cookies, which was both impressive and unexpected. "Look," he said, "I want to spend time with you, just the two of us, but not today. I barely saw my mom before I ditched her to come get you. I haven't seen my dad or Jace yet. Is it okay if we hang out at my house today, and then go off together tomorrow?" he asked.

"Yes, definitely. Your mom and dad have missed you so much. I didn't mean for you to leave them and come get me. I could have borrowed my dad's truck when he got home," I apologized, hoping Jerica didn't think I'd stolen her son away.

"Why are you apologizing? I couldn't have waited another second to see you. I've never been so desperate to see someone in my life. So, is my little brother used to the idea of us as a couple?" He didn't look very worried about how his brother would react. I think he rather liked the idea of causing a stir.

"I guess we'll find out," I replied, my stomach churning.

He grabbed my hand again the second we got out of his truck. I tried to pull my hand away when we went inside, but he wouldn't allow it. My stomach was in knots at the thought of Jerica's reaction to her son's display of affection. Sure, she knew the two of us had developed a close relationship, but I didn't know exactly what she expected. It would kill me if I saw even a hint of disapproval on Jerica's face. I'd hoped Bryce and I would kind of play it cool over the summer, and let everyone get used to the idea of us as friends before we tried to shove handholding and hugs down their throats.

The newly returned Alexander clearly had other ideas. Still grasping my hand in his and dragging me along for the ride, he went in search of his mother. We found her in the kitchen, which was convenient, because much like his younger brother, Bryce's eventual destination was always food. "Hi, Mom. Alisa made cookies. Do you want some?" He finally released my hand and pulled milk out of the refrigerator and cups from a cabinet.

"No. I'm making dinner. Save the cookies for dessert," she scolded. "Hi, Alisa. It's good to see you, sweetie. Abe, Jace, and Rachel should be here in a while. We'll have a regular welcome home party." Her back was turned to me as she said this, the knife in her hand moving at warp speed as she chopped vegetables. Bryce, I'd noticed, had completely ignored his mother's instructions to lay off the cookies. He ate a cookie almost in one bite and washed it down with a half a cup of milk. Abe and Jerica's grocery bill was about to increase substantially, I figured.

"Do you need any help?" I asked Jerica.

"No. I've about got it covered. Why don't you get my son out of my kitchen before he eats everything in sight and spoils his dinner?" Jerica suggested, turning around and waving the knife menacingly toward her son. Bryce, taking the hint, put the lid on the cookie container, stowed away the milk, and put his cup in the sink. He made a hasty retreat from the kitchen and I followed.

"So, do you want to go downstairs and go a few rounds in Dad's studio?" he asked, a wicked gleam in his eyes.

I remembered the last time we'd sparred and blushed at the memory of me lying flat on my back with Bryce on top of me. The huge smile spreading across his face alerted me to the fact that he was thinking along those same lines. And, that he knew what I was thinking as well. "Um, maybe some other time," I stammered.

"Okay, let's just go downstairs and hang out," he suggested, leading the way. He grabbed the remote for the TV and sat down on the couch. I sat down at the other end.

"Come sit by me," Bryce said. I moved a little closer, not looking at him. "Alisa, look at me. Why are so nervous around me? Did I do or say something to upset you? Have you changed your mind about us? Just tell me and I'll back off."

The idea of him backing off sent waves of pain and panic right through me. "No. You didn't do anything and I definitely didn't change my mind. You know I'm not good around people," I tried to explain, "I just don't know how to act around you. And, I'm not sure how this is going to work between us. You're so…perfect. You're older and more experienced and magically gifted." I began to tear up just thinking about Mordecai's insistence that the male Witch was drawn to the female's magic. I had none—how could Bryce possibly be attracted to me?

"Alisa, what you have is better than magic," Bryce said, wiping a tear from underneath my eye. "I have enough magic for both of us. Remember what I told you? You don't need magic to be special."

"But still—I'm average in every way possible. I'm short and plain and boring. I can't even carry on a normal conversation. I'm just waiting for the moment you'll realize you could have so much more than a naïve high school girl from Hicksville." I was on a roll now. That was one of my biggest problems; once I opened my mouth, everything I thought came pouring out unhindered by common sense.

Bryce actually laughed. He moved closer to me and put his arm around me, pulling me against his chest. I could hear his heart beating against my ear. "There is nothing average about you. And, Alisa, you are never, ever boring. You're beautiful…you really are. As for your height, I'm willing to overlook that. And, I mean that literally. Did you know that if I'm standing behind you, I can see right over the top of your head?" He started laughing again, and kissed the top of my head.

"Alisa, we're made for each other. We're the two most insecure, neurotic people on the face of the earth. We shouldn't be set loose on the streets of Oaktree; it's not fair to the rest of the population. It took me three flights to get home, and I worried through all three. I thought once you saw me again, you would remember all the times I made a total ass out of myself. I'm still worried the excitement will wear off once I'm around all the time. I'm worried any mystery surrounding me will be gone if I don't go back to training, and you'll just see me as an ordinary community college student with a bad attitude."

I was surprised by the depths of his insecurity. "I like your bad attitude. And, I've never found you to be mysterious, so that's not an issue. The 'short' jokes will have to stop if we're going to have a chance."

Bryce eased away from me, and looked into my eyes. He spoke seriously, "I think I know what part of our problem is. It's the anticipation. Maybe I should go ahead and kiss you now, you know, get it over with, then we can both relax." Bryce tried to keep a straight face. "It's for the greater good, Alisa. We can't risk letting all this tension spill over; it could infect the rest of my family."

"Well, if it's for the good of all," I said, hardly able to draw enough breath to say the words aloud. He leaned over and placed his lips on mine. It was different than the light kiss he gave me on New Year's Eve. I'd thought that was my first kiss, but I was wrong. This was my first real kiss and it was everything I'd always dreamed of and more. His lips were light and soft upon mine at first, then building in intensity. I melted into him, an act of complete surrender. When we finally pulled apart, we were both breathing erratically.

"I love you," he said, leaning into me once again.

"I love you too," I said. Bryce whispered in my ear, words unintelligible, yet beautiful. And though I couldn't decipher the exact meaning of each individual word, I understood in my soul. "What was that?" I asked softly.

"It's the language of the Fae. I can't give you an exact interpretation, but I can offer a rough translation," he said, pulling away from me and looking me in the eyes. "I promise to protect you and take care of you until you decide you don't want me anymore. I offer this honestly, willingly, with my heart and soul."

My body trembled in response. In sharp contrast to his earlier joviality, he now seemed unusually solemn and serious. The words he spoke reverberated in my heart, and I felt a deep connection as the words he spoke took root. I felt tied to him—claimed. He lowered his lips and grazed my neck. I heard heavy footsteps on the basement stairs. We sprang apart just as Jace entered the room, Rachel following closely on his heels.

"So, Bryce," Jace said, surveying the situation. It wasn't difficult for him to know exactly what had been going on before he came downstairs. I'm sure my cheeks were flushed and I had a guilty look on my face. "You and Alisa, huh?"

"Yes, I'm Bryce and this is my girlfriend, Alisa. You remembered our names. Good for you." I loved it when Bryce was sarcastic. And, I loved it when he called me his girlfriend.

"Hey, I don't have a problem with it. I'm just surprised by Alisa's bad taste, but if she's responsible for the generous mood you've been in since Christmas, then I'm all for it. Get married. It's fine with me," Jace offered magnanimously. "Mom said to come up in a few minutes. Dad's on his way and we'll be eating soon."

We all trekked up the stairs to wait for Abe, who undoubtedly would be anxious to see his newly returned son. Rachel gave Bryce a hug and told him it was good to see him again. Then she turned to me and said, "Alisa, I'm so sorry I haven't returned your phone calls"

"That's okay. I know you've been through a lot," I said.

"No it's not. That's no way to treat my best friend." She pulled me into a hug, and we both had trouble keeping our tears in check. I glanced at Jace just in time to see him roll his eyes in response to our female emotional moment.

Jace, I was relieved to see, seemed to be back in her good graces. He held her hand the whole time we sat in the living room, and she didn't punch him in the face. I thought that was a good sign.

The reunion between Bryce and Abe was joyous and touching. To my immense relief, the family seemed to accept the idea of Bryce and me as a couple. This was a good thing, because he didn't stop holding my hand or putting his arms around me all evening long. Abe and Jerica took it in stride. I guessed after raising three boys with dangerous and unpredictable magical powers, nothing fazed them anymore. Unfortunately, the same thing could not be said for us younger folks. When Jerica made her big announcement, we were floored.

"We wanted to wait until everyone was together again before we told you," she said, her face glowing with pure happiness. We're having a baby!" Complete silence met this announcement. Then, the room erupted with noise.

"Oh, Jerica. That's wonderful. A new baby!" This comment came from me.

"Seriously? When did you find out? Have you been to the doctor? Is everything okay?" Bryce was clearly worried about his mother's health.

"Aren't you too old? How did this happen?" From Jace, of course, who was clearly an idiot.

Rachel punched him in the arm and squealed, "Congratulations. I'm so excited! A new baby!"

Abe was largely ignored through all of this. I glanced at him and smiled at his obvious pleasure. "Thanks Alisa and Rachel. Bryce, of course we've seen a doctor; your mother is fine. She's in perfect health. Jace, lots of women have children in their forties. And, if you don't know how it happened, then we've failed as parents." Abe laughed at his son's embarrassment when he said this.

I fought back tears of joy. After everything this family had been through, Jerica deserved every bit of happiness that came her way. They all did.

***

"Bryce, it's after eleven," I said, looking at my cell phone. "I have to go home. I promise we'll see each other tomorrow."

"Just a few more minutes," he insisted. "Please."

"No. Now," I urged.

"Fine," he said, kissing me on the lips. "Let me tell my mom we're leaving."

He disappeared behind the kitchen door, and left me alone in the living room. I heard Jerica's voice, and I was surprised to hear her crying. "Do you realize what you've done, honey? I'm so worried for you, Bryce. If she refuses you…"

"How did you know?" he gasped.

"When you speak the Claiming Words, the initial ties form. I have Perception, honey. I can see what you did," she said. I couldn't imagine what she was talking about.

"I thought you'd approve. I thought you liked her," he replied. My heart sank. Jerica didn't want me with either of her sons. I almost ran from the living room and out the front door, but my pain held me in place.

"I love Alisa like a daughter. I couldn't wish for a better mate for you. But, it's too soon. Once you say the words, there's no turning back, not for you," she said.

"Don't tell Dad," he pleaded.

"Honey, I can't promise anything. You know why that is…" The sound of her voice trailed off, presumably because they'd moved further away from the kitchen door. I strained to hear them, but could not. Something told me Bryce's murmured, foreign-sounding words led to this discussion between them, but I couldn't be sure. I tried to latch on to the one thing that gave me comfort—Jerica loved me.

"Just tell me one thing," I heard Bryce say as their voices moved closer to the doorway. "Will it work between a Witch and a human?"

A long pause ensued. Even though I had no idea what they were talking about, I held my breath and waited for Jerica's response. Her voice was so filled with emotion, I closed my eyes against the anguish I heard. "Oh, honey. That's what I've been trying to tell you. It already has."

Seconds later, Bryce came back into the room, and the light of victory was in his eyes. Whatever it was that worried his mother so, brought him indescribable joy. There were so many questions I wanted to ask, but I couldn't figure out a way to do so without admitting I'd been eavesdropping. "Ready?" he asked, jangling his car keys.

I concentrated on retaining my composure, and followed him out the front door. He helped me into his truck, and leaned down to kiss me before he closed the door. Climbing into the driver's seat, he turned to me and asked, "Are you okay? You're really quiet all of a sudden."

"I'm fine. I just don't want to get in trouble for coming home after curfew," I said.

When we arrived at my house, Bryce put the truck in park and walked me to my front door. His kissed me until I had to lean against my front door for support. I sincerely hoped my dad wasn't on the other side of the door wondering why I was taking so long to come inside.

"I'll see you early tomorrow morning?" Bryce whispered in my ear.

"Sure, unless I'm grounded," I said, remembering it was past my curfew.

"Don't worry about that. If your parents give you any trouble, just let me know. I'll persuade them to back off," he promised. I suspected he spoke of the magical form of Persuasion, rather than the human variety. He lowered his lips within an inch of mine and whispered, "We can't be apart. Not anymore."

My soul reached out to his, and in my imagination, I could see the ties Jerica had spoken of. Ties, which bound us together. Ties, which stretched and grew thinner as Bryce walked away. I could hear the words he'd spoken earlier as a whisper in my heart. My soul reached out to his, and I knew Jerica was right. Whatever Bryce had done had obviously worked. There was no turning back—for either of us.

CHAPTER TWENTY
RACHEL

With my new security spells in place, I was able to fall asleep easier, but true restful slumber remained elusive. Sometimes when I fell asleep, I could still see the forest, could still hear the Demon's call. I worried Re'Vel would still try to take me, and I worried about my desire for him to do so. But, most of all, I worried my questionable lineage meant evil lurked within my veins. Maybe that's why Re'Vel wanted me so badly. Maybe that's why Nevare wanted me as well.

I felt an overwhelming curiosity about the family I'd never met, Mordecai in particular. I had a burning desire to know more about him. Bryce knew my cousin—Mordecai had been a guest at New Year's. I thought about asking Bryce for information, but I was nervous about approaching him. I didn't really know Jace's older brother, but from what I'd seen of him at Christmas-time, he was pretty hard to get along with. It had been a week since Bryce's return, and I still hadn't bolstered up the courage to talk to him.

"I can ask Bryce to talk to you if you're afraid to ask him yourself," Alisa offered after I confided in her.

"No. It's something I need to do on my own. When the time is right, I'll ask him." The idea of Bryce coming to *me* made me shudder.

"We're playing tennis later. You should come with us. Maybe you'll find a chance to talk to him then," Alisa said.

The Alexanders were tennis fiends, and although they hadn't managed to convert me, they often dragged me along for the ride. I didn't relish the thought of sweltering out in the heat while enduring an endless round of tennis matches, but Alisa was right. Maybe the subject would come up, or at the very least, maybe I'd find some common ground with Bryce and work up the nerve to talk to him. It was worth a shot.

I sat against the fence, watching from the sidelines. Waves of heat radiated off the tennis court, and I used some of the water from my water bottle to cool off my neck and shoulders. Jace and Alisa faced off, and I rolled my eyes. Those two wouldn't quit until there was a clear winner and loser, so it could be hours before we could pack up and go home. I sighed in resignation.

Bryce jogged over to where I was sitting and grabbed a water bottle, drinking most of it in one gulp. "I'm gonna go over to the playground and re-fill at the water fountain. Do you need more water?" he asked.

"I'll go with you," I offered, hoisting myself off the ground. I brushed off the small bits of gravel that stuck to the back of my thighs.

I followed Bryce to the small, deserted playground and tried to think of a casual way to bring up the subject of my first cousin, however, Bryce beat me to it. "So, my mom told me about your dad. That sucks." He reached for my water bottle and dipped it under the fountain.

"Yeah, it's weird having a whole family I don't even know." I waited breathlessly for him to take the hint and mention the one member of my family he knew very well.

"I went to WTB with your cousin, Mordecai. He was my training partner last year."

"What's he like?" I asked.

"Powerful," Bryce replied. That was a strange answer. I'd expected funny, or smart, or troublesome.

"He's an Nkaribo," Bryce said. "What can I say?"

I took the water bottle from him and followed him toward the tennis courts, hoping he would say something else. I was an Nkaribo, apparently, and that didn't mean anything to me. I struggled to speak, but there was something intimidating about Bryce. At last, I blurted, "What did you mean when you said he's an Nkaribo? You said that like it should mean something to me."

"I didn't mean anything against your family, Rachel. The Nkaribos are notoriously powerful. Your father was rumored to have worked for the Demon Re'Vel, but some say he worked for Nevare as well," he said, frowning.

My heart beat rapidly in my chest, and I felt lightheaded, like I was having a heatstroke. I swayed on my feet and staggered, missing a step. Bryce reached out to grab my arm before I fell. "You don't look too good. Let's sit in the shade." He guided me toward a picnic bench underneath a tall oak tree. We could see the tennis courts from where we sat, and I wondered if Jace and Alisa had noticed our extended absence. I hoped they didn't come looking for us. I had some questions for Bryce, and once Alisa came anywhere near him, he wouldn't be able to pay attention to anyone but her.

"I've seen Nevare," I blurted, without thinking. I'd never mentioned Nevare to the Alexanders. After Re'Vel tried to abduct me, Nevare took backseat in my mind. Bryce stared me down, his body tense, his eyes blazing with fury. He was the last person I wished to confide in, but it couldn't take back what I'd already said. With a shaking voice, I continued speaking. "I've seen him in my dreams. He was arguing with Re'Vel about claiming me. What does that mean? Jerica said my brother had Re'Vel's Claiming Words in his tattoo, but I don't understand how either of the Demons can claim me. I don't have a tattoo."

"You'd better tell me more about that dream," Bryce said, leaning over me.

I recoiled. I'd always thought Jace and Bryce looked quite a bit alike, but at that moment, Bryce seemed inhuman. I quickly explained my recurring nightmare about the castle. When I told Bryce about Re'Vel's insistence that his claim superseded Nevare's vendetta, his face twisted in rage. "My father killed Nevare's brother, and in turn, Nevare killed mine. If it wasn't for the Claiming Words, I'd hunt him down right now, and bathe in his blood."

His voice shook with fury, and the water bottle he held turned to crushed, cracked plastic in his fist. Bryce didn't seem to notice the water trickling from this clenched fist onto the pine needle strewn ground under the bench.

"Nevare's claim on me prevents you from pursuing him?" I asked.

Bryce glanced over at the tennis courts, and his face relaxed slightly. "No. It's *my* claim that prevents me from pursuing Nevare. But I don't regret it. One day, the Demon will come for us, and when he does, I'll be waiting."

Bryce's claim? What did that mean?

I watched Jace chasing Alisa with his tennis racket raised over his head. I snickered; I was used to their antics, but Bryce didn't seem amused...not in the least. Surely, he wasn't jealous. I mean, how could he be jealous of his own brother? They were just messing around. Like they always did.

Bryce advanced toward the tennis courts, and I mumbled something about going to the ladies room. I trudged toward the pavilion at the other end of the park. The sun beat down on me, and I slowed my steps. Kicking at gravel scattered across the pavement, I considered the implications of what Bryce told me. The Demon responsible for killing Jace's brother had claim on me. My father gave my brother to Re'Vel: that was certain. But, did he give me to Nevare? And, why? If the Claiming Words were in the necklace—a necklace I no longer wore—was the claim now void?

If only I could ask Re'Vel. But, that was impossible. I'd cut him from my dreams. He was dangerous. Nothing good could come from seeking out the Demon. Besides, I had little control over my dreams. What if I went in search of Re'Vel and found Nevare instead?

The relative shade under the pavilion provided some relief, but the humidity in the ladies room was stifling. Streaks of sunlight filtered in through filthy windows set high above the stalls. My phone vibrated in my pocket, and I pulled it out, glancing at the text message. My mother was wondering what time I'd be home. Soon, I hoped. I sent a quick reply, and put my phone down on the sink.

I splashed some lukewarm water on my face and neck, but it did little to cool me off. I swatted at a fly, turned off the water, and dried my face with a stiff brown paper towel. Exiting the ladies room, I remembered my cell phone. Just as I turned back to retrieve it, a strong arm snaked out and grabbed my wrist, pulling me backwards. My body collided against a rock hard obstruction.

I looked up into the eyes of my father. No. Not my father. These eyes were set against the backdrop of skin so dark it swallowed the light, and framed by midnight black dreadlocks. Full lips curled back to reveal a luminescent smile.

"Hello, cousin." His deep, accented voice washed over me. *Mordecai.* How he'd come to find me there, I could not imagine. I'd thought of little else but my cousin for over a week, and I found it disconcerting to see him standing in front of me.

"Please don't summon your lover," he urged. "If you do, I'll disappear."

My curiosity got the better of me. I nodded, and Mordecai released my wrist, He motioned for me to follow him down the trail and into the woods behind the building.

"I can't stay long, but I need your help, Rachel," he said.

"What sort of help do you need?" I asked. Prickles of apprehension shot up my spine when he turned his eyes on me. Hoping I wouldn't end up regretting my decision, I delved into his mind. I didn't get very far; his magical security was top-notch, and even his surface thoughts were closed to me. I felt darkness—the same darkness I'd once sensed in Bryce.

"What are you doing here?" I blurted. Maybe he'd come to visit his friend, but if that were the case, wouldn't Bryce have mentioned it when we were talking about him just moments ago?

"We're cousins. It is my duty to protect you. Rachel, this conversation must remain secret. Promise me you'll say nothing," he urged.

"Okay," I stammered feeling unsure.

"Swear on the Blood Bond we share," he insisted. "I can't talk to you until you promise."

"I promise." I couldn't bear the thought of Mordecai leaving without answering some of my questions and I didn't want to take a chance of severing all ties with him. The urge to form a relationship with my father's relatives was too strong to resist.

"Re'Vel became concerned when he could not find you in your dreams," Mordecai said.

Dear God, I thought. Did everyone in my family work for Re'Vel? Was it only a matter of time before I gave into him? So, that's why he wanted me to promise I wouldn't say anything about this conversation. How could I keep such a promise from the Alexanders? They needed to know he was working for the Demon.

"He wishes to speak to you once more," he continued. "He is concerned for your safety,"

"He's the biggest threat to my safety," I countered. "He tried to abduct me. Did he tell you that? He cut my neck. I think he took some of my blood."

"Not enough. That's why he sent me. I'm your first cousin. We share a Blood Bond. He wishes you to Transport with me. He merely wants to speak with you for a few moments; you can go home at any time. I can take you now," he offered, reaching his hand toward me.

"I can't. I...my friends are waiting," I said, taking a step away and gesturing toward the tennis courts. I could just make out the outline through the trees; I could hear Alisa's laughter on the wind.

"If I don't bring you with me, Re'Vel will punish me severely. We're family, Rachel. Trust me," he said. I knew better than to trust *my* family. I'd trusted my father, and look what happened. He lied to me. He lied to everyone.

"But, why? Why do you follow the same Demon who killed my father?" I stopped walking and he turned to face me.

"Your father left many debts," Mordecai said. "So did mine. My father spoke Re'Vel's Claiming Words at the time of my naming. Your father spoke those same words when you were born."

"How can I owe a debt to Re'Vel?" I asked. "My father gave Jeffrey and me to the Demon. What more could Re'Vel possibly want?" I asked tearfully, thinking about my poor brother whose magic now belonged to a Demon.

"He gave Jeffrey to Re'Vel, but you are a matter of dispute. He wants irrefutable proof that you belong to him. There is a way..." He reached toward me, but I twisted away. I could hear Jace and Bryce arguing, probably about some trivial matter, and I considered calling out to my boyfriend.

"You can't pay for your father's debts," I said. "Neither can I. I'm sure Jace's family could help you."

Mordecai's brows knit together and he shook his head. "I'm sure they cannot. Please, Rachel. If you don't come back with me, you must give me some token of your cooperation. I beg you. Re'Vel does not handle disappointment easily, and his anger toward me will be swift and unyielding. Cousin," he pleaded, reaching one hand out to me. "We are family. I know you will not let me come to harm if there is any way you can prevent it. And, I am afraid he will hurt your friends...and mine." He gestured through the trees toward Bryce.

"If you give me something—the necklace, perhaps—I can create a temporary link so Re'Vel can bypass your security and see you in your dreams one last time. It's just a dream, Rachel. He can't hurt you in your dreams. I would never let him harm you," Mordecai pleaded. My eyes caught his, and again, I was reminded of my father—his uncle. My cousin and I shared a Blood Bond. We were family. I wouldn't send him back to Re'Vel empty-handed. I wouldn't allow anyone to hurt my cousin.

"I don't have the necklace," I said, regret washing over me. "What can I give you?"

The metallic flash of a dagger caught me off guard, and I staggered backwards. "I won't hurt you. A little blood is all I ask. Perhaps some hair. It is just a token, really." It occurred to me that my cousin was a madman. What sort of voodoo was this? A lock of hair? My blood?

"Please," he pleaded. "If I don't return with you, I must have something I can give him."

A lock of hair wasn't too much to ask, but a blood offering? Well, that was going a bit too far. "Give me the knife. Quick. Before I change my mind." I unfastened the hair-clip at the back of my neck and sawed at one of the braids.

"Say nothing to the Alexanders, Rachel. Please keep my secret," he begged. I nodded. "We share a Blood Bond, cousin. You cannot break a promise—not to me."

"I promise," I whispered.

"Thank you, cousin," he said, leaning forward and kissing me on the cheek. "You've been very helpful."

A feeling of impending doom settled over me as Mordecai Transported away. I felt foolish, duped. But, most of all, I felt alone. I tripped through the woods, following the sounds of my friends. Twigs snapped as I left the trail and tried to step over clumps of vegetation. I'd probably end up with poison ivy, I thought. It would serve me right for making such a promise to my cousin. But, how would I explain why I'd decided to walk this way?

"Rachel." Jace's voice drifted across our link. "What's taking you so long?"

"I decided to take a walk in the woods. It's too hot out on the tennis courts." The partial truth flowed effortlessly. "I'll be there in a minute."

"Okay. I was just getting worried. I told Bryce he shouldn't have left you alone. It's dangerous for you," he said. He didn't know the half of it.

I spent the rest of the afternoon baking in the hot sun, pretending to enjoy my friends, wishing I were anywhere else.

"You ready to go baby?" Jace called. My stomach rumbled, and I was reminded it was getting close to dinnertime. Only food could prevail over tennis in Jace's mind.

"I'm kind of hot," I replied. "And hungry."

"Bryce, Alisa?" he asked. "Ready?" They began to gather up their rackets and tennis balls. I reached in my pocket for my cell phone, but couldn't find it. Then, remembered I'd left it on the sink in the ladies room.

"I'll go with you," Jace offered when I explained to him why I needed to go back to the pavilion. We left Alisa and Bryce to their own devices, and walked hand-in-hand to the other end of the park.

With each step we took, I longed to tell Jace about Mordecai, but each time I opened my mouth to tell him, the words felt as if they were trapped inside me. Even when I tried to form the words to send across our link, I discovered I was unable to do so. When I realized it had become impossible to me to spill my secret, panic began to set in. It was as if the promise I'd made to Mordecai had become a permanent and binding contract. What had I done?

We approached the pavilion and Jace asked, "Why are you so quiet?"

"Headache," I replied. It was true. My repeated attempts to confide in Jace resulted in a crushing pain in my temples.

I popped into the bathroom, grabbed my phone, and said a silent prayer of thanks that it was still there. Then the room went dark. Strong hands covered my eyes, and a deep voice whispered in my ear.

"Gotcha." My heart took a dive down to my toes.

"Why are you so jumpy?" Jace asked, removing his hands from my eyes, and spinning me around to face him. My breathing resumed and my heartbeat returned to normal.

"What are you doing in the ladies room, Jace? What part of "ladies" don't you understand?" I asked, punching him in the stomach lightly. He didn't even flinch. His abs were like granite.

"So, this is the ladies room. It's nice. Much cleaner than the men's room. No wonder girls spend so much time in here," he joked. I shot him a nasty look.

"Funny. Let's get out of here," I said, moving past him and out the doorway.

THE CLAIMING WORDS

"Kiss me," Jace demanded, grabbing my hand and spinning me around. "I never get to spend time with you alone anymore. Bryce and Alisa are always around. Kiss me." He wrapped his arms around my waist, and I reached up to place my arms around his neck. My eyes flickered shut as he lowered his lips to mine.

"Maybe it's a good thing we aren't alone very often," he said. "I have no self-control around you. We'd better get back to Bryce and Alisa…you know, witnesses…otherwise I won't be responsible for my actions."

"And, I won't be responsible for mine," a voice said. I jerked my head around to see Re'Vel emerging from the woods. "Step away from her, child, and go play with your friends."

Re'Vel reached his hand out to me, and without a second thought, I stepped away from Jace. I felt so drawn to Re'Vel. It was as if I'd lost my willpower the moment I heard his voice.

"There, there, my love. You missed me, did you not?" he whispered in my ear. "We have your cousin to thank for our reunion. Thanks to him, the spells surrounding you are void. The lock of hair was a nice touch." I heard the laughter in his voice, but I didn't care that he was mocking me. My relief at being near him wiped away any sense of self-respect.

"Rachel, he's using Persuasion. Fight him," Jace urged.

"Why don't you fight for her?" Re'Vel chuckled. "Why don't you help her, son of Abe? Can you win the love of an Nkaribo—a direct descendent of the Fae? Demons will fight for her; they will crave her like a drug. And you? You are just a child. By the time you grow up to be a man, she will already be mated with a child of her own. *My* child."

"I'll kill you before I let that happen," Jace shouted. "I'll tear your throat out. I'll…"

"Perhaps. But, others will come. Can you fight us all?" he asked, stroking my hair. "Can you fight Nevare? Your brother couldn't."

Jace charged at Re'Vel, who with one flick of his hand, sent my boyfriend flying halfway across the pavilion. Jace crumpled to the ground.

"Rachel," Jace screamed in my mind. "Don't listen to him. Please." Something in Jace's voice broke through my fog of confusion, and I twisted away from Re'Vel. He reached out to grab me, but I yanked my arm out of his reach. I stumbled and fell into a concrete picnic bench. Pain worse than any migraine assaulted my skull. And, then, the world went dark.

CHAPTER TWENTY-ONE
ALISA

"What's taking them so long?" I asked Bryce. Jace and Rachel had been gone an eternity it seemed.

"They're probably up to no good," he said, kissing my neck. I shivered in the ninety-five degree heat. "Maybe we should go back to the car and wait for them."

"It's too hot in the car," I said, pushing him away. His displays of affection embarrassed me. As much as I craved Bryce, I felt he was moving a little too fast. But, he was older than me. Probably more experienced too.

"It's too hot out here. Especially when I'm with you. *You* make me hot," he said, reaching for me and pulling me close.

"Stop saying that." I felt a deep blush creeping up my neck. I decided to change the subject. "Bryce, I have to tell you something. Promise me you won't get mad."

"Are you thinking of dumping me?" I shook my head. "Are you running away and joining the circus?" I laughed and shook my head again. "As long as you promise not to leave me, I promise I won't get mad." He seemed very serious all of a sudden.

"I overheard something," I admitted. "The night you came home from WTB, when you were talking to your mom in the kitchen. She was crying...she said something about seeing the ties. What did that mean?"

"Nothing," he said.

"It didn't sound like nothing," I pushed. Our relationship was still in the early stages, but I didn't want it to be based upon lies. Besides, I knew he did something...he changed me somehow, and I had the right to know.

"Okay. When I whispered in your ear...like this," he said, pulling me close and nibbling on my ear. My stomach flipped over and my vision went hazy. I pulled away and tried to give him a stern look. "It was a spell. My mom was upset because she thinks it's too soon for me to make a commitment. She thinks I should have waited until you were ready."

"You put a spell on me?" I gasped.

"No. I put a spell on *me*. I whispered the Claiming Words in your ear. I've tied myself to you. I've made a commitment to spend my life with you. But, you're under no obligation to me. Not yet," he said.

I turned away from him, trembling. Why would he do that? And, what did it really mean…to tie himself to me? Of course, I felt obligated now. How could I feel otherwise?

"Don't…" he said, putting his hand on my shoulder. "Don't freak out on me. It's just an initial tie, Alisa. It isn't a permanent bond. Don't you want to spend your life with me?"

I turned back around to face him. "I love you, but maybe your mom is right. Maybe it's too soon for you to make such a huge decision. I'm only seventeen. I'm still in school. You may not still want me in a year. Or, even in a month."

"That's impossible," he insisted. "I'll always want you." He pulled me into his arms. "If I wasn't sure about you, I wouldn't have whispered the Claiming Words."

"What does that mean? Claiming Words?" I asked. "Rachel said her brother's tattoo has Claiming Words."

"There are different kinds. Her brother's tattoo is a Demon Mark. It's permanent. The words I spoke are words of love…my intent to form the Bond with you."

"Bond?" I asked.

"Marriage," he replied. I couldn't believe he'd even thought about making such a commitment. It amazed me that he loved that much. But, still…it was awfully soon to speak of marriage. After all, he'd only been home a few days. A lot could change over the summer. And, while I couldn't imagine being with anyone but Bryce, I couldn't imagine him wanting to spend the rest of his life with me.

"Are you sure?" I asked.

"I…" his response was cut short by the sound of thunder. Not thunder. A deep rumble pierced the still, silent afternoon. The blacktop shook underneath our feet. My first thought was that we were experiencing an earthquake. Bryce peered into the distance, his eyes widening in horror. "Over there," he said.

I glanced in the direction of the pavilion and saw a wisp of smoke. "What is that?"

"Call my parents," Bryce said.

"But, I left my phone in the car..." He was already gone.

I dashed to the car and pulled on the door, but it was locked. A lone cell phone lay on the driver's side seat, taunting me with its inaccessibility. I hesitated for a second, then ran in the direction of the pavilion.

My sides were aching by the time I reached the empty parking lot in front of the pavilion. Bryce circled a pale, dark-haired man, a Demon, while Jace crouched in front of Rachel's crumpled form. I dashed forward to reach my best friend's side.

"Stay with her," Jace begged.

I nodded in response.

Jace leapt over a table. Placing both hands in front of him, he shot Fire at Re'Vel. The Demon stepped out the way effortlessly, while Bryce extinguished the flaming bushes behind him.

"Careful," Bryce warned. "Let *me* handle Re'Vel."

Re'Vel flicked his pale hand toward Bryce, and a bolt of lightning shot toward him. Bryce threw up his arms, and it sizzled into nothing. The Demon flew at Bryce, and had him in chokehold in a split second. Jace jumped forward, ripping the Demon off his brother, and throwing him across the pavilion. A concrete bench shattered from the impact, and I threw my body over Rachel to protect her.

Rachel began to stir. I yanked my terry-cloth wristband off and used it to wipe the blood from her forehead. I applied pressure to the wound, praying she hadn't suffered a concussion...or worse. "Talk to me, Rachel," I whispered.

"Shit!" Jace yelled. I turned just in time to see him drop to the ground, presumably to avoid a blue fire bolt. Shards of ice scattered across the ground, some of the pieces melting right next to me.

"Put up a block," Bryce shouted and grabbed the Demon. He threw him against the wall, leaving a dent in the thick, wooden panel.

"Don't let him Transport out," Jace said, appearing next to Re'Vel as if he'd come from out of nowhere. "He's mine."

The Demon leapt to his feet effortlessly. His cold laughter raised goose bumps on my arms. "Oh, yes. Stand down. Let the child fight me. Anyone want to wager bets on who will win?" Re'Vel shot Fire from each hand, causing Bryce and Jace to duck out of the way. He then Transported to the top of the pavilion. Bryce followed, but the Demon knocked him back down immediately. I gasped and cried out. Bryce staggered to his feet.

"Alisa..." Rachel's weak voice murmured.

"Shhh. Lie still," I said, removing the wristband and checking her forehead. The bleeding seemed to have stopped.

"Stop hiding from me. Come down here and fight me," Jace taunted. "I'll kill you before I let you put one hand on her again."

"I'd never harm her. I'll spend the rest of my days with her, while you're playing with the little humans you love so much," Re'Vel replied.

"You already *did* harm her," I yelled, shocking myself.

"Perhaps the human should fight me," Re'Vel said, jumping back to the ground and landing right next to me and Rachel. I jumped back in fright. The Demon didn't even glance at me, but crouched down next to Rachel.

Bryce appeared next to me in an instant. I reached out, but before I could touch him, Re'Vel leapt, snatched him by the throat, and threw him across the pavilion. He fell against a picnic bench, with a sickening crack that made me cry out.

Rage overtook me, and before I could even consider the consequences of my actions, I jumped to my feet, kicked the back of the Demon's leg, and was rewarded by his startled exclamation as his knee buckled. He spun on me and reached out to grab me, but I ducked out of the way.

Out of the corner of my eye, I saw Jace running toward us, but when the Demon put his hand up, Jace fell back and crumpled to the ground as if he'd smashed into an invisible barrier. The Demon turned his attention back to me and hurled a sizzling ball of fire. I fell to the ground to avoid incineration. The smell of burning hair made my eyes water.

Re'Vel crouched down beside Rachel and began to murmur something. I regained my footing, determined to protect Rachel with my life if I had to. The Demon turned his eyes toward me, and I froze. He surveyed me calmly, then grabbed my wrist, pulling me

THE CLAIMING WORDS

toward him. His other hand wrapped around my throat, and before I knew what was happening, I was lying flat on my back. His hand was on my windpipe, and I could hardly breathe.

Bryce's scream of rage seemed to shake the foundations of the pavilion. One minute, he stood over me—the next moment, he was gone.

"Don't come any closer," the Demon hissed. "If you choose to interfere, I'll kill her. I can sever the ties that bind in an instant. Better keep your brother in check, because if he takes another step, you'll have to find a new little human to hear your Claiming Words."

"Stay back, Jace," Bryce shouted.

"He's got Rachel," Jace raged. "Let go of me."

"I won't hurt her," Re'Vel said. He released me and I rolled over on my side, gasping for air. I pushed myself onto my elbow and the Demon gave me an icy stare. "Don't move, human, or you'll have to explain to Abe why he must bury his remaining sons." He turned back to Rachel and placed his hand on her forehead. His words were unintelligible, but oddly familiar.

"Let go, Bryce," Jace screamed. "What's he doing to her?"

I stared in shock as Rachel's wound knit together, leaving only dried blood behind. Rachel opened her eyes and stared at Re'Vel. He stroked her face tenderly, and she flinched away.

"I would never harm you," Re'Vel said. "Come with me, and I'll protect you. I can't Transport with you while Nevare holds claim—not unless you lend me your magic. Release your magic, my love." I watched in horror as Rachel's expression changed from fear to one of dreamy content. She seemed spellbound, enchanted.

"Rachel! Don't do it!" Jace yelled. His voice seemed to break the enchantment, because Rachel's eyes narrowed and she shook her head back and forth.

"I love you," the Demon said, running his fingertips over her lips.

"Get away from me," she said, knocking his hand away.

"Very well. But, there will come a day when you change your mind. I've seen it," Re'Vel replied. He turned to Bryce and Jace. "Until I return, be sure to guard her with your life. Only I keep Nevare away from her—and from your family. If any harm befalls her, you'll have not one, but two Demons to contend with." With a cold gust of air, the Demon was gone.

Jace was by Rachel's side in an instant, pulling her into his arms. Bryce lifted me off the ground, hugging me tightly. "Are you okay? Did he hurt you?"

"I'm okay. My wrist hurts a little. But Rachel…"

"I'm fine," she said.

"I would have died if I'd lost you," Jace said, holding her tightly. "I love you so much."

"I love you too," she said.

"We need to go," Bryce said. "If a Park Ranger shows up and sees all this, we won't be able to explain it." He gestured at the destruction surrounding us, the shattered concrete bench, an overturned trash can, the burn marks on the ground, and the ladies room door hanging by one hinge.

Jace lifted Rachel and began carrying her to the car. She pushed as his chest. "I can walk. I'm fine."

"You're hurt. We should get you to the hospital."

"And, what are we going to tell them?" Bryce asked, putting his arm around me and following his brother. "We'd better call Dad."

When we reached the parking lot, Jace placed Rachel in the backseat of the car and climbed in beside her. Bryce helped me into the passenger seat and pulled the seat belt around me. I flinched when his hand brushed against the emerging bruise on my wrist.

"Maybe you should both be seen by a doctor," he said.

"No," Rachel and I replied in unison.

"We'll go back to my house, and if my dad says you need to go to the hospital, then that's where you're going," Bryce said.

"You can't make me go," Rachel insisted.

"*I* can," Jace insisted.

Once we were inside the safety of the Alexanders' house, I began trembling as the shock of the experience began to wear off. Weak-kneed, I sat down on the sofa. Jace eased Rachel onto the loveseat, hovering over her protectively. Bryce called out to his parents and Jerica rushed into the living room.

"What happened?" she cried, her eyes settling on Rachel.

"The Demon…" Jace began.

"Oh, my goodness! You're hurt." Jerica descended upon Rachel, scrutinizing her injuries closely. "Abe," she called.

Within seconds, Abe joined us, his expression grim. Bryce explained what happened while Jerica bustled around, distributing ice packs and glasses of water.

"You said the Demon healed her?" Abe asked. Bryce nodded. Abe and Jerica exchanged a worried look.

"This is the second time he's tried to take her," Abe said. "How does he find her so easily?"

Everyone looked at Rachel. She shifted against the pillows on the sofa.

Bryce interrupted, "Re'Vel said he couldn't Transport with her while Nevare holds claim."

"Nevare," Abe gasped. The expression on his face was unreadable. "Re'Vel mentioned Nevare?"

"Rachel, I think you should tell my dad what you told me," Bryce said.

"I've seen him in my dreams," she admitted. "I used to have nightmares about him, but Re'Vel drove him away. I haven't dreamed of him in ages."

"What about Re'Vel? Has he tried to contact you since the first attack?"

Rachel stammered, "When I fall asleep, I can see the forest…the place where we used to meet. I always run the other way."

"Good," Jerica said firmly. "Don't speak with him—he's dangerous even in your dreams."

"Re'Vel is dangerous, but Nevare is lethal," Abe said. "If you ever dream of him again, let us know immediately."

I wondered what I was missing. The mention of Nevare seemed to unnerve the usually unflappable Abe in a way I'd never seen.

"Do you think he knows where we are?" Jerica asked.

"We're not in hiding. He knows," Abe replied. "He's waiting. Just like he waited for his opportunity with Royce. I killed Nevare's brother, and he took his revenge on my son. He'll keep coming for us until we stop him," Abe said.

"*I'll* stop him." Bryce stood with his arms crossed in front of him.

Jerica spoke softly, her voice filled with pain. "There was no evidence to link Nevare…"

"There's no doubt in my mind," Bryce said.

Bryce didn't often mention his older brother to others, but he'd talked to me about him. I knew about Bryce's pain, his descent into darkness after he'd lost his hero, his thirst to kill the Hunters responsible. He'd never mentioned Nevare.

Jerica took a deep breath and changed the subject. "Rachel's security spells aren't strong enough. Central might be able to help."

"No," Rachel said, beginning to cry. "I don't want anyone else getting involved. If my mother finds out…"

"Honey, you'll have to tell her soon. You can't keep this a secret forever," Jerica said.

"I will. I'll tell her. Just give me time."

"We'll talk about it later," Jerica said, smoothing Rachel's hair from her forehead and dabbing at the dried blood with a wet washcloth. "We don't have to make any decisions tonight."

Rachel let out a sigh and closed her eyes. She'd avoided yet another abduction attempt and managed to put off the eventual confession to her mother, but even I could sense the time of reckoning was drawing near. She couldn't run from the truth forever because the truth kept finding her. And, so did Re'Vel.

CHAPTER TWENTY-TWO
RACHEL

Danger found me everywhere, in sleep and in wakefulness. And, though it helped to know the Alexanders were on my side, I felt alone. Throughout the round of questioning and interrogation, the speculation about Re'Vel and how he'd found me so easily, I longed to speak of Mordecai, but could not.

I promised Mordecai I wouldn't tell anyone about him and that promise held my tongue. Our Blood Bond was more than a family tie, more than the heritage we shared. The Blood Bond was a magical contract and I entered into it without realizing it.

Each time I tried to speak of Mordecai, a debilitating migraine shattered my skull and ripped the words from my mouth. I was unable to speak of my cousin, held captive by my own magic.

Jace hovered over me all evening, checking me for signs of concussion, reassuring me he would keep me safe. I flashed him a smile of gratitude, but wondered if I would ever feel safe again.

"Rachel, you can go home when you're ready," Jerica said. "I'll have Abe drive you."

"I'm ready whenever he is," I replied.

Why delay the inevitable? Eventually, I'd have to return home, lie to my mother about how I'd spent my afternoon and evening, and make up an excuse for my disheveled appearance. I would have to enter my bedroom—a place where I felt safe once upon a time. And, eventually, I'd have to lay my head down on the pillow and fall asleep.

The forest would appear in the distance and the towering pines would rise above the mists, silent monuments to my altered existence. Re'Vel would whisper through the trees and I would shudder in revulsion, all the while struggling to resist the magnetic pull of the power he held over me.

"Rachel?" Jace's voice was laced with concern. "Are you okay?"

I wiped beads of sweat from my upper lip and pulled my teeth into a smile. "Yeah." I followed Abe and Jace out to the car, feeling helpless and hating myself for it.

Just like after the first attack, I was afraid to fall asleep, afraid of who might find me in my dreams? What other secrets were lurking around waiting to be discovered?

Alone in my bedroom, I thought about my brother and how lucky he was. There was a time no so long ago that I'd felt sorry for him for his loss of birthright, but now I envied his ignorance. Jeffrey remained blissfully unaware of the existence of the creatures who would stop at nothing to steal my magic, or the Demon who killed our father. But, was Jeffrey truly unaware? The presence of Hunters didn't go unnoticed; he had a nervous breakdown when he thought he was being followed.

I worried about Jeffrey almost constantly—more than I worried about myself. Should Re'Vel decide to target my brother, he would be defenseless. Jerica's vow to protect him, though well-intentioned, might not be enough. After all, Abe and Jerica had done everything to protect me and despite their best efforts, Re'Vel tried to abduct me twice. If the Demon's word could be trusted, only Nevare's claim kept Re'Vel from taking me. The fact that the two Demons were fighting over me didn't give a sense of comfort.

I longed for the days before I knew about magic, Demons, and Hunters. But, how could I possibly yearn for a life without Jace? He was everything to me, now. I thought about my boyfriend and the link we shared. Any sacrifice was worth having Jace in my life.

"Rachel, are you still awake?" Jace's voice drifted across our link.

"Yeah. I'm afraid to fall asleep," I admitted.

"Because of Re'Vel?"

"And Nevare."

"Nevare can't take you while Re'Vel holds claim..."

"Yeah, and Re'Vel can't take me because of Nevare. What happens when they decide to work together?" Panic began to set in, making it hard to breathe.

"They won't. Besides, I'm here to protect you," he said. "If you'll let me. Re'Vel can take you away if you allow it. You almost did. You have to learn to fight him."

Shame washed over me. It was true. I'd nearly given in to Re'Vel. As much as Re'Vel frightened me, I felt drawn to him. My willpower dissolved the moment he touched me and I couldn't understand why.

"I'm sorry," I said, "It's like I'm under a spell when he's around. I don't know how to describe it. My head feels foggy and the only thing that breaks through the haze is your voice."

"Then keep the link open tonight. You don't have to fight him alone. Let me help you."

"Thanks, Jace. I don't know how you put up with me."

"It isn't easy," he joked.

With Jace, I could face anything: the secrets of my heritage, my crooked family tree, the mystery surrounding my cousin, and the Demon who wouldn't leave me in peace. He would help me remain steady amidst the shifting sands of my constantly changing life. His presence in my mind eased me into a gentle slumber, bolstered my resolve to avoid the forest, and gave me the strength to resist the whispers on the winds of my dreams.

"Rachel," Re'Vel whispered. I took one step toward the forest, but Jace grabbed my hand and pulled me back. We walked away together.

CHAPTER TWENTY-THREE
ALISA

Long after the sun had set, Bryce and I sat outside on the porch swing, our bodies so close our legs were stuck together from the humidity. The late night breeze carried the smell of hydrangeas and some relief from the stifling heat.

Shock had finally faded to silent reflection, and I thought about everything that had happened that day. My mind drifted back to a time before Bryce, and I shuddered just thinking of my life before I'd met him: the loneliness, the isolation, the waiting for something to shake me from my apathy.

Jace and Rachel gave me a feeling of belonging and friendship, but Bryce gave me love. He gave me the confidence to stand up for myself against Becky, and the strength to go after what I wanted. He made me feel as if I deserved better than what I'd put up with all my life. With him, I was more than just the shy girl who stammered and blushed, more than the lonely girl who'd spent every Friday night at home, more than who I used to be.

"You're very quiet. Are you sure you're okay?" Bryce asked, nudging me softly.

"I'm fine. What about you? I don't know what I would have done if…" I trailed off, embarrassed. "I'm just glad you're okay. I don't ever want to lose you," I whispered.

"You won't," he said. He kissed me gently. I snuggled closer to him, not caring about the humidity, or the mosquitoes biting my ankles. My thoughts kept returning to the park. I nearly lost the only man I could ever love. And, I nearly lost my best friend.

"What's going to happen to Rachel?" I asked. "That Demon is going to keep coming back for her, and what if he catches her alone the next time?"

"She won't be alone. You heard my parents: she needs constant protection," he said.

"But, why does Re'Vel want her so badly?"

"He wants to take her for a mate."

"That's disgusting," I blurted.

"What is? Mating? It might be fun. We could try it." His hand moved upward on my thigh. I slapped it away.

"No. I can't imagine anyone mating with a Demon," I said, shuddering. "Wait. If Hunters are half-Demons, is that what Re'Vel wants her for? To create more Hunters?"

"Hunters are created when the Witch's magic isn't strong enough. But, Rachel is an Nkaribo, one of the strongest of her bloodline. She can create a true half-Demon, so Re'Vel hopes." Bryce put his arm around me and pulled me closer. "Now, about mating…"

"Stop that," I laughed, pushing his wandering hand away. "Is that all you can think about?"

"It is when I'm with you. Don't you think about it?" he asked.

My face burned with embarrassment, and I was grateful for the darkness, otherwise Bryce would have made fun of me. "We haven't been together that long. I don't want to move too fast."

"I'm not going to push you, Alisa. I'll wait as long as you want me to," he said.

"But your parents…" I said, remembering the time not so long ago that Jerica seemed upset to see Jace holding my wrist. I felt reluctant to explain this to Bryce…uncomfortable at the idea of openly acknowledging the huge crush I'd once had on my boyfriend's brother. "Your mom acted really weird one time when Jace and I were rough-housing in the kitchen. And, then the other night…I don't think she approves."

"My mom knew you were meant for me even before I knew it. She has the gift of Prediction. She knew you were mine the first time she saw you. That's why she told you our family's secrets," he said.

"Then why was she crying when she saw the ties?"

"Because once the Claiming Words are spoken, it sets events in motion. It will be impossible for me to stay away from you," he admitted.

"Then why did you do it?"

"Because my soul was already bound to yours. The words just made it official," he said. "I don't regret it. I love you."

"I love you too," I said. He leaned over and kissed my cheek. He whispered in my ear, and this time, the words pulled me in, wrapped around my soul. And this time, I knew what he was saying. This time, my soul called out to his, and somewhere deep inside myself, I made my own claim. "I'll never stop loving you."

"Promise?" he asked.

And, at last, I spoke my own Claiming Words—the human version, the only words I knew. "I promise." I looked up and saw my future in his eyes. Once again, I saw the ties. But, now they went both ways. And, now I was ready for whatever my future might bring…as long as Bryce was a part of it.

THE END

FOR NOW

About the Author

Tricia Drammeh is a wife and a mother of four children. Although she currently lives in Missouri, she has called many places home, including Georgia, Ohio, and California. She's worked in retail, customer service, sales, and accounting, but writing has always been her dream career. When she isn't writing, she enjoys reading, spending time with her family, and attending various Scouting functions. Tricia is currently working on her sixth novel.

CPSIA information can be obtained at www.ICGtesting.com
Printed in the USA
LVOW081147150912

298776LV00001B/9/P